THROUGH THE LENS

The Cedar Falls Series Book 1

S.A. Cantrell

Copyright © 2024 S.A. Cantrell

All rights reserved

The characters and events portrayed in this book are fictitious. Any similarity to real persons, living or dead, is coincidental and not intended by the author.

No part of this book may be reproduced, or stored in a retrieval system, or transmitted in any form or by any means, electronic, mechanical, photocopying, recording, or otherwise, without express written permission of the publisher.

ISSN-13:9798326706157

*To those who have discovered what it means
to love, and to all who are still searching.*

CONTENTS

Title Page
Copyright
Dedication
Chapter One | 1
Chapter Two | 13
Chapter Three | 23
Chapter Four | 32
Chapter Five | 43
Chapter Six | 55
Chapter Seven | 70
Chapter Eight | 83
Chapter Nine | 93
Chapter Ten | 107
Chapter Eleven | 116
Chapter Twelve | 126
Chapter Thirteen | 141
Chapter Fourteen | 150

Chapter Fifteen	160
Chapter Sixteen	166
Chapter Seventeen	175
Chapter Eighteen	187
Chapter Nineteen	195
Chapter Twenty	209
Chapter Twenty-One	222
Chapter Twenty-Two	236
Chapter Twenty-three	244
Chapter Twenty-four	252
Chapter Twenty-five	263
Chapter Twenty-six	270
Chapter Twenty-seven	281
Chapter Twenty-eight	285
Chapter Twenty-nine	290
Chapter Thirty	301
Chapter Thirty-one	309
Chapter Thirty-two	319
Bailey and Ezra's Snickerdoodles	322
About The Author	325
Books By This Author	327

CHAPTER ONE

I THOUGHT THE LOW point of senior year would be when the art teacher, Mr. Shultz, let everyone else in class make paper mâché masks, and I got stuck crafting a full-sized cow.

A cow!

I mean, don't get me wrong, *Milky White* was going to look great in this year's musical production of *Into the Woods*. It was so lifelike, and after talking to the drama teacher, Mrs. Hudson, I had figured out how to add a hinged jaw that opened, a false bottom so that the props "fed" to the cow during the show could be easily removed, and a hidden handle for the cast to move it around the stage easily.

Considering everything I'd had to do, I was pretty impressed with my design.

But seriously, why me?

With each strip of newspaper I'd dipped into the giant bowl of glue, I'd asked myself that question, silently wishing that he had chosen someone else—anyone else—for the job. I guess I should have been honored to design something for the school's fall musical, but come on, I didn't want my legacy at Cedar Falls High to hinge on a paper mâché cow.

That being said, I'd happily make a thousand more paper mâché animals if it meant I could have a different partner for the Through the Lens competition.

Mr. Shultz must have really had it in for me.

First, he'd stuck me with the cow in my 3D design class, and then he decided to ruin photography class, too. There was no other explanation for his constant need to fill my life with crazy art projects. All of which were starting to crush my future chances of getting into Providence School of Design, or PSD, as it was affectionately known among us artists.

Didn't he know how much this contest meant to my future?

I mean, forget about the prize money if I won—*which would be awesome*—but the prestige alone would be enough to push my college application over the top. You don't win a statewide high school art and design competition and not get noticed by the top art colleges. You just don't.

This was my shot to really stand out, but my chances had already been shattered, and I hadn't even started yet.

As soon as class was over, I marched straight up to Mr. Shultz's desk to express my fury, pushing my bottom lip out in a slight pout so he'd know exactly how upset I was. I know it was pathetic, but at that point I was not above begging.

"How can you do this to me?" I demanded.

He laced his fingers together on top of his desk and gave me a quizzical look. "Is there a problem, Bailey?"

"Sir, you partnered me with Ezra. You know he doesn't care about this contest. He doesn't even care about this class. Why would you pair us up for this? I need to do really well if I'm going to have any chance of impressing Providence. Please, you've got to give me someone else. Courtney and I work really well together, or even Dallas. He's got a good eye, but not Ezra. Come on?"

My heart pounded inside my chest as he took a very long pause. Glancing down at the papers on his desk, he finally said, "you know the partnerships were chosen by luck of the draw. There is nothing I can do."

My stomach felt as if someone had filled it with rocks. "Please, Mr. Shultz, there must be—"

He held up his hand, cutting me off. "Bailey, you are one of the best art students I've ever had come through this school. I was more than happy to help when you asked me to write recommendations for colleges. I believe in you and your future in the art world, but there are official competition rules that must be adhered to in this case. None of the other partners are up here complaining, and I'm not going to split them up just to make one student happy. This project will be a good learning experience for you. Trust me."

I clenched my jaw and blew out a hard breath. *Why was he doing this to me?*

He carried on as if he didn't care that he was ruining my life. "Besides, Ezra has never really stretched himself in this class, but don't rule out his ideas. There's talent there. Maybe you can help bring it out, and who knows, maybe he'll bring something out of you, too."

"Yeah, last place," I scoffed, slinging my backpack over my shoulder and sulking from the room.

This was a nightmare.

My chest tightened as soon as I rounded the corner into Senior Hall, but I knew what needed to be done. Steadying my nerves, I took a deep breath and marched into the fray.

Ezra O'Neill's locker sat smack in the middle of all the other jocks at the end of the hall. The wave of maroon jersey's enveloped me as I pushed closer to his locker.

There was a football game that night and all the players and cheerleaders wore their uniforms to school on game days. Like we needed another reminder that they were like gods and the rest of us were mere mortals. The smell of old sweat and stale body spray made my nose wrinkle and I fought the urge to gag.

They could at least wash the jerseys between games, couldn't they?

Shaking my head, I reached up and tapped Ezra square in the middle of his back. At first he ignored me, so I poked him harder, digging in with my fingernail. Finally, he whirled around.

"What?" He growled as he puffed out his chest and I swear he got an inch taller, as if he'd been expecting someone much bigger than me. Someone who might be picking a fight with him.

If he only knew the amount of rage I was suppressing at that moment.

When his gaze dropped to me, his face fell a bit. I tried not to take it personally. I mean, I didn't want to be there either.

"Oh...hi." He let out his breath and his shoulders dropped back to normal height.

"We need to talk." I put my hands on my hips.

"About?" He glanced to his friends who watched the two of us with huge smirks plastered on their faces.

I'm sure they would all laugh at me later. I wasn't part of their group. I didn't talk to most of them, and no one—I repeat, no one—approached the football players without a good reason.

But I had a *very* good reason to be there, so I didn't really care what they thought.

Trying to make myself a bit bigger as well, I pushed my shoulders back, focusing on Ezra and no one else. "The Through the Lens Competition. We're partners, remember?"

He ran a hand through his hair, making it stick up in what I'm sure most girls would find a really adorable coif, but I couldn't think about that right then. I was on a mission.

"Yeah, so?"

Fire rose up inside me. I suddenly hated his spiky hair.

"So?" I shrieked, my voice rising two octaves above normal. Clearing my throat, I counted to ten in my head before starting over. "So, when can we meet to discuss it?"

"Uh...listen, about that..." Ezra lifted his chin to his friends, who immediately scattered, leaving us alone. "I only took this class because it qualifies as a Fine Arts credit and I need it to graduate. I really don't have time for some stupid contest right now." He tried to push past me.

My blood boiled as I clenched my fists. This was totally unacceptable. Reaching up, I placed both hands on Ezra's chest, pushing him back against the lockers. He went wide-eyed as I dug my nails into the nylon maroon jersey. I know he had let me push him, but that didn't mean I didn't feel a bit powerful in the moment.

"Through the Lens is not a *stupid* contest. Now, I know you don't care, but here's how this is going to work. I was unfortunate enough to get you as my partner, but so help me, if you ruin my chances of getting into PSD, I will kill you. And it will be slow and very, very painful, I promise you."

His mouth quirked into a grin and I swear he rolled his eyes. Smoke erupted from my ears.

Maybe I'd just kill him right there and save us both the trouble.

A growl emanated deep within my throat. "We both have to participate to qualify and I can't do this on my own, so you agree to help me and I'll make sure you get a good grade. Okay?" I eased my fingernails out of his chest and stepped back. "Don't you care what this could do for your college applications?"

"Not really." He shrugged. "I'm going for an athletic scholarship. The schools who want me don't care if I can take pretty pictures."

I pasted a smile on my face, even though I was screaming inside. "This is not only a wonderful opportunity for both of us, but if we win, it's the kind of thing that will look great on *any* college application. Besides, it's a huge boost to our grade. Please?" I clasped both hands in front of me. I didn't care how many people were probably laughing at me. I was desperate.

"Are you seriously begging? You know I've never had a girl beg me for anything before. Do it again. I like it." He had the audacity to laugh as he brushed his hands over the finger-indention I'd left in his jersey.

I took a step closer to him and lowered my voice. "Death, slow and painful."

Leaning back against his locker, Ezra chewed on his bottom lip as if he thought it would torture me. Finally, he pushed himself off and said, "okay, here's the deal. I need some pictures taken for my own college applications. Shots showing game highlights and great moments of me on the field, that sort of thing. I've got a few newspaper clippings and my dad has tried to take some photos, but they're not very good. I need someone who knows what they're doing. Come to tonight's game against Rock Harbor and take pictures of me playing. If you can prove to me that you're as good as you think you are, I'll consider working with you. In exchange for you helping me out, of course."

"Now, wait a minute, I never said--"

"That's the offer, Grant. Take it or leave it." He ran his hand through his hair again like it would make me suddenly say yes.

"I—" I couldn't even speak.

I wanted to punch him in his perfect face. I wanted to rip his jersey to shreds with my bare hands. This was not supposed to be his negotiation, it was supposed to be mine. How had he managed to turn things around on me so fast?

I took a deep breath. "But, I hate football. Are you seriously going to force me to go to the *stupid* game and take *stupid* pictures of you like I'm your crazy, *stupid* girlfriend or something?"

"Who said anything about being my girlfriend?" He smirked, eyeing me up and down in a way that made my skin crawl. "I'll have to think about that one. I've never dated an art girl before."

"Aren't you dating Casey Turner?" Last year they had been the "it" couple, even winning king and queen at the Junior Prom. Or, so I'd heard. Tori and I had left before the official crowning so we could go bowling with some of her theater friends.

"Not anymore." His jaw tightened. "Why, you want the job?"

"I'd rather kill you." I seethed.

"If you kill me, you can't do your little contest. But, if coming to my *stupid* game is that far beneath you, then forget the whole thing. I mean, it seems a fair trade to me for what you're asking, but hey, what do I know?" He stepped past me, clutching his books to his chest. "Listen, I gotta get to Algebra. What's it to be?"

I'm sure smoke was rolling from my nostrils, but I had no choice but to huff a very frustrated, "fine. I'll do it."

"Great." He grinned. "Meet me tomorrow at ten at The Magic Bean. If I like what I see, you might just have yourself a partner. By the way, this is my best side." He gestured to the left side of his face. "And hey, you might actually enjoy yourself tonight if you took your nose out of the air for two seconds and give it half a chance." He winked and gave me a ridiculous thumbs up before turning and jogging down the hallway.

"Don't bet on it." My words trailed after him. "And my nose is not in the air."

I spun on my heel and marched to my third

period Chemistry class. When I slumped down next to my best friend, Tori Whittaker, she wrinkled her brow and cocked her head. "You look like you're ready to punch somebody. What happened?"

"Wanna go to the game tonight?" I asked through clenched teeth.

Reaching over, she pressed the back of her hand against my forehead. "Nope, no fever."

"Stop." I swatted her hand away. "I'm serious."

"Did you get hit in the head or something? Why would you want to go to the game?" She lowered her voice as the teacher, Mrs. Shepherd, walked in.

I groaned, "it's a long story."

After giving me a very quizzical side-eye, she finally shrugged. "I'll go as long as we can get *Taylor's* for dinner. I want a cheeseburger."

That right there was one of the things I loved most about Tori. She would agree to almost anything as long as there was food involved.

"Thank you." I mouthed, pulling my safety goggles onto my head. I tried to convince myself that my life wasn't over just yet. Going to one football game wouldn't be so bad if it made Ezra agree to work with me, right?

I'm thinking that's a big fat nope! He had acted like a big jerk because he was cool, and popular, and I wasn't. That was what his kind did to mine. But what choice did I have?

After Tori and I moved to the back of the

classroom and claimed our microscope for the day's experiment, I told her everything, but the more I talked, the angrier I got, until I almost spilled hydrochloric acid in my lap. Tori took over the experiment at that point and I was left to record our results, but I ended up doodling all over the paper and had to go ask Mrs. Shepherd for a new one because I was so distracted.

The rest of the day was even worse.

I ended up in the wrong line at lunch and instead of chili, which I actually liked, I had to eat chicken and noodles that was slathered in the mysteriously green-tinged gravy that makes me want to gag.

In Home Economics, I sewed the wrong seam on the outside of the pajama pants I was "*this close*" to finishing and had to spend the whole rest of the hour ripping it out.

In English, I read the same page of *Hamlet* six times and still didn't understand anything.

It didn't help that Ezra was in my English class. I kept glancing over at him, imagining all the ways I could kill him with nothing but a book, and maybe a pencil.

By the afternoon, my mind was a raging battle of anger vs worry, but neither seemed to be anywhere near a victory. My body wasn't any better. Between fits of a racing pulse and sinking stomach, I was on edge, moody, and exhausted. I couldn't wait for the last bell to ring so I could go home and shower off that horrible day.

By the time it did ring, I didn't know who I hated more, Mr. Shultz, for choosing the partners for Through the Lens, or Ezra, for thinking he could make deals with me.

Unfortunately, this was one deal I was forced to say yes to. My entire future depended on it.

Did I mention how much I hated Ezra O'Neill?

Yep, I think he just moved to the top of my list.

CHAPTER TWO

PULLING MY HOOD DOWN across my eyes so far that no one would dare talk to me, I walked home in a huff.

The town of Cedar Falls, Rhode Island was small enough that most of us walked to school, even though we could all drive. There wasn't much point when you could get there just as quickly on foot, and the parking lot only had a handful of student parking spaces, anyway.

Turning onto my maple-lined street was usually enough of a reason to make me smile, especially then, during autumn—my favorite time of year. But even the falling leaves and crisp air couldn't lift my mood. Halloween was still weeks away, and yet the houses were already covered in corn stalks, straw bales, pumpkins, and terra cotta pots brimming with different colored mums. Black cats and ghosts hung on windows, orange and black bunting adorned street lamps and porches, wreaths were displayed on every door, and yellow and orange twinkle lights were dispersed in between. One house even had a huge blow-up jack-o-lantern in the front yard that swayed in the breeze.

Normally, I took it all in, feeling immediately inspired to draw, or paint something, but that day, I hated it all. Every pumpkin made me scowl, every twinkle light forced me to grit my teeth. It was awful. To make things even worse, the ground was wet from the rain we'd had earlier that afternoon, and everything smelled like rotting leaves and damp earth.

I guessed if my life was over, the world might as well smell like death and decay, too.

Things improved slightly when I opened the front door of my house and the delicious aroma of cinnamon and apples filled the air, making my stomach rumble. Mom didn't work, so she was always around when I got home from school; and that day, my older brother, Mike, was there, too. He was a freshman at Connecticut State and finished early on Fridays, which meant he would beat me home from school if he was coming back to do laundry, hang out with his friends, and eat mom's cooking all weekend.

"Why are boys such jerks?" I accosted him as he emerged from the kitchen in a tee shirt and gym shorts, holding a fresh, steaming apple turnover in his hand.

"What, no hello? No how's college? No I missed you, bro?" He paused, taking a bite.

I glared at him.

"Guess not. Okay, what happened?"

"So you know I've been looking forward to the Through the Lens Competition for months, right?

He nodded his head, chewing slowly.

"Well, I really thought I had a shot at winning this year, but Shultz stuck me with the worst partner ever and now I don't know what to do. Reps from PSD will be there. They look for stuff like this on applications, and I'm going to fail. I know it. This is a disaster." I flopped down on the couch, covering my face with a pillow.

Mike sat down on the other end of the couch, shoving more turnover into his mouth. "Come on." He mumbled with his mouth full. "It can't be that bad. Who'd you get?"

"Ezra O'Neill." I growled against the pillow.

"O'Neill's in an art class?" He snorted. "Oh, I'd pay good money to see that guy draw something."

I lifted the pillow. "It's photography class, you idiot. He said he just took it to fulfill his Fine Arts credit. He doesn't even want to do the contest, but if he doesn't do it, I forfeit the whole thing. It has to be a partner project. End of story."

Mike took another huge bite. "Did he say he wouldn't do it?"

"Not exactly." I sat up, hugging the pillow to my chest. "He said he needs some photos of himself playing football for his own college applications. I guess the schools he's applying to like to see you in action, or something" I shrugged my shoulders. "I don't know. Anyway, he told me to come to the game tonight and take some pictures of him. If he likes them, we'll make a trade and he'll work with me."

"Wow, whatever will you do?" Mike tapped his finger against his chin.

"Come on, you know Ezra's just baiting me. He probably doesn't even need the pictures. He's just going to make me grovel and beg and then let me down. There's no way he'll agree to do this." Pinching the bridge of my nose, I finished telling him everything that had happened after class that morning.

"Listen, Ezra may not care about art, but he's not a bad guy. He probably does need the photos. I remember Tony obsessing over his application because of the same thing. I'm sure he's just messing with you. I mean you did threaten him in the hallway in front of the entire football team. That's a lot for a guy to deal with."

"Oh please? I only did what was necessary." I pounded my fist into the couch.

Mike's eyebrows shot up. "Really?"

I took a deep breath. "Okay, I might have gotten a little carried away, but it's only because this is so important to me."

My brother reached over and patted my knee. "Just don't go crazy on the guy. He's just trying to get into college, too. Maybe this deal isn't so bad. I mean, if you both get what you want out of it, what could go wrong?"

I leveled a gaze at him.

He pursed his lips. "You want me to come to

the game with you?"

"No, Tori's meeting me at *Taylor's* and then we're walking over together. I don't want him to think I need my brother to protect me from the big bad football game." I smiled for the first time all day.

"Good, because I was thinking of asking Marina to the movies tonight, but you know I'd go with you if you needed me too."

"I know." I got up and grabbed my backpack. "Have fun on your date."

"Oh, I will." Mike winked at me, taking the last bite of his turnover.

I rolled my eyes as I trudged up the stairs to my room. After finishing my homework, I changed into warmer clothes and told Mom where I was going.

"Be careful," she called from the kitchen.

"I will." I pulled on my jacket and made sure I had an extra battery and memory cards for the camera in my purse before heading out the door to meet Tori.

❖ ❖ ❖

Taylor's Cafe had been a favorite town hangout since the mid 1800's—or so the sign outside claimed. Although, I don't think those early patrons kept coming back for the best cheeseburgers and milkshakes in the state, like we did. But even the cheeseburgers weren't the real reason people flocked to *Taylor's*.

They came for the pies. *So many pies.*

Fruit, custard, pumpkin, cream, topped with either meringue or a scoop of homemade vanilla ice cream.

Did I mention the pies?

Tori was already sitting at a table near the door when I walked in, her hair piled on top of her head in a messy bun, and a half-empty glass of *Coke* on the table. She had a pen stuck over one ear and a highlighter between her teeth.

"Hey." I plopped down across from her and read the announcement board above the counter which showed that the BLT on wheat was the special of the day.

"I ordered us some cheeseburgers and fries," she said without lifting her gaze from her script of *Into the Woods*.

"You're the best." I said.

"I know." She finally looked up and closed her script. "So, we're really going to do this?"

As the waitress sat our food on the table, I sighed. "I don't have a choice."

"You know, a lot of girls would kill for one of the football players to personally invite them to a game, and ask them to take pictures of them." She raised her eyebrows suggestively.

I threw a french fry at her. "I take it back, you're not the best."

"I'm just saying, maybe there's a silver lining here you're not seeing." She sipped her drink.

"The only silver lining to this will be convincing Ezra to do the project with me so that I can win and impress Providence. So, as long as he does everything I say, and we can turn in the best project in the state, that's all I want. I don't care that he's popular, or a football player, or whatever. To me, he's just the means to an end. Period."

"There is something seriously wrong with you." She shook her head, lowering her voice. "We're talking Ezra O'Neill here. Star of the football team, Prom king, gorgeous."

"Just because I'm not getting all swoony because a hot football player spoke to me, how does that make me crazy?"

Tori grinned. "So, you do think he's hot?"

I almost spit out my bite of cheeseburger. "Who cares if he's hot? I've got more important things to worry about than hot guys. I have to get into Providence. That's what matters. That's what's important. I don't need some stupid boy messing that up."

She leaned forward, eying me with concern. "Look, I know you, and I know college is important to you. It's important to all of us right now, but don't get so short-sided that you forget to let yourself have a little fun, too. Come on, we're seniors. Live a little. You haven't done anything fun all year. We've barely hung out. This isn't you."

"I'll live once I've gotten into PSD. I'll breathe

when everything I have to do gets done." I wiped my mouth with a napkin. "And we've both been busy. You've got play practice practically every night, and you're constantly with Marcus. Besides, I've got portfolios to put together and applications to fill out."

"Don't blame this on me, or Marcus. It's not the first year I've had play practices. We've always managed to hang out, no matter who my boyfriend was. You know you're shutting yourself off and working too hard. You're going to regret being so uptight about this. Believe me," she said. "You don't see me so obsessed with NYU that I'm not letting myself enjoy my last musical at Cedar Falls."

"I'm not being uptight. I'm being realistic." I huffed. "No matter how hot Ezra is, he's football and I'm art club. We don't mix, and for good reason. So why let myself think about things that will never happen?"

Tori leaned back in her chair. "If things could never happen, then why was he flirting with you this morning?"

I gasped. "He was not. He was making fun of me and messing with my head. How can you even say that he was flirting? That was not flirting."

She stood up and pulled on her jacket. "Maybe, maybe not, but why would he tease you about being his girlfriend then?"

"Because he was trying to humiliate me," I

said after we had paid our bills and walked outside.

"I don't think so. He's actually a nice guy when you get to know him. He's in my history class and we've worked together a couple of times. He's really smart and he has good ideas. One of the other guys would have been trying to humiliate you, but not Ezra. I just don't see him being that way."

I threw my hands up in frustration. "Why does everyone keep saying he's so nice? He's not. He's a jerk."

"Because it's true. You just don't want to see it."

I knew she was trying to help me gain some perspective, but I didn't need perspective. I knew what I wanted, and I would do anything to get it. Even if it meant taking pictures for Ezra. Heck, I'd become his personal paparazzi if it meant impressing Providence. What was Tori thinking? Just because she'd had lots of boyfriends, it didn't make her an expert. So what if she thought he was so nice, or that he was gorgeous? It didn't mean *I* had to.

Who had time to think about the way Ezra's brown hair curled a little around his ears, or how tall he was? Who cared if he had cute dimples that marked his cheeks when he smiled, or if his blue eyes mimicked the colors of the Caribbean Sea?

Not me.

Nope.

I didn't have time for such ridiculous thoughts.

Art school, and winning this contest were more important. They had to be. Nothing, and no one—not even someone with great eyes—was going to stand in my way.

That prize was mine.

End of story.

CHAPTER THREE

THE CHEDAR FALLS FOOTBALL field was already abuzz by the time Tori and I paid for our tickets and found seats near the sidelines. I had hoped from that position I'd be able to get the best pictures of Ezra. I also really hoped that no one else would have a clue what I was doing at the game. I cringed at the thought of what the other kids at school would say on Monday if they saw me taking random pictures of one of the senior football players. It wouldn't be a pretty sight, believe me.

Announcers in the PA box tested the microphones, making the speakers hanging above the stands pop and crackle, as an off-kilter musical chord came from the band as they warmed up their instruments on the far left of the field. The cheerleaders practiced cartwheels and lifts at the edge of the bleachers, while the smell of roasting hotdogs and old grease from the concession stand tainted the air around us.

Parents and students filled the empty bleachers, carrying homemade signs and banners while dressed like crazy, obsessed fans. I almost felt out of place because I wasn't plastered from head-to-toe in our school colors. One girl even had maroon and white ribbons woven through her braids while a huge number eleven was painted on her cheek—*in glitter*. The only thing that made me feel a bit better was that neither Tori or I were wearing even a speck of green—Rock Harbor's color.

I would never admit it to anyone—especially Ezra—but my pulse fluttered a bit at the sight of it all, as if I expected something exciting to happen. Was this how he felt before every game? Like the atmosphere itself was enough to make your heart race inside your chest.

It was the same feeling I got every time I began a new art project. Staring at the blank canvas, or design sketch, was exhilarating. My heart would flutter and my hands would shake with the knowledge that what was before me could become anything I wanted it to be. It was up to me to mold and shape it, but until I touched it with a paintbrush, or took the first photo, I was filled with the same "what will happen" elation that I felt at that moment. Butterflies even fluttered in my stomach.

When both teams ran onto the field, I pulled out my camera and took a few photos to test the lighting. I hoped that the large floodlights would be bright enough to capture the moments of the game, without casting harsh shadows over the players. That's really all I needed. Decent lighting and a good vantage point. I had both.

What more was there?

The Cedar Falls Tigers gathered around the benches on our side of the field forming a sea of padded maroon boys. I couldn't see Ezra's face beneath his helmet, but the number five on his back was easy enough to spot. When I was confronting him in the hallway, I'd at least paid attention to the number I was digging my fingers into. I wondered if my half-moon nail imprints were still over his heart?

All I had to do was track that white number five through my lens and take as many pictures of him as I could. *Easy peasy*.

After Ezra and the team won the coin toss, **(PHOTO #1)** they ran out and formed a line that stretched across the center of the field.

I'd sat in the same room with my dad and Mike on enough Sunday afternoons to know that this meant the game was starting. It was usually at that point that I would leave the room, or pick up a book or sketch pad, and ignore the rest of the game so I had no idea what to expect after that, but I didn't have to understand the game to photograph it.

Standing up, I moved closer to the railing, where I crouched down, balancing my elbow on my knee for stability. Tracking Ezra's every movement, I watched as he caught the ball and ran with it towards our end zone. **(PHOTOS #2-#6)**

He was way harder to follow than I'd thought

he'd be.

Who knew Ezra could move so fast?

The crowd behind me was on their feet, screaming and shouting his name over and over again like a battle cry. I pressed my eye to the camera, snapping furiously as he dove across the end zone and landed with a thud, clutching the ball to his chest. The crowd erupted with cheers.

Ezra jumped to his feet as if he hadn't just nosedived onto the ground, and lifted the ball high above his head (more cheering) while the rest of team rushed into the end zone, jumping on him and slapping him on the back. **(PHOTOS #7-???)**

So many photos.

The rest of the game was pretty much the same thing on repeat. Ezra was obviously the star of the team like Tori had said, or else he was just the fastest runner. He carried the ball up and down the field like his shoes were on fire, scoring another touchdown before halftime.

My legs were cramping up from squatting for so long, so I turned the camera off and flopped back down next to Tori, as a sinking feeling began to wedge itself deep between my ribs.

"Having fun yet?" Tori shoved a nacho, dripping with hot cheese, into her mouth. I hadn't even noticed her leaving to go to the concession stand.

"It wasn't too bad until I realized Ezra isn't the nice guy you say he is. He has to be doing this to humiliate me. He's the big cheese out there. You can't tell me there aren't photos of all this somewhere." I gestured wildly with both hands. "He does everything. I don't even know why he needs the rest of the team. They should just call themselves Ezra's Tigers."

As if to prove my point, the crowd erupted in cheers again, and when I glanced onto the field, sure enough, Ezra had the ball and was running it towards the end zone…again.

"See." I reached for one of Tori's nachos.

She held the dish closer so I wouldn't drip cheep everywhere as I chose one and shoved it into my mouth.

"What are you going to do about it?" She asked.

"I don't know." I stretched my legs out in front of me, chewing. "I guess I'll meet him tomorrow, show him what I've got, and then do whatever it takes to make sure he agrees to be my partner."

"What if he hates your photos?" She licked cheese off her finger.

"I appreciate your confidence." My chest felt like a balloon with a slow leak. Deflated.

"I'm not saying your pictures are going to be bad. I just mean, what if it is all a big game to him, like you said? What if he just did all this because you embarrassed him in the hallway and he's trying to get back at you?" She took another bite. "I don't think that's what's happening, but what if it is?"

"Then I'll be screwed." My throat tightened.

I'll be screwed.

I didn't want to admit the worst to myself, but there it was. If Ezra didn't agree to work with me, there was nothing I could do about it. Participation in the project would earn us a better grade in Photography Class, sure, but it was ultimately our decision whether we wanted to take part in the contest, or not.

He could say no, and if he did, that would be the end of it. There was no other partner I could work with, unless someone else's partner quit on them, and hoping for that was a long shot. Everyone else was excited about the contest. It's why we'd all taken the class in the first place. No one was about to quit on something as big as Through the Lens.

My only hope at winning was Ezra O'Neill—or nothing.

So, what did I do?

I turned on the camera and took more pictures of him, catching every moment for the rest of the game, pressing down the shutter as if my life depended on it. I hated every minute, but I did it anyway. I didn't even care what was happening on the field. If Ezra was out there, I captured it on the memory card.

Cedar Falls won the game, which I guess was a good thing. *Yay! Woo hoo! Big deal.* The stands seemed to come apart at the seams when Ezra scored the final touchdown, but I was just so relieved that it was over that I breathed a long sigh and stretched my stiff muscles.

I never wanted to sit through another football game. *Ever again.* I couldn't believe people actually did that for fun. It was uncomfortable, and cold, and smelled like stale grease and armpits. *No thank you.*

As soon as I saw the opportunity, I grabbed Tori by the arm and pulled her out of the stands. I didn't want to wait around for Ezra to find me and risk him strutting over to laugh at the fact that I was so gullible and naive that I had actually shown up.

Limping away from the high school, my sore legs didn't loosen up at all on the way home. When we stopped at Tori's house, she turned to me and said, what I'm sure was meant to make me feel better, but didn't. "At least it wasn't an away game."

There it was.

The only consolation for the terrible day was the fact that at least we hadn't had to drive to another town for Ezra to humiliate me. I was supposed to be thankful that he'd done it here, at home.

"Right," I said through clenched teeth, before limping the rest of the way home.

Mike's car was gone, which meant he was still on his date with Marina. I could have used his advice, but instead I got Mom and Dad. Not that they were bad with advice, but Mike knew Ezra. Maybe he'd have some sort of inside *guy-knowledge*, or an idea about what I should do.

"Have fun?" Dad asked from the couch where he and Mom were watching one of their favorite crime dramas.

"Not really. I only went to the game because I had to take some pictures." I plopped down in a chair without taking off my jacket or shoes.

"Was it an assignment for photography class?" Mom sipped a cup of tea, her floral pajamas peeking out from beneath her fluffy bathrobe.

"Something like that." I didn't have the energy to tell them the truth. I just wanted to go to bed and forget the whole day had ever happened.

Upstairs in my room, I flicked through the pictures on my camera. I'd taken so many, but I had no idea what Ezra needed. I wanted to trust him. Give him the benefit of the doubt. I mean, Mike had said he wasn't a bad guy, but he and I had never been friends. Even growing up together in the same small town, he'd had his crowd and I had had mine. I think our conversation that morning at his locker was the most we'd said to each other in years. I couldn't remember the last time I'd even glanced his way.

Didn't he understand how easy Through the Lens would be? That all he had to do was say yes and I'd do all the work?

If he was willing to trust me, I'd set up the photos so they were perfect. I'd edit them like a pro. I wouldn't need him to really do anything except sign his name to the piece once I was done. I would make sure we won. But, getting that yes out of him might just be the hardest thing I would ever have to do.

So many things hung in the balance and he was the only one who could help me catch them, but that would mean putting my trust and my future in the hands of another person. I didn't know if I could do that.

Especially not with someone like Ezra O'Neill.

He better say yes if he knew what was good for him, because if there was something I was even better at than art, it was holding a grudge.

CHAPTER FOUR

THE NEXT MORNING, I sat inside The Magic Bean coffee shop, my hair in a high, messy bun because I hadn't had time to wash it that morning, a flannel shirt, jeans and my favorite boots. When I'd arrived, the first thing I'd done was order my favorite autumn drink—a pumpkin spiced latte—and was sipping away at it's pumpkin-y goodness when the bell chimed on the door.

Again.

I didn't even bother to turn around that time. Ezra had said to meet him at ten o'clock, but I'd stopped expecting him to show up when the hands on the clock moved past ten-twenty.

He's doing this on purpose.

I mean, come on, if you tell someone you'll meet them at a certain time, you show up at that time. It's not that hard.

"Hey, Grant, sorry I'm late. Overslept," said a deep voice behind me.

Glaring, I wiped whipped cream off my upper lip, while he slipped around the table and wedged himself against the wall across from me, plopping his own whipped cream-topped, syrup-drizzled drink on the table in front of him.

"I was going to give you another ten minutes. Then I was out of here." I crossed my legs beneath the table and tapped my fingernails against my mug.

"You would have walked out on me?" His gaze narrowed, an adorable smile playing on his lips. "If you were really hoping for that girlfriend spot, that's not a good way to start out."

My mouth dropped open. I couldn't decide if he was cute, or if I wanted to kick his chair out from under him, but every time I heard the word "girlfriend" from his lips, it sent me into a flutter of mixed emotions I couldn't untangle. Was Tori right? Was he flirting with me?

I stared at him for a long moment. I knew I shouldn't. I mean, what would he think if he saw me blush? What would he say next? Especially since me turning bright red was probably the exact response he was hoping for. But I couldn't help myself. With his cheesy grin and messy I-just-woke-up hair, he looked even hotter than usual.

Oh, I can't believe I just thought that. What is wrong with me?

Taking a deep breath, I shifted my gaze to the table and composed myself enough to form words. "Trust me, you're not my type. And, yes, I would have left. Did you think I was just going to sit around here wasting my Saturday, waiting on you to show up. I've got more important things to do."

Ezra clutched his chest in feigned injury. "Ouch, you wound me."

"Gee, and here I was thinking a big, tough football player like you would be used to pain by now. Especially since, from what I saw last night, you spent the whole game getting tackled and rolling around on the ground." I wrapped my hands around my mug, glaring at him.

"I did not spend the whole game rolling around on the ground." He leaned back in his chair, stretching and then placing both hands behind his head. Another smug grin plastered to his face. "So, what is your type?"

I gasped. "We are not having this conversation, so if that's all you came for then I'm out of here."

His grin remained. "Did you at least enjoy the game last night?"

I glared at him. "What do you think?"

Ezra took his arms down, resting his hands on the table, and lowered his voice. "Not even a little bit?" His face fell and he stuck out his pouty bottom lip.

I sighed. "Look, it really doesn't matter what I thought about the game. Do you want to see your pictures, or not? Or was this all part of your big plan to humiliate me, and now is the moment when you laugh and tell me it was just a big joke."

"What are you talking about?" Ezra's brow creased as he sat up straighter in his chair. "Why would you think this was a joke, or that I would ever do that to you?"

I ignored his face. His sad puppy-dog face.

"Oh, I don't know," I said, "because you didn't want to do this project in the first place, and even though you know how important this is to me, you've decided that, instead of shattering my dreams of getting into Providence in one fell swoop, you're just going to mess with me until I crack."

Leaning forward, Ezra laced his fingers together around his mug. "You're right, this contest isn't something that I'm very interested in doing, but I also know how important it is to impress colleges right now. That's why I asked you to take the pictures. I thought we could work together. You help me. I help you."

"Oh."

Lifting the mug to his lips, he took a long slurp. "Can I see the photos?" As he pulled the mug away, it left behind a huge whipped cream mustache. He didn't bother wiping it off.

I handed the camera across the table.

"What do I do?" He held it like he'd never seen one before. The mustache was still there.

I stifled a laugh. "Uh…push the right arrow."

"Got it." Ezra's eyes bore into the display screen of the camera, but they showed nothing of what he might be thinking. With each press of the right arrow button, my stomach twisted into knots.

Soon, his mustache was annoying me. *He's got to know it's there.*

"Ezra."

I repeated his name three more times before he finally glanced up.

"What?"

I swiped my forefinger across my own top lip.

"Huh?" His forehead wrinkled with confusion.

"Wipe your face," I said, handing him a napkin.

"Oh. Thanks." He wiped off his cheeks and mouth, while continuing to press the buttons on the camera. When he was finished, he turned it around, grinning. "This isn't me."

The final photos on the memory card were ones I'd taken while waiting for him to arrive that morning. They were shots of my pumpkin spiced latte from different angles. One had the wall blurred behind the table. Another was shot from above. In another one, I'd placed the pumpkin decorations from the table around it.

"You were late. I was killing time," I snapped, snatching the camera from his hands.

"They're really good." He grinned. "I like the flat lay one best."

I choked on my coffee. "How do you know what a flat lay is?"

He tilted his head and lifted one eyebrow. "Come on, Grant, I may not be obsessed with the class like you are, but I still want to get a good grade. I do pay attention once in a while."

"I'm not obsessed with the class." I chewed on my lip. *Okay, maybe I was, but how dare he point it out.*

"Whatever. The pictures are good." There were those dimples again. *Dang it.* Why did he have to be so cute?

"You think so?"

"Yeah, I mean, there's definitely a difference between the ones of me and the ones of your coffee, but I can see that you have talent." He leaned his chin on his hand.

My ears burned. "Well, of course there's a difference. One is of a person and the other is of a beverage." I shoved the camera back into my purse, grinding my teeth.

"I know. That's not what I meant." He took another sip of coffee, remembering to wipe his face that time.

"What did you mean, then? Never mind. I don't care." I had had about enough of Ezra. All I needed to know was if he was going to work with me, or not. "So, what's your decision?"

"Decision?" He stroked his chin.

I threw up my hands in exasperation. "Are the pictures good enough for you? Will you do the project with me?"

Ezra sat there, staring at my face for several long seconds. My cheeks began to burn and I had to break eye contact with him before I either slapped him or started to like him. I'm not sure which would have been worse.

"I'll do it," he finally said.

I let out a huge breath, meeting his gaze again. "Really?"

"Yeah, if you'll keep coming to my games and taking pictures."

"What?" I squealed. There was no way I could stand to go to any more of his ridiculous games. "Surely I got enough decent shots last night for you to use in your application, didn't I?" My shoulders began to knot up.

"You got decent ones, sure, but I need better than decent. I need good, and those weren't good." He scooted his chair back and crossed his ankle over his knee.

"What do you mean they weren't good?" I grit through my teeth.

How could he be so insulting? What did he know about good photography? He never did anything in class.

"I said what I said." He took another sip.

"How many more games?

"I don't know. I'll keep you posted." He trailed a finger around the rim of his mug, getting more whipped cream on his finger, which he then proceeded to lick off. My eyes trailed every movement and I hated myself for it.

"What do you want from me, Ezra? Why are you doing this? Those pictures were fine." I huffed.

"Let me see the camera again." He reached

across the table.

I didn't know why he wanted it, but I gave it to him. After several long minutes of him going back through each picture again, he sat the camera on the table and turned it around so I could see the picture he had chosen. It was one of the team running the ball down the field.

"See, right here. How is any college supposed to know this is a picture of me? You got one of the whole team running. You can't even tell that I'm the one holding the ball. They need to be more obvious. This looks like you didn't want to be there and just took pictures of anything and everything that moved." His gaze met mine.

My chest tightened and I wanted to growl. "Of course I didn't want to be there, but you already knew that." I hissed.

Holding up a hand, he cut me off. "I can't hope to impress colleges if the photos I send them are crap. If you want me to do something I don't want to do, then you have to do the same. You can't come to the games and take pictures if they look like you were hating every minute of it. If you do, then you're no good to me."

My hands clenched in my lap. "Who are you to criticize how I take pictures? It's not like I can put you in a flat lay and set up the shot with props and great lighting. You wanted action shots. I gave you action shots. What else do you want?"

"I want your best work. Is that too much to

ask?" He shoved the camera back across the table.

I held it in my hands but didn't look at it. I didn't understand. It's not like I ran out there on the football field last night and told him how to catch a ball. Art was my thing. He had no idea what he was talking about.

He pushed back his chair and stood up. My gaze lifted to his face as I waited for more insults to come spewing out.

"You've got yourself a partner, but you have to uphold your side of our bargain, otherwise, I'm out," he said, shoving his hands into the pocket of his hoodie.

He had several twisted leather bracelets around his right wrist and I wanted to pull every one of them off and strangle him with them.

"Are you kidding me, after you talk to me like that, you expect me to work with you?" I asked in my most mocking voice.

He actually had the nerve to laugh. I glared at him.

Leaning down, he came eye to eye with me. *Why did he have to smell so good?* "I was being honest with you, and I have a feeling you don't get that a lot. I need pictures for college and you're my best shot at getting them. If you're willing to help me, then I'll help you."

My eyes narrowed into tiny slits. "Fine," I spat.

He held out his hand. I cringed at the thought of touching him, but I bit back my revulsion and reached forward, shaking his hand for the briefest of seconds. Jerking my hand back, I wiped my palm on my jeans.

Ezra didn't seem to notice.

"See you at school on Monday, partner." Turning on his heel, he left the coffee shop without another word.

I was fuming. *Fine, okay*, he had agreed to be my partner, but I felt like I'd still lost the contest anyway. How in the world was I going to work with Ezra if he criticized and insulted everything I did?

I turned the camera back on and three things hit me all at once, each one knocking the breath out of me as if I'd been punched.

1. Ezra had deleted every single photo I'd taken of him at the game.

2. He had secretly snapped a picture of me when I wasn't looking. In it, I was holding my coffee to my lips, my eyes sparkling with sheer joy as I took a sip. The background of the coffee shop was slightly blurred, making the whole effect of the photo feel cozy. Anyone could tell I was in pumpkin-spiced bliss.

But, the most infuriating, and surprising thing of all…

3. Ezra O'Neill was good at photography.

Like, really good.

I flung myself back in my chair, unable to move. I thought I'd be the one in charge of this project. Once we found out what the theme and required photos were, I'd planned to sit in my room and sketch out the entire design—*without* him. He was just supposed to tag along on the photoshoots, do exactly what I told him to, and not question my opinions at all.

My stomach twisted in even more knots. *Ezra was not going to play along the way I'd envisioned, was he?*

Any guy who would delete my photos like that was not going to just sit on the sidelines and wait until I told him he could play. This boy had the guts to fight against me and good ideas inside that pretty head of his, and I hated him even more for them.

His dimples were stupid.

His hair was stupid.

Everything about him made me want to vomit.

As I watched the rest of the whipped cream melt into a slimy sludge in my coffee, I became more determined than ever to make sure Ezra did not ruin this chance for me. Even if he did have an eye for photography, *I* was the artist.

This was *my* project.

If he was going to mess with me, then I'd make him regret it.

This was not over.

Not by a long shot.

CHAPTER FIVE

I SLAMMED MY BACKPACK down on the large black table in the art room the following Monday morning so hard, the pencil cup that sat in the middle, fell over, scattering drawing pencils everywhere.

"How dare you," I growled.

Lowering his pencil from where he'd had it poised against his upper lip, Ezra turned to look at me. "I get the feeling you're mad at me."

"Good guess, Sherlock. You come up with that one all by yourself?" I crossed my arms over my chest, my blood pounding in my ears.

Leaning on his elbow, he studied my face. "Well, I can't read your mind, Grant, so you might as well tell me what I did."

I pulled the camera out of my bag and waved it in his face. "You deleted them. All of them."

"Oh, that." He turned back to the math homework he'd been trying to finish before next period.

"What do you mean, oh that?" I demanded. "You don't delete photos off of someone else's camera. That's like...criminal."

"They were pictures of me. I had every right

to delete them if I didn't like them." He refused to look up from his notebook.

I reached over and slammed it shut.

Flinching, his head whipped towards me, eyes mere slits that cut across his face. He scowled. "What's your problem?"

I threw myself onto the stool next to him. "You're my problem. You said you'd only work with me if I took pictures of you at the game. I did. And you had the nerve to delete them so I would have to go to more games. How dare you?" I wanted to scream.

"I told you, they weren't good. I didn't want to use them. That's why they're gone." He tapped his pencil on the table.

I locked eyes with him and glared.

He continued to scowl too, somehow maintaining eye contact for longer than I expected, before turning and opening his notebook again. "You didn't say what you thought about the one picture I left behind."

I let out a high-pitched huff. People turned to stare at us, so I lowered my voice and leaned closer. "You mean the one you took of me?"

"So, what did you think, pretty good, huh?" Raising his eyebrows, he had the audacity to smirk at me.

"I guess it didn't completely suck." I admitted, as Mr. Shultz walked in.

Ezra didn't need to know what I really thought about his picture. I would go to my grave denying that it was anything more than *okay*. But the truth was, it was more than good. It was really good. *Beginner's luck, no doubt.*

"Okay class, if you're not already sitting with your contest partners, I suggest you get there. I have the official rules here, as well as the theme and photo list. One of you come get the details and then start planning your design. If you and your partner have opted not to participate," His gaze found me with a questioning look. "then continue the work on the black and white collages we started yesterday. You know where the cameras are." He dropped a stack of papers onto his desk.

Everyone started moving at once, gathering the forms and rearranging to work with their partners. I glanced at Ezra, waiting to see if he'd changed his mind.

Raising a hand, he gestured to the front of the room as if to say, "what are you waiting for?"

Letting out a huge breath of frustration, I marched up to Mr. Shultz's desk and snatched up both papers. When I returned to Ezra, he'd gone back to his math homework. Shoving the papers under his nose didn't seem to get his attention, so I dropped them on top of his notebook.

He closed his eyes and clenched his jaw, letting a slow series of breaths in and out. I was making him mad, but I didn't care. He was going to play ball with me. Or else.

"Okay." He opened his eyes, closed his

notebook and glared at me. "What do we do, group leader?"

His mocking tone didn't phase me at all.

Smiling, I read out the rules, quietly. The other teams had dispersed around the room, some were even sitting on the floor, so I could have talked as loudly as I wanted, and none of them would have overheard anything, but from that moment forward, they were our competition, and I was taking no chances.

"The annual Through the Lens competition will be held on Saturday, November 27th from 2:00-5:00 p.m. at the Providence Civic Center. All entries must be presented no later than a week prior to the judging. Each design entry must be completed with a partner, and both participants must be present at the judging to qualify. Three sets of partners will be awarded the prize for runners-up, each partner receiving a trophy and $500. The winning team will receive the grand prize trophy, $1000 each, and the honor of having their design piece placed on display in the Providence School of Design Museum for three months."

I paused, lifting my head to see if Ezra was still paying attention. He was staring at me, so I kept going.

"All photographs must be original and taken by the participating team members only. Each of the required theme photos must be included in the design. The theme must be adhered to completely. The dimensions of the final project can be no larger than four feet by three feet. Any additional desired mediums may be used in conjunctions with the photographs, so long as the photographs are the main focus of the piece. Color-grading is allowed. Failure to comply to these rules will result in a forfeit from the competition."

"Well, that sounds easy enough," Ezra said, once I'd finished.

"Are you kidding me?" My mouth fell open. "There are so many things to decide. Everything has to be perfect. Don't you get that?"

"Sure, but you can't have everything figured out before we even start. You have no idea how this is going to go, so how can you determine what perfect is going to look like?"

"Because this is my project. Mine. If I say it's going to be perfect, then it is. Just give me until tomorrow and I'll know exactly what we're doing." I leveled him with a hard glare that I hoped would convey my complete authority over the project. Or at least intimidate him.

What did he do?

He laughed.

I couldn't believe it. The jerk laughed in my face.

Something primal came over me then, and before I knew what I was doing, I backhanded him across the arm. *Hard.* So much so that my own hand was stinging.

"Ow." He reached for the spot on his bicep, a look of shock plastered on his face. His mouth was open when he said, "what is wrong with you?"

"You! Why are you trying to ruin this for me?" I hissed.

"Ruin it for you? How could I ruin this for you? By telling you you're not in charge, that this isn't just *your* project?" He scoffed, edging away from me.

"Yes."

"And, why's that?"

"Because this is my thing. You have no idea what you're doing. You're not an artist. I don't need your help in any way except to put your name on this and stand with me on the day." The words were out of my mouth before I could haul them back in.

Ezra jumped to his feet. "Mr. Shultz, can Bailey and I step out in the hall for a minute? I need to discuss something with my partner." He spit out the last word as if it tasted bad.

"Um, sure. Go ahead." Our teacher waved us towards the hallway.

Ezra marched for the door, wrenching it open. He held it, glaring at me while I walked past him.

"Look," he growled after closing the door and turning to me, "I know this thing is important to you, but you're not the only one involved here. I'm not going to put my name on anything that I'm not a part of, so if you think for one second that I'm just going to roll over and be your lapdog, you've got another thing coming. We're partners in this. You and Me. Together. This isn't just *your* project. It's ours. So, if you want a partner who's going to let you make all the decisions and not offer any input, or tell you when they think you're making a bad call, then you can march yourself right back in there and tell Shultz that we're done."

Breathing heavily, rage rippled from his tense shoulders as he clenched his fists at his side. I took a step back from the intensity with which his eyes were boring through me. No one had ever looked at, or spoken to me, like that before.

Who does he think he is?

I puffed out my chest. "Oh, this is exactly what you wanted, isn't it?" I took a brave step forward. "You get me so angry that I quit for you and then you can walk away and no one will blame you for calling it quits? You know, I was totally prepared to carry on with our partnership, but I should have known you'd do everything you could to sabotage it."

"Aahh! You are so selfish. Not everything is about you." He held both palm against his temples.

"Actually, when my future is on the line, it kind of is. If PSD is involved, I get to be selfish." I crossed my arms over my chest and clenched my teeth.

Ezra flung his arms wide. "PSD, PSD, PSD. I'm so freaking sick of hearing about that school. It's all you talk about. What do you do, cuddle up with their college catalog every night? Make out with the glossy pages? That's gotta be one hot relationship, Grant. No wonder you don't have a boyfriend."

I gasped. "How would you know that I—"

"It's not that hard to figure out. You blush every time I tease you about it, and after spending time with you, I can't imagine any guy could stand having you boss them around all the time?" He glared at me.

Fighting back the tears that threatened to spill out, I said, "how dare you. You don't know anything about me and you don't have the right to judge my choices, romantic or otherwise. Providence is my dream and I'll do whatever it takes to get there. Maybe you don't have dreams, but I do, and nothing you say is going to stop me, or stand in my way, you conceited *jerk*." I held my head high, despite the way I was starting to shake all over.

"Excuse me, you think *I'm* the jerk? I have dreams, thank you very much. Big ones. But I'm not hanging all my hopes on one thing that might not even happen. Tell me, what will you do if you don't get in there? What becomes of the great Bailey Grant and her perfect plans, then?" He inched towards me, forcing me to back up slowly.

"There is no other option." I swallowed hard. "I have to get in."

"You are the most infuriating person I've ever met." He growled.

"Right back at you." I growled back.

"Do you hear how idiotic you sound, right now? You've got your heart so set on one thing that you're not even open to the possibility that something really good might staring you right in the face, but it's not what you want so it's not even an option." He moved closer and I had a feeling we weren't just talking about colleges.

His words were hitting too hard, but I couldn't back down. "Because there is no other option. It's PSD, or nothing."

Ezra's eyes zeroed in on me. "That's the most ridiculous thing I've ever heard."

"Why?" I backed up, the intensity of his gaze making it hard to breathe. "Why do you even care?

"Because I...I care, okay?" He advanced towards me. My back pressed up against the line of lockers as he paused, placing both his palms against the wall on either side of my head. "You always need to have a plan B. Plan A's don't always work out and if you've got everything riding on them, then you have nothing to catch you if they fail. No one walks onto a football field without pads or a helmet because they're so confident in their own skills that they don't protect themselves. That's just asking for trouble."

Ezra was only a hands-breadth away from me by that point. His closeness made my pulse shudder. My mind whirled. If Tori had been there, she would have told me to kiss him. Just lean forward those last few inches and kiss him. Maybe it would make us both forget what we were fighting about.

As if he knew what I was thinking, Ezra licked his lips, drawing my attention to them even more. I wondered if they would feel as soft as they looked. Inching forward a fraction, I debated for another half a second, before his mouth turned into a taunting smirk.

Clenching my jaw tight, I shoved away any romantic feelings that might have been bubbling the surface. Why had I ever thought he was cute, or *kissable*? Ezra was just the guy I needed to help me complete this project. Nothing more.

I leveled him with a hard glare. "We're not on the football field, so save your little pep talk for someone who needs it."

Closing his eyes, Ezra dipped his head. When he lifted his gaze back up, his eyes locked with mine, but softer that time. "Are you applying anywhere else?" His voice was pitched low.

"Of course. I'm not as stupid as you think I am. But, Providence is the dream. I have to get in there, and winning this contest would surely guarantee me a place." I pushed off the lockers, forcing him to straighten up and drop his arms to his sides.

Stuffing his hands in his pockets, he hung his head. "I don't think you're stupid. I think you're scared."

"Why would I be scared?" Ice dropped into my stomach. *How can he know me so well?* Was I that easy to read?

"Because you're not used to coming in second best. You think your ideas are the only ones that matter, because you've always won. But now, you're afraid that maybe PSD won't see you as the best. Otherwise, you would be confident that your application, and the portfolio I assume you already sent them, will be enough to win them over. Instead, you're hanging everything on this competition. If you were as sure of yourself as you pretend to be, you wouldn't need it, and yet, here we are, arguing in the hallway because you're too scared to let anyone else have a part in this. You think I don't know anything about photography. You're convinced that my ideas will be horrible, and so you've already decided you won't even consider them. Tell me I'm wrong."

I'd had enough. Tears were beginning to form behind my eyes and I wasn't about to stand in the hallway and cry in front of Ezra. So, even though he was dead right, I opened my mouth and lied to him. "You have no idea what you're talking about."

"Oh, I think I do." His voice dripped with

sarcasm.

"No, you don't." My voice finally broke.

Ezra leaned in again, so close that time that he and I were sharing the same breath. "Fine. You're not scared, but this is still a group project. You and me. Together. The next time you try to take over, or tell me I don't know anything, it's over. Got it?"

"Got it." I whispered, dropping my gaze to the floor.

Ezra turned around and began pacing back and forth across the hall for what felt like an eternity, clutching his head and taking deep breaths. Finally, he stopped. "Okay, what's on the list? What do we have to do?"

I pulled the crumpled paper from where I'd shoved it into my pocket. Unfurling it, I read to him the list of required photos, along with the theme.

He groaned. "Oh, you have got to be kidding me."

CHAPTER SIX

20TH ANNUAL THROUGH THE LENS COMPETITION

ELIGIBILITY: HIGH SCHOOL STUDENTS AGEd 15 18
THEME: AUTUMN IN NEW ENGLAND

REQUIRED PHOTOS

1. CAMPFIRE
2. FOLIAGE
3. PUMPKINS
4. APPLES
5. CORN MAZE OR HAY RIDE
6. APPLE CIDER OR OTHER THEMED HOT BEVERAGE
7. BAKED GOODS
8. FLANNEL
9. FOOTBALL
10. HALLOWEEN
11. ACORNS
12. S'MORES OR ROASTED MARSHMALLOWS
13. DECORATED STREET SCENE
14. FALLEN LEAVES
15. LOW LIGHT/NIGHTTIME WITH FOCAL

POINT LIGHT SOURCE

"There's no way we can get this all done" Ezra growled. I've got football. I don't have time for this."

"What do you want me to do about it?"

"I don't know. I mean, I thought the theme would be something like historical buildings, or life in a coastal town. You know, something we could get done in like, a weekend, but these things are so specific, like Halloween, that's weeks away. I wouldn't have agreed to this whole thing if I'd known it meant having to spending so much time—" he cut himself off, his face going bright red.

"So much time with me? That's what you were going to say, wasn't it? You don't want to do this project because it means spending time with me." Tears welled behind my eyes again. "You already insulted me for having dreams and for *not* having a boyfriend; and you certainly like telling me what you think I'm thinking, but this is cold, even for you. Do you really think I'm that horrible?"

"That's not what I meant. It's just that..." His face had deepened to a dark crimson and he fumbled about with his hands like he couldn't decide where to put them.

"I know exactly what you meant." I turned away from him so he wouldn't see the tear slip down my cheek. I wiped it away quickly. "If this is how it's going to be working with you, then you'd probably be doing us both a favor if you did quit. I don't need this."

Ezra sighed and stepped closer behind me. I could almost feel his breath on the back of my neck.

"No." He paused so long that I though that was all he was going to say, but then he cleared his throat and continued, "if I tell someone I'm going to do something, I do it, whether I want to, or not."

I turned around slowly, causing him to take a step back. "Somehow, that doesn't make me feel any better, but if we're going to do this, we've got eight weeks. We can't spend the whole time fighting. We've got to make a plan."

"I know." His gaze fell to the floor.

The door to the art room burst opened at that moment, causing us both to jump.

Mr. Shultz was staring at us. "Bailey, I just got an email from Mrs. Hudson. The cast is ready to start rehearsing with the cow tonight and I think the finishing touches you put on it yesterday have dried by now. Ezra, you don't mind helping her carry it across the courtyard to the theater do you? Thanks." He disappeared back in the classroom before either of us could answer him.

Ezra stood with his mouth hanging open. "Uh…what was that about a cow?"

"Forget it. I can move it by myself." Walking down the hall, I eased open the door to the supply closet, where we'd been keeping *Milky White* when I wasn't working on it.

"I'm sorry, did he just say *cow*? Carry the *cow* across to the theater?" Ezra followed closely at my elbow.

I let out a huge sigh. "Yes, that's what he said. The drama club needed a life-size calf for *Into the Woods*, and I got the unfortunate task of making them one. Go ahead and laugh if you want. I'm sure it will give you a great story to tell all your buddies later." I turned on the light, basking the cow in question in the eerie glow of an ancient light bulb.

"Whoa, there really is a cow in here." Ezra walked past me into the closet, examining the animal from every angle.

"Yep." I leaned against the doorframe, wishing he'd go away. This would be a lot easier without him mocking me at every turn.

"This is really good, Grant." He glanced at me. "Can you do any other animals: elephants, horses, giraffes?"

I wished I could slap the grin off of his face, but I didn't think hitting him again would be the best idea. "Shut up. This is what they asked for, so it's what I made. Now, it really isn't that heavy, so please move so I can take it over to the theater."

I walked in and wrapped my arms around the cow's middle. I had added a handle for moving it short distances across the stage, but I didn't want to chance carrying it very far that way. I grunted, picking it up, and realizing it was much heavier than I thought it would be.

"Wait, no, I'll help. Here." Ezra reached for the cow, grabbing it by the head.

"Careful, the mouth opens." I warned him, just as the jaw unhinged in his face, causing him to shriek.

Grinning with satisfaction, I grabbed the back end, and we walked the cow out of the closet. I kicked the door closed behind us. Ezra walked backwards down the hall, pushing open all the doors with his back unit we were outside. The air was cold and it was starting to rain.

"Hurry," I urged "the paint will run if it gets wet."

Ezra started moving more quickly, and I had to get a better grip as I tried to keep up with him. Even backwards the guy was fast. When we got to the grey metal door at the back of the stage, he pushed, but nothing happened.

"You got a key for this thing?"

"No, it should be unlocked. It's just a little sticky sometimes." The rain was starting to come down even harder. We had to get inside.

"Here." Ezra handed me the cow and pushed his whole body into the door. After three strong shoves, it flew open, causing him to stumble inside. Luckily, his time on the football field seemed to have trained him to have good balance so, whereas I would have fallen flat on my face, he merely took a couple of steps to steady himself.

Turning, he grabbed the front of the cow again and we hurried inside, the door slamming shut at our heels. The stage was dark and creepy with the set pieces for the show sitting in odd places behind the curtains and in the wings.

I knew where most of them were since the Art Club—of which I was president—were the ones who came over after school to paint them. However, with no lights on, and the wind whistling through the old, high windows as the rain pelted the metal roof high above our heads, the shadows of the set pieces and exposed wooden frames were enough to make my spine tingle.

"This way. Follow me." My voice echoed in the cavernous space.

"Follow you where?" Ezra asked. "I can't see anything."

Closing my eyes to let them adjust to the darkness, I said, "Up the stairs and then we'll just set it in the middle of the stage. They can do what they want with it tonight."

"Okay. Lead the way."

We both moved slowly up the stairs.

"Ow." Ezra winced and I felt the cow shudder on his side. "Ow," he moaned again, knocking his shin into the stairs.

"Just two more." I said in between his yelps of pain. I almost felt bad for him. Almost.

"If you say so—OW!" He moaned.

I had to stifle a laugh. "How are you able to play football if you can't even walk up the stairs without tripping over everything?"

"I don't play football in the pitch black." His voice shook the curtains around us as we slipped through the wings and emerged onto the center of the stage where the emergency lights made it a lot easier to see. He stopped, his mouth falling open. "Wow, this is amazing." He breathed.

"Have you never been here before?" I gently lowered my end of the cow down to the floor.

Ezra did the same, stepping past me and moving to the front of the stage. "No. Not since the second grade spelling bee, which I lost, so not a high point for me."

Cringing at the memories he'd just stirred up, I approached him, gazing out over the empty auditorium. "Oh, I hated those spelling bees. I never won either."

"Looks like we have at least one thing in common." Ezra turned his head towards me.

I met his gaze. Something inside me sparked and I wasn't sure what to do about it.

"Look, I'm sorry for what I said to you. I had a fight with my dad this morning and I guess I'm still a bit on edge." He turned towards me. "I didn't mean that I didn't want to work with you, I just meant that I didn't realize it would take up so much time." He paused, running a hand through his hair. "And, I'm sorry about the whole boyfriend thing. I really don't have much room to talk since I'm single myself."

"So did Casey dump you?"

Pain etched his face. "She cheated on me, okay. Apparently, I'm too nice and she wanted someone bad…so she spent her summer with…and I… well, here we are."

"I've heard that about you," I said, immediately wanting to take it back.

His head snapped to me. "What? You heard she cheated on me with some college guy? Great! It's probably all over school by now."

I took a step towards him. "No, I heard that you were a nice guy." I licked my lips and took another step. "I've been complaining about you a lot over the past couple of days and even my brother said that you weren't the type of guy who'd be trying to humiliate me."

"I'm not." He shoved his hands in his pockets, shaking his head.

"You're not a nice guy?" I asked.

A smile broke across his face. "No. I wasn't trying to humiliate you. I'm still not trying. And, about the nice guy thing…well, I guess you'll have to figure that one out for yourself."

I thought for a moment. "I'm starting to see it, and I'm sorry too, for the things I said. I think I got mad because I've just been so stressed."

"No? You're stressed? I couldn't tell." He smirked.

"Yeah, well." I glanced around the stage. "You said you and your dad were fighting this morning. Are you okay?"

He seemed thrown by my concern. Turning away from me, he began to walk among the set pieces. "Yeah, I'm fine. You're not the only one stressed about college right now."

"Is that what you argued about?"

Why was I so interested?

"It's what we always fight about, but no this morning it was actually about you." He stopped walking and looked at me.

"Me?" I shrieked. My stomach dropped.

"Well, not you exactly, but this contest. I told him I was going to do it and he told me I was being stupid and to tell you no. But I told him I'd already promised, and I don't break my promises."

I didn't know what to say. He really was a nice guy and I'd yelled at him. "Thank you." I felt like I should hug him or something, but I didn't move.

"Forget it." He shoved his hands into his pockets as he walked behind Rapunzel's tower. "Did you help make all this?

"Yes, the Art Club always makes the sets."

"Art Club. Right." He headed towards a fake tree in the corner.

"They're good." He ran his hand along the low, painted branches. "I might have to come see this play. Are you going?"

The cold theater was suddenly way too hot. "Of course. I always do. Tori's in it." I cleared my throat. "Um, we better get back. Class is almost over."

"Right." He let out a sigh, as if leaving was the last thing he wanted to do.

I couldn't help smiling to myself.

Back at the stairs, I was stepping down when a hand latched onto my shoulder.

"Eep!" I shrieked.

"Sorry." Ezra was so close his breath tickled the back of my neck. "I can't see and really don't want to fall down the stairs. Coach would kill me if I broke my leg and couldn't play. I can't even imagine what my dad would say."

My heart began to race. I kept my steps slow, reaching for the handrail to steady us. Ezra's fingers dug into my collarbone and after we'd gone down two steps, he wrapped his other hand around my arm, stumbling behind me.

"You okay?" I asked.

His grip tightened and I stopped walking for a moment trying not to think about his hands on me.

I failed miserably.

"Yep, I'm good." I could almost hear a grin in his voice.

When I reached the bottom, I thought he'd let me go, but he didn't. Holding my hands out in front of me, I fumbled for the door. As my fingers met cold metal, I pulled on the handle, but the wind outside was keeping the door shut. I tugged and tugged, grunting.

"What's wrong?" Ezra was practically pressed

up against my back.

"The door's stuck." I yanked on it again.

"Let me try." His arms came around me. Hands, big and rough grazed over my fingertips. I jolt of electricity shot through my veins. "On the count of three. One...two...three."

We both pulled as hard as we could. The door flew open, causing us to stumble backwards. Ezra's back hit the side of the stairwell with a loud thud as I fell against his chest. His arm came around me, a hand landing on my stomach, keeping us both upright.

He let out a low moan.

"Sorry." I pushed myself off him. "Are you okay?"

"Yeah," he wheezed, straightening up and then bending forward, holding his side. "I got the wind knocked out of me. I think I'm okay now."

"You ready to go?" I tried to make my voice sound as if I hadn't been at all phased by his hand on my stomach, but I'm not sure it worked.

"Lead the way." He clutched his side.

I moved to the door and groaned. The rain was coming down in sheets by that point and neither of us had worn a jacket.

"I hope you're okay getting wet, because we're about to be drenched."

I was very, very thankful that I'd gone with the orange t-shirt that morning, and not the white one I'd been considering, especially since I'd put on my floral bra.

"I've been wet before." Ezra laughed. "Come on."

I hesitated.

He stepped out, then turned around, rain dripping from the ends of his hair. His blue shirt had instantly plastered itself to his chest which was way more muscular than I would have thought. Not that I'd been imagining Ezra's toned abs. Heat rose to my cheeks as stared at him.

"Let's go." He reached for me, fingers closing around my wrist. Pulling me along next to him, we ran across the courtyard. I slipped once on the slick stones, but his arm went taut, his hand gripping like a vice to keep me from falling.

"Thanks." I panted once we'd reached the other side and made it safely through the doors. We stood breathless, dripping on the tiles. I wrapped my arms around myself for warmth, and to cover my chest as soon as I saw Ezra's gaze drift in that direction.

"Any time." He shook the water from his hair and tugged his shirt away from his chest with a squelch.

Awkward silence followed, as it became obvious that neither of us was going to say anything else. Walking back to the art room, we made it just as the bell rang. No one seemed to notice how wet we were as they pushed past us to get out.

"Here," Ezra said, as we hurriedly gathered up our things.

I glanced up through stringy, wet hair to see him holding a hoodie out to me.

"What?"

"You need it more than I do." He gestured to my soaked shirt.

I glanced down, gasping. The floral bra was very, very visible. I wrapped my arms around myself.

"Take it. You can give it back to me later." He was trying very hard not to look at my chest.

I snatched the hoodie from him and turned around, throwing it over my head. Pushing the sleeves up so I could reach the hair tie from my wrist, I pulled all my dark hair into a soggy, wet bun on top of my head.

When I turned around, he tilted his chin towards the hoodie, smiling. "It looks good on you."

Glancing down, I realized that Ezra hadn't just handed me any old hoodie. He'd given me his team hoodie. The ones that only the football players—or their *girlfriends*—wore. I sucked in a breath. Everyone was going to see me in it, but what choice did I have? Even if I only wore it to my locker and swapped it for my jacket, too many people would know, and I'd have to show the entire Senior Hall my bra in order to make the switch anyway. No, I had to leave it on until I dried off. I had no other choice.

"Of all the hoodies." I groaned.

"Sorry, it's all I had with me. It's clean if that's

what you're worried about. My mom just washed it."

"Everyone's going to be staring at me." I rolled the sleeves up so I could pick up my books.

"They'd be staring even more if you walked out there without it. Trust me." He started laughing.

"This is so embarrassing." My whole body grew hot.

"But funny."

"Maybe for you. You're not the one who's wearing crazy underwear for the whole school to see." I followed him out the door. "I'll give the hoodie back to you tomorrow."

"Fine." He grinned.

"Or later today."

"Fine."

Fear gripped my heart and I grabbed his arm. "Please don't tell anyone it's yours."

His brow creased. "Why not?"

I didn't have time to explain it all to him. "Because everyone will be asking questions anyway, and it will just be easier if it's our secret."

"I don't understand?" His shoulders hunched and he stared at the floor.

"Everyone will be talking about us."

He lifted his head. "So? Is that a problem?"

"Yes."

"Why?"

"Because they'll all think we're—" I gestured back and forth between us, hoping he'd get the hint.

"Oh. Well, we wouldn't want that, now would we?" Ezra's expression turned hard, the smile that had been there a few seconds before, now completely gone.

"No." I swallowed hard. "Especially since it's not true."

"Right." Ezra turned, backing me up until I was against the wall. Leaning forward and lowering his voice, he said, "I guess Casey's not the only one who doesn't want a nice guy, because that's all I was trying to be, but don't worry, I won't ruin your precious reputation."

My chest clenched. "Ezra, I didn't mean—"

He shook his head, but didn't say another word as he turned and disappeared down the hall.

CHAPTER SEVEN

MORE THAN ONE SIDEWAYS glance and opened mouth greeted me as I walked down the hall to my locker, but no matter how many people whispered my name, I couldn't shake Ezra's words:

I guess Casey's not the only one who doesn't want a nice guy, because that's all I was trying to be.

That's not what I'd meant at all. Didn't he understand that wearing his hoodie was like wearing a huge neon sign that screamed: *Notice me*?

Sure enough, before I'd even had time to pull my Chemistry book from the top shelf, head cheerleader and Ezra's ex, Casey Turner, appeared at my elbow.

"Where'd you get that?" She demanded, sucking on a tooth.

I jumped, my heart leaping into my throat. "None of your business." I closed my locker.

She stepped in my way. "It's not yours."

My jaw clenched. "And yet, here I am wearing it."

How could she cheat on Ezra like that? I wanted to cause her much physical pain.

She had probably worn that hoodie many times before me. And here she was feeling all territorial towards it. But I wasn't going to let her get to me. She didn't know it was his. I could be anyone's.

Over her shoulder, I watched Ezra opened his own locker, pulling out books as he threw glances at me. I know I'd asked him not to tell anyone that the hoodie was his, but I wished he would just march down here and tell Casey to back off.

He didn't.

As he slammed his locker shut and walked away, Casey's eyes narrowed. "Just tell me where you got it."

"Um, no." I tried to move around her.

She blocked my path again.

"What is your problem?" I pushed the sleeves up. "I didn't steal it, if that's what you're worried about."

"I don't believe you."

"Too bad."

Her eyes roved over me. "You really expect me to believe that one of the football players gave it to you? That's the stupidest thing I've ever heard."

"What's the matter, Casey, jealous that you don't have one of your own to wear anymore?" I smirked. It felt good defending Ezra for some reason.

"Ha," she scoffed, "I can have one any time I

want."

"Then go get one." I stepped to the side and walked past her.

"Which one did you have to sleep with to get it?" She called after me.

Anger rose up so fast I thought I was going to explode. I whirled around, but Tori caught my elbow.

"Don't. Just leave it." She pulled me across the hall and into the Chemistry classroom.

I was speechless. I couldn't believe Casey had said that to me. In the hallway. In front of everyone.

"But, she…"

Tori wrapped her arm around me and led me to our seats. "It'll only cause more of a scene. Just ignore her. She jealous, and jealous people are always stupid. Don't stoop to her level."

I sat down, taking deep breaths and wishing that none of this had ever happened.

She leaned in close, whispering, "How *did* you get Ezra's hoodie?"

My head whipped to her.

She gave me a long side-eye. "I told you he was flirting with you, but this is fast, especially for you."

"Not now." I grit through my teeth as I pulled the hood up over my wet hair and wished I could disappear into the floor.

All day long, I fielded questions:

Whose hoodie was it?

Where had I gotten it?

Was I was having a secret romance with one of the football players?

I told everyone that it wasn't their business, and left it at that. Too bad they all knew I was hiding the truth, and my refusal to spill the beans only seemed to fuel them with more questions.

Walking into fifth period English, however, was the worst. Ezra was sitting in his seat, his jaw tightly clenched. He had an arm resting on his desk with a fisted hand propped against his mouth. Glancing up when I walked in, his eyes instantly locked with mine. He flinched, his entire body stiffening before he turned, and looked away.

Taking my seat, I pulled the strings on the hoodie so tight I almost choked myself. Coughing, I glanced at him again. Ezra was leaning back in his chair, not smiling, but still staring at me. There was so much tension between us in that moment, it was like neither of us could break free. For the rest of class, I kept finding my eyes wandering in his direction, while he stole glances of me. If we happened to look at the same time, he would either hold the gaze and bite his lip, or turn away so fast I had to question whether he'd actually looked at me at all.

It was pure torture.

I tried to catch up with him after class to

give him back the hoodie and talk to him, even though I had no idea what I was going to say, but he ran off—*literally*—he jogged across the room and out the door so fast I couldn't follow him. I waited around at the lockers after school too, but he never showed up there either. I didn't know what I was going to do.

Soon, Casey appeared, again. "What's the matter, did your little football player tell you to meet him here? Ah, poor thing. He's just messing with you. All the boys are at practice."

I closed my eyes, biting my tongue.

She giggled, her friends Courtney and Shawna laughing right along with her.

I wanted to die. I was so humiliated, I turned and ran down the hall and out of the school, their laughter chasing me.

How had little old me putting on one maroon hoodie caused such a shift in the space time continuum. I mean, it was just a hoodie for crying out loud.

Luckily, when I came in the door at home, Mom didn't ask too many questions.

"Well, that was very nice of him," she said, after I explained to her what had happened.

"I know. I would have been really embarrassing to have had to walk around soaking wet all day."

"I'm sure." A huge smile broke out on her face.

"What?"

"So, do you like this boy?" She turned around,

adding garlic and onions to a large pan on the stove.

"Mom, no, he's just my project partner. That's it. I swear." I couldn't control the shake in my voice.

"Mm-hmm." She stirred the sizzling pan with a large wooden spatula.

"Seriously. I mean it." My pulse was racing and I felt like pulling my head inside the hoodie and hiding forever. Mom had that uncanny ability to make any prying into my social life feel like I was on trial. Like I should be ashamed of things I hadn't even done yet.

"If you say so, dear," she said, pulling a huge package of hamburger from the fridge.

When she stepped out of the door to take the wrappings to the outside trash can, I grabbed a leftover apple turnover from the container on the counter and ran upstairs before she could ask me any more questions. I didn't want to talk about Ezra, or the hoodie, ever again.

Inside my room, I tore it off, hugging it to my chest and trying not to cry. My shirt was still a little bit damp and felt cold against my skin. Since the moment I'd put the hoodie on, I had gotten more attention than I'd ever had at that school in my entire life. People had noticed me when I wore it, but they had also thought things about me.

Things that weren't true.

Things I didn't want them to think, which

was why I would never wear it again.

Ever.

The only good thing about it was how comfortable it was... and also the smell.

While I would have thought the hoodie was something Ezra slung on after practices or games, I had honestly expected it to carry the scent of a sweaty, musty guy, but *oh my word* was I dead wrong.

Ezra O'Neill smelled so good.

I inhaled deeply as I clutched it to myself. Whatever cologne he wore was about the finest thing I'd ever had near my nose. It was intoxicating.

When I finally stopped sniffing it, I threw the hoodie over the chair by my bed and grabbed the big, chunky cardigan I wore around the house when it was cold. Mike always said it looked like someone had tried to shave a teddy bear, but I didn't care. I loved it.

Even with the comfy familiarity of my old cardigan, trying to focus on my homework was like trying to breathe underwater.

Impossible.

I kept glancing over my shoulder and seeing Ezra's hoodie on the chair, mocking me. I couldn't shake the look on his face that morning when he told me what had happened with him and Casey. It made me wonder how many people he'd confessed that to.

But then, I also thought about the looks

he'd worn during English class. I replayed all the conversations I'd had that day in my head, over and over again. I cringed at all the hateful, mean things that Casey had said to me.

Tori just said she was jealous, but of what? It's not like she knew it was Ezra's.

Halfway through my math homework, I couldn't take it anymore. Picking up my phone, I texted Mike.

> do you have Ezra's number

no why

> do you know where he lives

candy apple house

> really??

yep what's going on?

> tell ya later thanks

Running downstairs, I pulled on my boots and was out the door before Mom could stop me. I ran down the street and then two more blocks behind our house. Although I hadn't known it at the time, Ezra's house had been a favorite trick-

or-treating stop for Mike and I when we were little. His mom's candied apples were legendary.

I made it to the tall hedge that ran next to his driveway before I paused, still having no idea what I was going to say, but I couldn't turn back now. I was committed. Taking a deep breath, I turned into the driveway...and ran right into Ezra.Like literally ran into him. So hard that I actually lost my balance and fell, landing hard on my butt in the middle of his driveway.

"Ow," I moaned.

"Hey, watch where you're—oh, it's you." He bent forward, catching his breath and clutching his side. I wondered if he was still sore from where he'd smacked the handrail in the theater. "What are you doing here?" He growled.

Standing up, I brushed myself off, hoping my face wasn't as red as other parts of me probably were at that moment. "Are you okay?"

Ezra straightened up, his face going rigid. "Don't worry, you can't hurt me."

Somehow, I didn't think we were just talking about the way we'd plowed into each other. "I'm sorry," I said.

"It's fine. What are you doing here?" He grabbed the trash bin he'd been pulling down the driveway, and wheeled it out onto the curb.

"I came to apologize." I swallowed around a lump in my throat. "About this morning."

"Don't worry about it. I'm a big boy. I'll get over it." He shoved his hands in his pockets and wouldn't look me in the eye.

I had hurt him worse than I thought.

Taking a step forward, I reached out, wanting to touch him, but instead, put my hands in my pockets, too. "When I asked you not to tell anyone about the hoodie, it wasn't because I was ashamed to admit you'd given it to me."

He glanced up. "Then what did you mean, because all I heard was that you'd be embarrassed if anyone found out it was mine?"

Sighing, I took another step closer. "Aren't you worried?" I blurted out.

"About what?" He pulled his hands from his pockets and crossed his arms over his chest.

"Being seen with me." I hung my head, unable to make eye contact. "Letting people know that you gave me your hoodie."

"*Loaned*." He paused. "I loaned you my hoodie. I do want it back at some point." Stooping to meet my gaze, he continued. "Why would that bother me?"

Turning away, I bit my lip. "I don't know. I just thought that maybe you'd want to keep this whole project thing a secret. I mean, if people start seeing us together they might get the wrong idea."

"You mean like we're...dating?" His voice shook a little.

"Yeah." I finally turned, looking up at him. "Or worse. Casey practically attacked me when she saw it."

He looked anywhere but at me. "Does she know?"

"No, I didn't tell her." I kicked a pebble with my shoe. "Ezra, you're not a girl, so maybe you don't understand, but the only people at the school who wear those hoodies are you guys… and your girlfriends. No one else. Wearing it today said something. It wasn't just Casey who wanted to know which football player I was…" I couldn't say the rest, at least not without feeling sick to my stomach.

"Oh." His eyes grew wide. "*Oh.*"

"Now, do you understand?" I hoped my cheeks weren't as red as they felt.

"Yeah. I think I do." His face was scarlet, too. "I didn't think about that. I swear. Listen, don't mind Casey. She's crazy, but basically harmless."

"And your ex."

His jaw clenched. "Don't remind me."

"What did you ever see in her anyway? No offense, but she's kind of terrible."

Ezra flinched. "I don't know. Our families are really close and we grew up together. It was easy to be with her I guess. I don't know."

"Did you love her?" I slammed my hand over my mouth, wishing the ground would open up and swallow me whole.

He snorted. "No! I didn't even care when we broke up. I was more upset that she'd cheated on me than I was hurt. I should have broken up with her way before that."

"Still." I dropped my hand and took a step towards him. "You didn't deserve to be treated like that."

Ezra gave me a tight-lipped smile. "Thanks." He paused, his face becoming serious. "And, hey, just so you know, I didn't tell anyone about the hoodie because you asked me not to. But, I'm not embarrassed of you, or this project, or having anyone know it's mine."

"You're not?" My insides were heating up all at once, like molten lava had been poured over me.

"No, why did you think I would be?" He took a step closer.

"Because you're football and I'm Art Club. I know where I stand on the school's popularity charts and it's nowhere near you, believe me." I met his gaze, which softened the more I talked.

A grin spread across his face. "That didn't seem to bother you when you jumped me at my locker the other day."

I laughed. "Yeah, sorry about that. I was a little worked up."

"I know. I've never seen anyone with such a wild look in their eye. I can't stop thinking about it." He cleared his throat like he hadn't meant to say that. "Um...look, I don't care what people think about any of this, and working with you is not going to ruin my street cred or anything. Everything's cool, okay?"

"Okay. Hey, can I have your number?"

Ezra raised an eyebrow.

My pulse quickened. "In case we need to discuss the project, or something. I was going to call you tonight instead of coming over here, but I didn't have it."

"And yet, you knew where I lived." He stroked his chin. "Should I be afraid?"

"I asked my brother. He told me." I pulled out my phone.

Reaching for it, Ezra typed his number into it. "Oh, right. Tell Mike I said hi."

"I will." He dialed his number from my phone.

Pulling his own phone from his back pocket, he saved my number too, which I must admit, made my stomach flutter a little.

Ezra O'Neill had my phone number.

"Well, I better get home for dinner." I put my phone back in my pocket and turned around. "See you later." I took a few steps before turning back around. "You really are a nice guy, just like everyone says."

"You're not so bad yourself, Grant. When you're not yelling at me."

"Bye."

"Bye."

I grinned all the way home.

CHAPTER EIGHT

SPAGHETTI AND GARLIC BREAD were waiting for me when I walked into the kitchen.

"There you are. We were starting to get worried," said Mom, as I plopped into my usual chair at the table.

"Sorry, I had to do something real quick." I reached for the tongs and dropped a heaping mound of pasta on my plate, before grabbing two slices of garlic bread.

Mike and I used to fight over the last slice of bread, but with him off to college, it was just me, Mom and Dad—on week nights, anyway—so no one stood between me and the last slice that night. But, it did make me miss my brother. I hadn't quite gotten used to him being gone yet.

After dinner, I went back upstairs, and that time, I was able to focus and get my homework done. I hopped in the shower, and had just finished blowdrying my hair when I noticed a message blinking on my phone.

My heart jumped into my throat when I saw that it was from Ezra.

want to go to the farm tomorrow

> ???

pumpkins are on that list right

> yeah

you want pumpkins

we got pumpkins

I had forgotten that Ezra's grandparents owned the big orchard and farm outside of town. In the autumn, they sold pumpkins, gourds, apples, and thousands of potted mums. We'd be sure to get a lot of good photos if we had the run of the place.

> are you kidding ????

> yes

great

see ya tomorrow

> tomorrow

The next day in Photography Class, Ezra and I discussed the layout of the farm and where we thought we might get the best photos for our project.

"There are these really rustic crates we could stack the pumpkins in, and wheelbarrows, if we want to go for that kind of thing. Or, my dad just got this old red chevy that we fixed up over the summer. Right now it's full of mums, but we could rearrange things if you like that idea better." Ezra babbled on and on about all the different photo-ops at his family's farm. He kept running his hands through his hair and playing with the bracelets on his wrist.

"I like the rustic crates idea." I rested my chin on my hand as he continued.

"Good. That will be much easier than moving everything out of the truck. Although, it is really cool. Maybe we could find a way to use it somehow. The red would stand out in the photos." He chewed his lip and made notes on a piece of paper.

"I like the idea of going rustic. It's popular right now and very autumnal-feeling. We could use wood as our background aesthetic for all the pictures even. I mean, we do have to have some sort of frame, or canvas to attach the photos to. It might look really cool." I paused for a moment as the wheels turned in my head. "Oh, oh, brilliant idea. What if we used the actual crates in our design? It would add a lot of texture and visual interest. Do you think your grandparents would let us have a couple to break apart and use?"

Ezra shrugged. "I don't see why not. There's always a few that are too broken to hold the pumpkins anymore. We keep them in the barn."

The large red barn was the centerpiece of the O'Neill family farm. Lots of kids went there to take senior pictures. It was iconic in our town.

"What if we kept something from every shoot we do, too? Not just the crate pieces, but a little piece of the photo itself. We could arrange the pictures with the wood scattered around in sort of a wacky frame that holds all the other objects as well." I was so excited, but Ezra's face was pinched.

"I'm not sure I see what you're talking about?"

I grabbed the pen from his hand and turned his notebook to a blank page. "I'm thinking this." I sketched what I had in my head, or at least a rough estimation of it.

"Oh." Ezra leaned forward. "I like it."

"You do?" Maybe getting him to agree to all my ideas wouldn't be so hard after all.

"Yeah, I think it will look really cool." He glanced up at me, his eyes more blue than usual.

I smiled, wondering why we'd been at each other's throats the day before when we could clearly work so well together. His smile turned into a laugh the longer we stared at each other.

"What?" I handed him back his pen, my cheeks growing hot.

"Your face just goes all crazy when you're creating things in your head."

Yep, my cheeks were on fire. "It does?"

"Yeah, but it's kind of cute." He chewed on his pen.

Cute, did he just call me cute? What is happening? Now, my whole body was way too hot. "Really?"

"Uh-huh."

I turned away. "Well, I bet you get goofy looks on your face when you're playing football."

He leaned against the table. "Okay, first of all, I never look goofy, and second of all, even if I did, I wear a helmet, so no one would ever see it."

"Sure, whatever you say."

"You don't believe me?" He grinned.

I ginned back. "Nope."

"What do you want to bet?" He laced his fingers together.

"Huh?"

"What do you want to bet that I do not get a goofy look on my face when I'm playing football?" He repeated.

I tilted my head to the side. "Nothing, because there's no way to prove it. Like you said, you wear a helmet."

"Okay, next game I'll go without a helmet. Then you'll see that I'm right."

"Yeah, like they'd let you do that." I tucked the design sketch into my bag. "It's too dangerous."

"Aw, Grant, you worried about me getting hurt?" He pursed his lips.

"No, I just—" My mouth went dry. Why were his lips so mesmerizing?

"You are worried. Just admit it. But, you're correct, it is against the rules, so I guess you'll just have to admit I'm right and leave it at that."

"Not gonna happen." I shook my head.

"I can't believe you don't trust me." He turned

away.

Patting him on his back, I said, "oh, I trust you. Just not about this."

His head whipped towards me and he went wide-eyed.

Shoving his pen into my hand, he said, "wait, hold on a second." Opening his notebook to a clean page, he tapped the paper. "Can I get that last statement in writing please. I feel like I might need to remind you of it later."

I rolled my eyes, laughing "Be serious."

"I am serious. This is a big moment for us. I can feel it, and it needs to be documented." He pushed the notebook closer to me.

Us. Did he say us? A big moment for *us*. Ezra and I didn't have moments and there certainly was no *us*.

He stared back at me, raising his eyebrows and pushing the notebook even closer. "I'll tell you what to write if you can't remember." He winked.

I was not getting out of this. I could tell. "Fine. What do you want me to say?"

"Well." He rubbed his chin. "I'd start with something like, Ezra is the best. Ezra has great ideas. Ezra is the hottest football player in the whole—"

I cut him off with an elbow nudge to the ribs. "I didn't say any of that."

"It doesn't mean you weren't thinking it." He pushed the paper closer. "You said you trust me." Laying his chin in his palm, he tapped the notebook with his forefinger. "Right there."

"You think you're so funny." I said, writing the words on the paper.

"Yes, I do." Closing the notebook, he shoved it into his backpack.

"So, what time should I meet you at the farm?" We hadn't discussed it and I wasn't sure when his football practice would be over.

"Oh, I brought my car today, so we can leave as soon as school's out. Why don't you meet me at my locker," he said.

My breath caught in my throat. Everyone would see us leave together. They'd talk. They'd know it was his hoodie I'd worn the day before.

He leaned forward, scanning my face. "Is that okay? Or are you still worried about what we talked about yesterday"

My palms started to sweat. "No, it's okay. I'll meet you after school."

"Great," he said. "I'm sure no one will notice anyway."

My stomach was in knots by the time I met Ezra at his locker that afternoon. I wished I had his hoodie to hide inside as we walked out of the school together.

I was right. People did stare at us. Casey Turner glared at us so hard I swear there was fire behind her eyes.

Ezra didn't seem to notice at all.

But I did.

Now, everyone knew it was his hoodie, and were probably thinking the same things Casey had.

Through the Lens was supposed to be about me impressing Providence School of Design. That's it. It was never supposed to do anything for my social life. No one was even meant to know about the contest, and when I won, they wouldn't know about that either. A new trophy would simply appear in the display case by the office, and no one would stop to look at it.

But like this... with Ezra.

Nothing was happening the way it was meant to. I had suddenly become painfully aware of everything I said, wore, or did because I knew everyone was watching and criticizing me.

I wished I had Ezra's confidence to not care what people thought about me, but I didn't. I had grown comfortable being invisible. It was all I'd ever known. Art was my voice, and I was used to letting it do all the talking.

I didn't know how to be the girl who was seen, and talked about, and stared at.

The more time Ezra and I spent together, I feared what being seen might do to me. Of all the people in class I could have been paired with, this partnership wasn't turning out to be anything like I'd planned.

Then again...

Glancing up at the boy walking beside me—and smiling down at me—I decided that being seen might not be so bad. Especially if he was the one doing the seeing.

CHAPTER NINE

AS EZRA DROVE US to his family's farm, I couldn't help thinking about my mom. She was one of those people who loved buying mums every autumn, but could never keep them alive from year to year, no matter where she planted them around our yard.

She'd even tried leaving them in pots and bringing them into the garage to keep them from freezing in winter.

She'd killed them all.

Every year.

Every single one of them.

Which meant that, every September, she would buy new ones and announce her big plans for keeping them alive that year. Dad, Mike and I had given up trying to convince her otherwise, but so far, in the seventeen years I'd been alive, her plans had never worked.

Despite Mom's black thumb, she and I had made annual trips to the O'Neill Farm to buy each year's victims ever since I was little. While there, we would also choose our pumpkins for the town carving contest, which was always held on October twenty-fifth and trust me, was a very big deal.

To win it meant you were basically royalty in Cedar Falls. There was even a picture of the winner and their pumpkin which went up on the wall at *Taylor's* where everyone could see and admire it.

I had always loved the O'Neill farm, but up until that moment, I had never associated it with Ezra. In fact, I'd never really given any thought to him at all. But that had all changed, and now I was driving to the farm with the O'Neill heir, himself.

Ezra didn't bring us in through the front entrance like I'd always done with Mom. He knew a back way that avoided the line of cars coming in to buy up all the pumpkins, and I liked his way even better.

The trees were still a couple of weeks away from full brilliant color, but as we drove through the bright red covered bridge that crossed a small stream, I couldn't help but stare at the side mirror, watching the wind from his jeep stir the fallen leaves on the road behind us. It was magical, like we'd entered an enchanted forest. I half expected fairytale creatures to appear from behind the tree trunks.

When the forest opened up and we got out first glimpse of the farm in the valley, it was so beautiful, I almost pulled the camera out and started taking pictures. Leaning forward to gaze out the windshield, a "Wow" escaped me.

"Like the view?" Ezra glanced sideways at me.

"It's amazing," I breathed, "I never knew this road was up here."

Laughing, he put on the most awful British accent I'd ever heard, and said, "that's the big O'Neill family secret, my dear. We don't mingle with the commoners unless absolutely necessary."

I covered my eyes with my hand. "That was terrible."

"What are you talking about, love, my accent is amazing." He carried on talking like that until he stepped on the brake as we came down a steep hill into the valley.

I tried to ignore the fact that he'd called me *love.*

He continued, back in his own voice, "actually, this was the old road into the farm before my grandparents turned it into a business. The delivery trucks couldn't get through the hills very well when the roads were washed out in the spring, or were icy in the winter, so they put in the other road. Now, only the family really uses this one."

"Well, I love it."

Ezra pulled the jeep up behind the big red barn in the middle of the farm. The paint was fresh on the outside, but the wooden beams were worn and weather-beaten. He led me over to the farm shop, and through the back door. The scent of baked goods wafted over us like a comforting blanket. I closed my eyes and inhaled deeply, my stomach growling.

"Come on." He tugged on my arm, leading me deeper into the shop.

Entering the kitchen, we saw three older women, covered in floured aprons, chopping apples and rolling out long sheets of pastry.

One of them glanced up from where she was peeling apples and her face lit up. "Ezra, what brings you here. It's not your day to work."

"Hey, Grandma." Ezra walked over and wrapped his arm across his grandmother's shoulders. She was much shorter than he was, but neither of them seemed to mind. "What would I have to do to get my hands on some of these?" He raised both eyebrows repeatedly in question as he jerked his head toward the trays of fresh-from-the-oven apple strudels.

"Introduce me to your friend, and you can have all you want." She pinched his cheek.

The cheek in question—and the other one—turned bright red as everyone in the room turned to stare at me. I felt my own face heat up in response.

"This is Bailey. She and I are doing a project for photography class at school and we need to take pictures and get some of the old crates from the barn," he said, running his hand through his hair.

Ezra's grandma acted as if she didn't really believe him, but she smiled anyway. "Ed is in the barn. He can help you with the crates. Take him a cup of coffee, will you?" She gestured to the machine on the counter.

"Sure." Ezra moved over to fill a mug with hot black coffee. "Want one?"

It took me a minute to realize he was talking to me. "Oh, yes, please."

"Here." He handed me a full cup and nodded to the tray next to the machine, which had a bowl of sugar and a jug of cold milk sitting on it.

I added both to the cup and stirred vigorously.

"Can you do mine too?" he asked, sitting another full cup in front of me before walking across the kitchen and grabbing two apple strudels from the tray on the counter. "Two sugars, lots of milk," he added.

Handing me a hot strudel, Ezra shoved the other one into his mouth and grabbed two of the cups off the counter. "Thanks, Grandma," he mumbled as we walked back outside.

"She seems nice," I said, taking the extra cup from him so he could pull the strudel from his mouth.

"Yeah, she's great. Have you ever had these before?" He gestured to the strudel.

"Are you kidding. Who hasn't? They're amazing." I took a bite. The hot, apple cinnamon filling hit my tongue with a pop as the buttery, flaky crust crackled between my teeth.

"Bet you've never had one this fresh,though.

I guarantee it. By the time they hit the shop, they're barely warm. Hot is the best way to have one of these bad boys." He took another huge bite.

"Wow, I feel so honored."

"You should. I don't share my grandma's strudel with just anyone." He winked.

I was in the middle of overanalyzing his words when we stepped into the barn and he called out, "Grandpa?"

"Ez, is that you?" A voice came from the deep recesses of the barn.

"Grandma sent coffee for you."

"Did you bring a strudel too?" His grandpa called back.

"Uh, no they weren't finished yet." Ezra turned to me, whispering, "eat fast."

I'd planned on savoring the strudel, but I shoved the last bite in my mouth and chewed frantically, instead. Brushing crumbs from my face and shirt, I took a sip of coffee to hide the grin that Ezra and I were sharing.

"Oh well, I'll head over in a bit. She always saves me one." Ezra's grandpa appeared, taking the coffee and looking me over with a lifted brow.

I had a feeling that Ezra didn't bring many girls to the farm. I couldn't imagine Casey ever wanting to come here. She might get her perfect clothes dirty.

"Grandpa, this is Bailey. We're doing a project for school and need some old fruit crates. You got any here that we could have?" He leaned against one of the wagons they used for the hayrides, crossing his feet at the ankles.

"Sure. There's some in the loft if you want to crawl up there and get them. They're all broken up, though." His grandpa sipped his coffee.

"Oh, that's actually better. We were hoping to break them apart for the wood" I chimed in.

Ezra's grandpa shrugged his shoulders. "Well, doesn't make any sense to me, but help yourselves. Be careful on the ladder."

"We will. Thanks, Grandpa." Ezra led the way to the back of the barn, where an old wooden ladder stood propped up into the hayloft.

"Not scared of heights are you?" He grinned, hoisting himself up.

"No." I couldn't say that heights were my favorite thing in the world, but I wasn't about to seem like a scaredy-cat in front of Ezra.

Slowly, I followed him up to the hay loft.

"Watch your step," he said as I came off the ladder.

"Whoa," I coughed from the dust we'd scattered, "and I thought Mike's room was a mess. This is…"

"An O'Neill family trait, I'm afraid. We keep everything." He kicked at the crates nearest us. "What do you think of these?"

I stepped closer to have a look. The crates all had the farm's logo stamped on at least one of the slats on each side. They had seen better days, but that didn't matter.

"They're great." I reached down and picked one up, examining it more closely.

"How many do you think we need?"

"Let's take four. If we need more, we can always come back, right?" I asked.

"Sure." Ezra bent to pick up three crates and stacked them together.

I'd never noticed the tight, corded muscles on his arms before that moment. Rolled up shirtsleeves suddenly moved up my list of things that made a guy look hot. Staring at Ezra lifting and moving the crates around made my stomach fill with butterflies.

"Can you carry any of these going back down?" He hoisted them all into his arms.

I forgot the question.

"I'll take that as a no." He laughed, moving back over to the ladder and balancing the crates in one arm while maneuvering down it with the other.

"Oh, be careful." I rushed over to watch him climb back down.

"You worried about me again, Grant?" He chuckled.

"They look heavy, that's all."

"I've been carrying stuff up and down this ladder since I was a kid. I'll be fine." He winked.

I composed myself before following Ezra. Halfway down the ladder, when I glanced over my shoulder, I felt a small twinge of pride at the way he was watching me slowly climb to to meet him.

After packing the crates in the back of his jeep, we returned to the barn for the cups of coffee we'd left on the wagon. Ezra suggested a walk around the farm and I wasn't about to say no.

Everyone who worked on the farm seemed to be busy preparing for the annual Apple Cider Festival that was coming up that next weekend. The apple orchard was being picked clean. Hundreds of baskets full of red, juicy fruit were being loaded onto the backs of tractors and wagons.

In an empty field, workers were arranging straw bales among very large pumpkins, tying corn stalks together, and setting up empty concession stands. A tent was being erected in the center of the field. That's where all the cider would be served. I imagined tray after tray of Ezra's grandma's apple strudels adorning long wooden tables inside the tent, as well as the famous sugar donuts that everyone went crazy for.

"So, where should we start?" Ezra waved his arm over the expanse of the pumpkin patch.

People were everywhere, and the afternoon light was beginning to fade behind the hills. It was going to be hard to get any decent shots of the pumpkins at that rate.

"Well, I like how the pumpkins look stacked

in the crates like that." I gestured to the stands on either side of us. "If we could get near enough to take some close-up photos, that might work. The list just said a picture with pumpkins, but I think the more we can get in the shot, the better."

Walking among the many rows, dodging customers, Ezra fell silent for several minutes before stopping abruptly, and turning to me. "Do they have to be orange?"

"What?"

"Well, I was just thinking, we have some white pumpkins in the field still. If we mixed them in with the orange ones, it might look kind of cool." He stuffed his hands into his pockets.

"You have white pumpkins?" The farm hadn't had any of those before, and I'd always wanted to see if they were as cool as they looked in magazines. "Show me."

"Okay, but first, I've got another idea." Ezra took off running. He appeared at my side a few minutes later pushing an old rusty wheelbarrow. "Stick some orange ones in here. Small ones." He grabbed a few from the stands and put them inside. "We'll make our own arrangement in the field."

We added several more pumpkins to the wheelbarrow before he lifted the handles and led me away from the stands. Around the other side of the barn, I spotted the white pumpkins, looking as if someone had dropped huge white marshmallows in the field.

"We'd better hurry before we lose the light," I said.

"Right. Gotcha." Ezra took off running into the field. He bent down and picked up a small white pumpkin. "Go long, Grant. Go long," he called.

I didn't have time to protest before he hauled back and lobbed a pumpkin at me.

I screamed, praying I would catch it. When it landed in the cradle of my arms, I gasped. "Ezra! This is not a football. What if I'd dropped it?"

"Then you would have dropped it, but you didn't, so we're all good." He picked up another one. "Try again."

By some miracle, I caught that one too. "Ezra!"

"Oh, come on. You know, you're not half bad. Maybe I should talk to coach about getting you a spot on the team." He teased, tossing yet another pumpkin my way.

"If I drop one of these I'm going to tell your grandma it was your fault." I placed the pumpkin in the wheelbarrow.

"Oh no, not my grandma." Ezra pretended to cower in fear. "She'll hug me and force-feed me more strudel. Please, don't tell my grandma. Wait, on second thought, go ahead. I'm still hungry."

"Stop it, and quit throwing pumpkins at me." I put both hands on my hips, finally noticing the ground around Ezra's feet. "Hey, grab some of those vines, too. We can drape them around the pumpkins for some texture, and I'll dry them for our display."

Ezra pulled up a handful of vines and picked three more pumpkins.

"Don't you dare throw those at me." I warned him.

"What, don't you like pumpkins?"

"I like pumpkins, just not when they're being thrown at my head." I helped him arrange the final three in the display I'd created in the wheelbarrow.

Ezra wiped some dirt off the top white pumpkin with the hem of his shirt. "I wasn't throwing them at your head. Come on, give me some credit. Do you really think they'd let me on the football team if I couldn't even aim?"

"So, if you *had* wanted to hit me in the head?" I pulled the camera out of my backpack and took a couple of sample shots to test the low lighting.

"Oh, you'd be lying unconscious with pumpkins guts in your hair right now." He elbowed me in the side.

"Well, thank you for not choosing that scenario." I pulled him away from the wheelbarrow where he was casting a harsh shadow.

Squatting down, I took several shots.

"What can I do?" He asked.

"Could you get a shot from above, like a flat lay? I'm too short without standing on something." I handed him the camera.

"Sure." He stood over the wheelbarrow and lifted the camera as high as he could, snapping a few pictures.

"Let me see."

Together we scanned through the photos, while I shielded the screen from the late sun so we could see better. Ezra leaned so close his hair tickled my ear.

"How'd we do?" His breath warmed my cheek.

"Um…" I swallowed hard, trying not to think about how close he was. "I think we got some good shots, but we won't know for sure until we get them on the computer to edit them."

"Cool." Ezra lifted the handles of the wheelbarrow and pushed it back towards the pumpkin stands. People kept stopping us and asking where the white pumpkins were, and he would point them in the direction of the fields.

I had to admit, if Ezra hadn't suggested using the white pumpkins, I wouldn't have considered them at all. Normally, white things add no contrast and wash out pictures, but against the bright orange ones, and the rusted wheelbarrow, they actually stood out really well.

Maybe having him as a partner wasn't going to be so bad, after all. He had already come through with props and ideas. And he did have the ideal location for taking lots of great pictures.

Yes, that must be the reason I was smiling. Because my partner's family owned a pumpkin farm.

Yep.

Sure thing.

It had nothing to do with the boy beside me, or how hot he looked pushing a wheelbarrow. And those arms of his with the rolled up sleeves. It had nothing to do with those. Nope, not a thing.

The butterflies in my stomach knew I was lying.

CHAPTER TEN

THAT FRIDAY, the football game was in the neighboring town of Lawton. Ezra insisted that I come to take more photos for him and so, per our bargain, Tori and I drove the forty-five minutes upstate to go to the game.

"I can't believe he's making you come to the away games, too. Why can't you just do the home games?" Tori put her feet on my dashboard and pulled out her script for *Into The Woods*.

"Because he asked me to, and besides, I made a deal with him." I reached over and flipped on the headlights, as the sky was growing darker.

"Whatever. He better be worth it." Tori wiggled in her seat to get more comfortable, pulling out a highlighter and making notes in her script.

I thought back to the way I'd felt the week before. I'd been so nervous about Ezra being my partner, my stomach had been all twisted into knots. The bleachers had been freezing. My legs had cramped up, and I hadn't even tried to get good shots of him on the field. I'd only tried to take as many pictures as I could—all of which he'd deleted.

This time would be different. I was starting to see Ezra in a newer light, and he was becoming someone I'd consider to be a friend. I didn't mind going to the game so much now, even if I'd had to bribe Tori with the promise of a trip to *Dunkin'* on the way home to get her to go with me. I wasn't brave enough to go alone, yet.

At the football field, we found seats near our team's end zone. I figured the lights were brighter there and if Ezra performed like he had the week before, it was where all the great action shots would happen. The night air was much colder than I'd expected, so I wrapped my scarf tighter around my neck, pulled my beanie down over my ears and put on the fingerless gloves that I'd picked up at the store that week, hoping they'd help me not to freeze while taking pictures.

Almost immediately, Tori ran off to buy two large cups of hot chocolate. While she was gone I glanced around the stands. Most of the people were sitting on large wooly blankets, or had them wrapped around themselves like giant cocoons. I made a mental note to bring one to the next game.

If Ezra insisted on there being a next game, that is. I still had high hopes that I would get the pictures he craved very soon, and he'd let me off the hook.

Tori returned before I completely turned into a human icicle, pressing a white styrofoam cup into my hands. "Extra marshmallows, just the way you like it," she said, as I curled my fingers around the cup for warmth and inhaled the thick chocolate scent, letting the heavy steam rise up to warm my cheeks.

"Hey, you made it." A deep voice made me jump.

Ezra was standing on the other side of the bleachers, leaning against the rail, looking completely...adorable...if I were being honest with myself. A wide grin spread across his face as he wedged his helmet beneath his arm.

"You told me I had to come." I reminded him.

"Yeah, but I didn't think you'd actually do it." He turned his attention to my best friend. "Hey, Tori."

"Hi." She slurped her hot chocolate loudly and pulled out her script again, turning away from Ezra.

"Thanks for coming," he said to her.

She didn't take her eyes off her script. "I didn't come here for you, pretty boy. I'm in it for the donuts."

He mouthed a silent "what?" to me with raised eyebrows.

I giggled. "We have a date with *Dunkin'* on the way home."

His eyes went hazy. "Oh, I'm so jealous."

I shrugged. "That's what you get for riding home on the bus." I moved over the the rail, squatting down so that we were eye to eye.

"So, any particular shots you'd like me to get tonight?"

"Just try to catch anything that makes me look good." He smiled.

I rolled my eyes, giving him a mocking salute. "Yes, Sir."

"Oh, I like it when you call me sir." He puffed his chest out. "Let's make *that* your official name for me."

I gave him a light shove in the shoulder. "Get over yourself."

His gaze fell to the cup in my hand. "Hey, is that hot chocolate?"

"Yeah, want me to get you one?" I didn't know if I could make it to the concession stand and back before the game started, but I could try.

"No, but I'll have a sip of yours, if that's okay?" He reached for the cup, pulling it from my hand.

I'd never shared a drink with a boy before—except Mike—and that was not the same thing, believe me. Ezra put my cup to his mouth and took a long sip, his eyes on me the whole time. When he handed it back, he licked his lips and I suddenly felt hot and flushed.

"Thanks. I gotta go before coach gets upset. Enjoy the game." He jammed his helmet on his head, gave me a quick wave and jogged back over to join the team.

I held the cup in my hands for a few seconds before taking a sip myself, surprised to find the rim still warm from his lips.

"Okay, what the heck was that?" Tori demanded when I sat back down.

"What was what?"

"All that flirty stuff, and sharing your drink with him. I thought you said you two weren't flirting." She scoffed.

"We were not flirting. Come on, I was just asking him what pictures he wanted me to take." My cheeks flamed.

"And the cup thing?" She tapped my hot chocolate with her chipped green polished fingernail.

"He took it from me before I could say no." I took another sip.

"Yeah right. You like him, just admit it," she leaned in close. "I knew you would."

"I do not. He's my project partner. That's all." My gaze flitted over to where Ezra was standing on the field. He turned, catching my eye and smiled, as if he knew we had been talking about him.

I turned away quickly.

"Oh, I'm sorry. I'm gonna need to go sit over there so when lightning strikes you for lying, I don't get hit by it." Tori pretended to scoot farther away from me. "I've got a show next month and I'm not missing it."

Biting the inside of my cheek to keep from smiling, I said, "stop. I swear, there is nothing going on between us."

Tori leaned closer and lowered her voice to a

whisper. "I didn't say there was anything going on between you. You came up with that all by yourself. I only said that you liked him, which you totally do."

"No, I don't. You just don't get it." I tried to convince both of us that she was wrong, even though my heart was pounding faster with every word I spoke.

"I told you this thing would be good for you." She leaned back, a smirk on her face.

Pulling out my camera, I checked the settings. "What are you talking about?"

"I told you that you should find a silver lining and maybe try to live a little in the process. Remember that conversation?"

"Vaguely."

"Well, I think you've found your silver lining, and he's wearing a white jersey with a big maroon number five on the back." She stretched her legs out in front of her and crossed her feet at the ankles.

I finally met her gaze. "Okay, here's the thing. Even if I liked Ezra, it doesn't mean he'd like me back. It's not like with you and Marcus. We have nothing in common."

She leaned close and whispered, "he likes you."

"He does not. You don't know what you're talking about." *Come on, there's no way Ezra O'Neill would like me. He's just a nice guy like everyone says.*

Tori shook her head. "If he didn't like you, then tell me why, of all the girls sitting in these bleachers, he only came over to talk to you?"

What was she talking about?

Glancing around, girls behind us were staring at me—with scowls on their faces. Even the cheerleaders on the field were giving me sideways glances, in between shaking their pompoms and jumping up and down to keep warm. Casey's gaze kept shifting between me and him, as if she was finally putting the pieces together. Although there really was nothing to put together. Ezra and I were project partners. I wore his hoodie, and he just drank my hot chocolate. But that was all there was.

"This is crazy. He does not like me." My voice crackled, like the fire that seemed to be blazing around me.

"Bailey, are you seriously telling me you don't see it?" She laughed.

"See what?"

"Ezra O'Neill is the most popular guys in the senior class. He's the star football player and he's been single since the beginning of this year. Everyone wants him, and he's paying *you* all kinds of attention."

I suddenly felt like my heart was going to rip out of my chest. I hadn't been this nervous filling out my PSD application.

Tori sipped her hot chocolate, before turning and lowering her voice even more. "You can deny it all you want, but there's something there. Trust me. Spend a little more time paying attention to your partner and a little less time obsessing about the project and you'll see it."

I had fully intended to keep arguing with her, but the game started. I couldn't believe what she was saying. I mean, sure, Ezra was hot, and popular, and super cool, but there was no way that I could like him. I was only setting myself up for disappointment if I let myself feel something for him. He was so out of my league. I shoved the emotions down deep inside, even though Ezra's face was all I could think about.

After snapping a few photos, I dropped the camera into my lap.

Who was I kidding?

I *was* starting to think of Ezra differently. Whenever I saw him, my pulse raced and my hands got all sweaty. Every night since we'd gone to his family's farm, I'd gone to bed thinking about how much fun we'd had, and replaying every conversation in my head.

I'd never spent that much time thinking about anyone. But it wasn't just all in my head. At school, I couldn't wait until I could see him every day. Photography class was becoming my favorite hour because I got to spend it with him. My stomach would twist when I passed him in the hallway, and in English class, every time my glance wandered in his direction, he was staring at me, too.

Even watching his game had my heart pounding inside my chest. Ezra had been tackled twice already, and both times I had found myself gasping and clinging to the camera as tight as I could until I knew he wasn't hurt.

The week before, I didn't care at all when he got tackled. He could have broken his leg and I would have simply taken a picture of it and moved on.

But now...

I was taking pictures with feeling. I cared about what I was shooting, because in some small way, I now cared for Ezra. He'd been getting under my skin since that day at his locker. But now, instead of wanting to punch him, I...well, I didn't know what I wanted to do to him, or with him. I just knew I liked spending time with him, and I liked myself better when he was around.

As I watched him run the football down the field and dive across the end zone, securing the win for Cedar Falls, I stood up and cheered. Me, Bailey Grant, actually cheered at a football game.

It wasn't because of the atmosphere, or the team.

It was because of the boy.

The boy that I was maybe, just maybe, starting to have feelings for.

CHAPTER ELEVEN

THE NEXT MORNING, I was halfway through buttering my toast when Mom cornered me in the kitchen. "Do you have any plans for today?" She had way too much energy for a Saturday morning.

"No, not really." I yawned, wiping the sleep from my eyes.

"Want to go to the Cider Festival with me? Jean was meant to go with me, but little Esme's got a sore throat, so she can't. I know you don't usually go to these things, but I've got two tickets and don't want them to go to waste." She asked, excitement written all over her face.

I yawned again, a little sad that my perfectly-planned Saturday of doing absolutely nothing had just been shattered, but I couldn't tell her no. She looked too excited. "Sure, sounds fun."

"Great." She poured her second cup of coffee that morning—hence the extra perkiness.

"No problem." I slathered a generous amount of strawberry jam onto my toast and took a bite. "I need to get some pictures of apples and cider for my project anyway. I'm sure Ezra won't mind."

"Ezra? Is he the boy who loaned you his hoodie?" Her voice did that mom thing it does when she senses a juicy bit of gossip coming her way.

I paused, my toast halfway to my mouth. "Yes, he's my partner for Through the Lens." I tried to act casual, but I could feel her eye's attempting to bore into my soul. I decided to change the subject. "So, are we going to Duncan's Farm?" It was where she and her friend, Jean, went every year.

"No, I've got tickets for the O'Neill Farm. I heard they're going all out this year, and you and I haven't picked out our pumpkins yet. Did you know they have white pumpkins? How interesting would that be? I wonder if the insides are white too?" She sat down at the table, flipping through the morning paper.

"Uh, yeah." I swallowed the bite of toast that had turned to sandpaper in my mouth. It dawned on me that if I didn't say something, I was sure to embarrass myself later. "So, Ezra…he's the O'Neill's grandson, and he and I went out to the farm the other day to take some photos of the pumpkins. The white ones are cool."

"Really?" Her voice was going higher at the end of her words. Yep, she was in full gossip mode. My life was over.

"Yeah, it was no big deal. We needed some old wooden crates, and he mentioned they had a bunch at the farm that we could use. While we were there, we took some pictures of the pumpkins." I tried to steady my racing heart. "The light was really good."

Focusing my full attention on my toast and glass of water, I prayed that Mom had no indication that I might...maybe...possibly...like Ezra, because if she did, she would never let it go. I couldn't let on that he meant anything to me. Not a single thing.

"I bet." I could hear the disbelief in her voice. "Well, I want to leave in about half an hour, so eat up."

"I better get dressed, then." Hopping up, I placed my plate and glass in the dishwasher, and then ran up to my room.

Closing the door behind me, I leaned against it and shut my eyes. There was no way to get out of going to the farm, which meant there was also a possibility of running into Ezra's grandparents—or Ezra himself—so I might as well make the best of it. I'd play it cool if we saw him, telling him Mom dragged me there, and just do a quick introduction.

The one thing I knew for sure was that I needed to look good. Not that Ezra hadn't seen me at my worst, looking like a drowned rat with mascara smeared down my cheeks, but there was no excuse for appearing like a slob.

Running into the bathroom, I brushed my teeth, washed my face and ran the straightener through my hair, before applying my usual amount of makeup. That's where things fell apart, because standing in front of my closet, I forgot what clothes were.

I knew I'd be wearing my jacket and no one would see what I was wearing underneath, but just in case, I chose my favorite sweater and jeans. Grabbing the school's camera, I threw it in my purse and ran downstairs.

Thankfully, Mom didn't question me any more about Ezra as we drove to the farm. I almost told her about the secret back entrance, but I figured that would be a sure-fire way to send her over the edge. Besides, I kind of liked that it was just our thing, mine and Ezra's. It felt like a secret that only we shared, and I wasn't about to ruin that.

The huge field they set up for parking was packed by the time we got there. I couldn't believe people got up at the crack of dawn for an apple cider festival. I mean, I thought Mom dragging me out at eight o'clock was over-the-top, but apparently lots of other people were crazy, too.

Mom opened the trunk of her car and took out two oversized burlap shopping bags. I cringed, but she handed one to me anyway. At the entrance gate, Ezra's grandpa was sitting on a stool, a steaming cup of coffee in his hand.

"Hey there, missy, I remember you." He took the tickets from my mom and ripped them in half. "Did those old crates work out for you?"

"Yes. Thank you so much for letting us have them." I tried to keep my voice from shaking.

"They were just taking up space in the loft. You and Ez did me a favor by getting rid of them." He winked. "Have fun today, and make sure you get one of Gloria's strudels. They are to die for."

"Oh, I know. I had one the other day," I said without thinking.

Mom gave me a sidelong glance, and I pushed her on through the gate, thanking him for all his help.

"How do you know that man?" She asked.

"He's Ezra's grandpa. He helped us get the crates from the barn," I deadpanned, "he's really nice."

"Yes, he seems to be." She stopped to admire a stand of the famous white pumpkins. The sight of them made me think of Ezra—I almost found myself missing him.

What was happening to me?

I followed Mom through the farm. Booths and stalls were everywhere, selling homemade wreaths, autumn garlands, Christmas decorations, wooden carvings, hand-woven baskets, wind chimes, potted flowers, and even autumn-themed t-shirts. Food stalls sold everything from roasted nuts, kettle corn, honey, baked goods, and saltwater taffy. An area had been set up with old-fashioned carnival games for the children, and there was even a bandstand, where a jazz band was warming up.

The cider tent was huge, with cornstalks wrapped around each of the many poles that were holding it up. Giant metal vats stood in the back, brimming with hot apple cider, and on the tables in front of them were hundreds of steaming cups, not to mention the platters piled high with warm sugared donuts.

Tables and chairs were scattered all throughout the tent, but most people took a cup and donut to go. As mom and I approached the table for our cider and donuts, I very familiar group of women greeted us.

"Bailey." Ezra's grandma reached across the table and grasped my hand. "I'm so glad you changed your mind and came today. It's lovely to see you again."

My mouth was hanging open. "Changed my mind?"

"Ezra said you weren't going to be able to come because you'd made other plans. Is that not correct?" Her brow creased.

I was speechless. Ezra had told his grandma that he'd invited me to the festival, but that I couldn't come. He hadn't invited me at all, and clearly didn't want me there, but I didn't want to tell his grandma that. So, I set my jaw and said, "Yes. I thought I might be doing something with my friend, Tori, but she had to cancel."

It was a lie, but one she—and more importantly, my mom—would believe. I was always hanging out with Tori.

Silver liquid rimmed my eyes as she turned to my mom and extended her hand. "Hello, I'm Gloria. We met your daughter earlier this week. She and our grandson are really adorable together if you ask me." She said that last part in a whisper, but I heard every word.

"You think so?" Mom played along, eyeing me with suspicion.

I couldn't meet her gaze.

"Oh, yes. We all thought so." She gestured to her friends, who nodded in agreement and gave me tight-lipped smiles.

I couldn't decide if I wanted to burst into tears or crawl into a hole and die. My face was on fire and my throat closed off, making it difficult to speak. Holding my donut and cider, I stood there like an idiot while they talked about Ezra and I as if I wasn't even there. As if it was no big deal.

As if he hadn't lied to them.

About me.

"Amanda," someone called from across the tent.

Mom and I both turned to see one of her friends waving as she came to join us at the table.

"Linda, how are you?" Mom grinned.

The two of them began chatting. It gave me the perfect opportunity to disappear.

"I'm gonna go check out the pumpkins," I said, as she and Linda strolled off in the direction of a table where more of Mom's friends were already sitting.

"Sure. I'll find you later." Mom didn't even turn around.

I practically ran from the cider tent, stifling the tears that had wanted to escape so badly. They finally slipped out as I ran for the unoccupied straw bales scatted beneath a large tree on the edge of the pumpkin patches.

Sipping on the cider and munching on the donut, but not really tasting either one, I sat under that tree for who knows how long, feeling like a complete idiot. *How could I possibly have thought that Ezra might like me?* He didn't even want me at his family farm and had lied to his grandma about it.

My quivering jaw suddenly went rigid and set. My eyes narrowed into angry slits and I clenched my teeth. *Why do I care if he likes me?* It's not like either of us had ever said anything about our feelings. If I'd never listened to Tori, I wouldn't have even started thinking of the possibility that he and could become something more. That he might actually like me.

She was so wrong.

I almost pulled out my phone to call Tori and tell her just how wrong she'd been, but I couldn't do it. Not without admitting that I did have feelings, which had turned from a butterflies-in-the-stomach level of giddiness and excitement, to a twisted jumble of pain and humiliation.

I was so stupid?

Guys like Ezra didn't like girls like me. Football and art didn't mix—and for good reason. We weren't meant to coexist.

Why had he lied and told his grandma I couldn't come?

Why did he want me to stay away from the farm?

I mean, he hadn't even said anything, and I had never once implied that I wanted an invite to the cider festival. If mom hadn't dragged me out, I would have been up in my room at that moment, enjoying a quiet Saturday, not aware that he had lied about me. Had Ezra planned to ask me and then changed his mind? Had I done something wrong?

Was I wrong?

Wrong looking.

Wrong acting.

The completely wrong type of girl for a boy like him. Wrong in every way.

Wallowing in my own misery, I got up and wandered around the pumpkin patch for a long time, not really paying attention to anything. The bins of orange pumpkins blurred together as I looked, but didn't really see.

Mom was expecting me to be choosing a pumpkin for the town carving contest, but I couldn't focus. I felt so disconnected, a wedge of pain driving itself deeper into my chest with every step.

When I walked past the stand full of white

pumpkins, tears burned the backs of my eyes again. Closing them, I took a deep breath and begged the tears not to slip out. I wasn't the kind of girl who got her feelings mixed up over a boy, and I certainly didn't cry over one.

I would not shed another tear for Ezra O'Neill.

He wasn't worth it.

He wasn't worth it at all.

CHAPTER TWELVE

"I'D CHOOSE THAT ONE if I were you."

I whipped around so quickly, I almost punched Ezra right in the stomach.

"Easy there, Grant." He caught me by the shoulders. "What's got you so jumpy?"

I jerked out of his grasp, my jaw clenched so tightly that my cheeks burned.

"Are you okay? What's wrong?" His gaze narrowed.

I backed away from him. "I talked to your grandma.

"Oh yeah? Did she force-feed you donuts?" He shoved his hands in his pockets.

"Why did you tell her that you invited me here, but I couldn't come?" I blurted out.

Ezra's mouth dropped open and his eyes grew wide. He stumbled backwards. Actually stumbled, until his legs met the pumpkin bin. "Um…I…um…" he stammered.

"Well?" I put my hands on my hips and waited.

His gaze fell to his shoes and he rubbed the back of his neck with his hand. "Okay, here's the deal. Ever since you came here the other day, she's been on my case about when I was bringing you back. I told her that I was going to invite you to the festival, which I was. I had thought maybe we could get some more photos and stuff, and maybe just hang out a bit. I almost said something at the game last night, but then I chickened out. I didn't want you showing up here and have her treat you funny, so I lied and told her that you couldn't come. I had no idea you'd show up anyway." He chewed his bottom lip. "I hope she didn't say something to upset you."

"Oh, you mean like tell my *mom* how adorable we were together." I repeated her speech with the most sarcasm I could muster.

Rubbing his hands over his face, Ezra let out a low moan. "She didn't?" He squinted at me between his fingers.

"Oh, she did. I can't wait to field all those questions on the ride home." My stomach clenched just thinking about it.

"I'm so sorry." He reached for my arms, but halted, pulling back and shoving his hands back in his pockets.

"For lying, or for getting caught?" I crossed my arms over my chest.

"Bit of both." He cringed. "Listen, the last thing I wanted was for this to happen. I know I already messed up with the whole hoodie thing. I didn't want you to come here, and have her jump all over you, too. I was trying to protect you from being embarrassed again."

I sighed. *This nice guy thing was really starting to bite me in the butt.*

"Ezra, we already talked about the hoodie, and I apologized for freaking out. I might not be used to having so many people notice me and talk to me." My gaze dropped, unable to meet his eye. "But, you don't have to keep protecting me. I'm okay. We're okay."

That time he did reach for my arm, his grip warm and gentle. "I am sorry."

My heart began to melt at his words and the small smile that worked its way onto his face. I smiled back at him. "I'll forgive you if you help me pick out the pumpkin that will win the carving contest." I waved my hand over the pumpkin stalls.

"I don't know, that's a lot of pressure to put on a guy. How will I ever choose a winning pumpkin." He gripped his chin, gazing over the selection before us.

"You just point me in the direction of the best pumpkin here and I'll work my artistic magic on it." I inched closer to his side.

Warmth radiated from him as he reached for a medium-sized, round, white pumpkin. Turning, he presented it to me as if it were a prized treasure I'd just won. "This one is perfect, don't you think? You know, most people are a bit scared of the white ones, so they don't choose them for carving. It'll make a statement."

Taking the pumpkin in my hands, I weighed it, turning it over to examine it from all angles. "When did you become such a pumpkin expert?"

He placed his palm on his chest. "Hello, family business. Ask me anything about pumpkins and apples. I know it all."

"Did you list that as a special skill on your college applications? Pumpkin genius."

"Of course. It's what all the great schools want. Who cares about what I could do for their football team? It's that farm knowledge they really want." He smirked as he added. "Makes that girls go crazy, too."

I snorted, feeling far more confident than I knew I could be when I said, "Oh yes, tell me more about those pumpkins. Ooh baby, baby."

That got us both laughing so hard my sides hurt.

Ezra wiped tears from his eyes. "Nothing makes a girl fall for you like a good conversation about gourds."

"And apples, don't forget the apples." I was still laughing.

"That's a second date thing. Don't want to reveal all my moves right from the start." He bent over, grasping his knees.

When I had finally stopped laughing I held up the white pumpkin. "How much is it?"

"Oh, don't worry about it." He waved his hand, drying more tears from his eyes.

"Come on, I have to pay for it."

"After what my grandma and I did, it's the least we can do. Take it, please. I won't take no for an answer." He gave me a cheesy grin that showed all his teeth.

I had no idea what came over me in that moment but I did the unthinkable. I sat the pumpkin down and flung my arms around his neck. "Thank you," I said.

He stood stone still for half a breath, before his arms came up and wrapped around my back. "Wow, I didn't realize this carving contest was so important to you," he whispered against my hair. "Or that giving you a pumpkin was all it would take to get you to hug me."

Suddenly, fully aware of the fact that all of me was pressed up against all of him, I pulled away, blushing. "I didn't just mean about the pumpkins."

"I know." He suddenly seemed to not know what to do with his hands. They clenched and unclenched at his sides.

I had to get us out of this awkwardness. Fast. "But if my mom wants one too, we're paying for it."

"Deal." He sighed deeply.

I held open the burlap shopping bag mom had given me, and Ezra gently placed the pumpkin inside.

"So, did you bring the camera?"

"Don't I always?" I pulled it out of my bag and slipped the strap over my head, letting the camera dangle against my chest.

Ezra took the bag with the pumpkin in it from me. "Want to try and knock out the apple and the cider pictures, then?"

"Sure, but I don't know if the styrofoam cups are the best thing for a photo." I squished up the side of my mouth, thinking.

"Well." Ezra paused, scratching his head. "Off to the kitchens, then."

The farm shop kitchen was dark and quiet, a complete opposite to how it had been the last time I was there. Ezra flicked on the lights while I began opening cabinets and drawers, searching for anything that would make our pictures look better.

"What do you think of these?" He held up two dark green, spotted, metal mugs, similar to the ones my dad and Mike used when they went camping.

"Perfect. Very rustic."

On the large work table in the middle of the room sat a basket of apples and jars of spices, which I assumed would be used to make the next batch of his grandma's famous strudel. Lifting the jars, I found one with whole cinnamon sticks inside it.

"Could we borrow these?" I asked, gesturing to the items on the table.

"I don't see why not, as long as we return them." Ezra shrugged.

I stuffed the cinnamon sticks into the bag,

along with the two mugs and a couple of red plaid napkins that I'd found in one of the drawers. "Can you carry that basket of apples?"

"Yeah." He raised an eyebrow. "Where are we going?"

"Oh, I know a place."

I led him back out to the spot where I'd been pouting earlier. No one was sitting there, which I took as a good sign. Spreading the napkins out on the top of the straw bale, I took special care in overlapping them, while trying to make them look like I'd just thrown them down.

"Do you want to go fill these with cider, or should I?" I asked, holding up the mugs.

Ezra snatched them from me. "I'm on it." He took off for the cider tent while I finished staging the photo.

Placing the cinnamon sticks around the napkins, I reached up into the tree above my head and plucked several bright orange leaves. I wanted the rich color from the ones still on the tree, as opposed to the more dull-hued ones that had already fallen to the ground. Scattering them around the straw bale, I searched for anything else that would add depth and texture to our photo. Acorns were lying on the ground nearby. I picked them up, as well as a few twigs.

When Ezra returned with the mugs of cider, we took a few sips each, before arranging them in the middle of the scene I'd created.

"Should we use any pumpkins? We have some

really small ones around here someplace," he asked, as I began to test the lighting.

"I thought about it, but this photo is supposed to be about the apples and the cider. I don't want to have it competing with the pumpkin ones we already took." I reached for the basket he'd sat on the ground.

Pushing my hand aside, Ezra chose three apples and polished them with the hem of his shirt so they wouldn't show any smudges or fingerprints. When he deemed them perfect, he carefully placed them around the mugs, moving them around, until he was satisfied with their placement.

I thought it all looked great…except for the lighting.

Sunlight was floating through the tree overhead, casting strange shadows and light patches on our display.

"Ugh." I moaned.

Ezra leaned towards me. "What's wrong? Is the setup bad?" He blocked out most of the light.

I held up my hands. "Stop. Don't move."

His froze. "Why?"

"I need you to block the weird light."

Leaning forward on my side of the straw bale, the rest of the display went into shadow. Positioning the camera against my eye, I was very aware of how close Ezra's face was to mine at that moment. Risking a glance up, it was as if he was feeling the same tug, because when our eyes met we were so close we shared the same breath. His blue eyes were all I could see, and they sparkled as he blinked. I could have counted his eyelashes if I'd wanted to.

We stared at each other, neither of us moving. My pulse raced through my body, and when Ezra's eyes flicked to my mouth, I sucked in a harsh breath.

I'm not going to lie, I've dreamed about my first kiss many times, and I'd certainly imagined it with Ezra, but at that moment I was terrified. I mean, let's face it, Cedar Falls was a small town and there just weren't that many boys to choose from. None had really ever made me feel anything. *Until now.*

Plus, I didn't know what to do. *Was I meant to keep my eyes opened or closed? What did I do with my hands? If we both tilted our heads the same way, would we mash our noses together?*

I shuddered.

Ezra was looking and smelling so good that day, and his lips were so close, I wanted to shut my eyes and let him lean in, but I froze with even more questions.

What if I was a bad kisser?
What if it ruined everything?
What if I wasn't as good as Casey? What if he compared the two of us?

No, I couldn't do it. *Not now. Not like this.*

Blinking, I found my voice. "That's great, just hold still while I get the shot."

Turning away from him, I placed my eye against the camera again, working to soothe my ragged breathing. Ezra let out a shuddering sigh too, but I couldn't look at him again. Not until the photo was finished and I'd moved well out of kissing range.

When I finally did met his gaze again, he was grinning like he knew a secret I didn't. Rubbing his thumb against his bottom lip, he gestured to the camera. "How'd we do?"

He was trying to make me stare at his lips. He knew exactly what he was doing and I was falling for it like a fool. I stared at them and wondered if they were as soft as they looked. I felt stupid for pulling away from the moment we'd just had, but it was over now and I didn't even know how I'd start it back up again so I handed him the camera.

He flipped through the photos. "Oh, cool." He threw the strap around his own neck. "I've got an idea for the apple picture."

"But..." I gave him a questioning look.

"Need I remind you that I have it in writing that you trust me?" He raised an eyebrow.

I groaned. "I knew that was going to come back to haunt me."

"Come on." He took hold of my arm and pulled me closer to him.

My heart jumped into my throat.

"Hold out your hands." He reached down to my other arm and pulled my hands close together, turning them so they were facing upward.

My blood tingled as his rough fingers grazed over mine. He ran his thumbs down the insides of my palms, causing me to shiver. The smirk on his face told me he was doing that on purpose, too.

He bent down, picking up the apples we'd used in our last photo and set them in my hands, gently. He worked carefully, stacking them in a way so they wouldn't fall. Then he added another one from the basket we'd brought from the kitchen.

"Now, hold still," he said, moving around me and snapping pictures from every angle.

"There." Ezra took the apples from my hands and showed me the pictures he'd taken.

The photos he'd shot were really good.

I was becoming more and more impressed with my partner's eye for flair and design. I was also very glad that the polish on my fingernails wasn't chipped, since he'd zoomed in very closely on a couple of the shots.

Handing me one apple, Ezra stepped back, saying, "now, hold this one up with your fingers curled around it."

"Like this?" I was pretty sure I knew where he was going with the next photo, and if we could pull it off, it would look amazing.

"Uh, not quite." He dropped the camera to his chest and took my hand in his—again.

Fire ignited in my stomach.

"Twist it a little bit more." He turned my wrist slightly. "Perfect. Now lift your hand up so it covers your face."

Moving my hand into position, I was careful not to untwist my wrist. Ezra snapped several more pictures, making me feel super self-conscience, even though my face was completely covered.

As we walked back to the kitchen to return all the things we'd borrowed, Ezra said, "take one of the napkins for the display."

"Won't your grandma miss it?"

"Nah, there are so many of them, she won't notice if one's gone." He heaved the basket of apples higher into his arms.

Those arms!

Once everything was put away, we walked around the farm, playing some of the carnival games, sampling the food and wandering among the craft stalls.

"I'm glad you came today," Ezra bumped his hip against mine as we walked back into the cider tent, hoping to swipe a couple more sugar donuts from his grandma.

"Me too." It had been the best day I'd had in a long time.

"Um…are you going to Homecoming next weekend?" He stuffed his hands into his pockets and stared straight ahead.

Was he getting ready to ask me to the dance?

And was he nervous?

"Yes. Are you?" My palms grew sweaty.

"Oh, I have to. It's pretty much expected that all the players will be there. Also, Casey is in the Homecoming court and I'm escorting her at the game. We also have to dance the first dance together you know, but maybe we could spend the rest of the night together, if you want?" He ran a hand through his hair, then stopped abruptly, his face going bright red. "Unless you've already got a date, or something."

My heart stopped beating. He was escorting Casey? *How did I not know this?* I felt as if someone had punched me in the gut. "You're escorting your ex-girlfriend at Homecoming?"

It was as if all the air had been sucked out of the tent.

"Yes. The court has to be escorted by senior varsity players and she asked me weeks ago. I was going to have to escort someone. All us seniors do. It's kind of expected."

"Why are telling me this?" I blurted, gripping the nearest tent pole to steady myself.

"Because you asked, and I wanted to be honest with you." He searched my face. I'm not sure what he saw there.

"No, I mean why tell me about Casey, and why ask me to meet up with you at the dance if you're basically already going with her?" I was shaking.

"I'm not going with her. I just have to walk her down a carpet at the game and suffer through one dance with her."

"Is that how she's going to see it?" My legs felt like lead.

"I don't care how she sees it. This is all for show. I'm not getting back with her. I thought my feelings about this were obvious?" He stepped closer, lowering his voice.

"What?"

"I want to go with you to Homecoming. I'd pick you up and take you, but I've got to go so early for football stuff that it would probably be best to meet you there. But, I also need you to understand what I *have* to do—and how much I don't want to do it—before I get to do what I *want* to do." He was so still I wasn't sure if he was breathing.

"You want to dance with me?" My voice broke.

He nodded his head as if he was afraid to speak.

"Are you sure?" My hand was gripping the tent pole so tight my knuckles were turning white.

"Very." He stepped so close I had to look up to meet his gaze. "Will you go with me?"

"Bailey, there you are." Mom called, walking towards us. "You ready to go?"

"In a minute" I turned to Ezra. "Yes."

He smiled so wide his teeth showed. I think I did, too.

"Bye," I said, turning quickly and heading

towards Mom so she wouldn't want to talk to him.

"See you later," he called after me.

I didn't turn, but I could feel his eyes on me all the way to the car.

To my surprise, the drive home was without an interrogation. Considering all the things Mom had heard that morning, I was shocked. But, her friends had given her enough gossip that she either forgot about me, or my relationship with Ezra was no longer a priority for her.

Ezra had asked me to the dance. Or I should say, he'd asked me to meet him there, but still, it was something I'd never had before.

A date to a dance.

It was something I couldn't stop thinking about for the entire next week.

CHAPTER THIRTEEN

THE NEXT DAY I did something I'd never done before. I bought a formal dress for a school dance. The navy blue midi-length gown I'd found was simple, but nicer than anything else in my closet. I'd fallen in love with it the moment I saw it, and Mom approved, which I took as a sign that it was meant to be.

Fate, if you will.

Tori had actually jumped up and down when we met up the next afternoon to go shopping, and I told her what had happened at the farm.

"I knew it," she'd said, over and over, "I told you he liked you."

I was about to start jumping with her, but Casey Turner walked by at that moment, talking loudly, clearly for my benefit. "I'm super excited about the game. Ezra and I look so good together, I don't see how we won't win. And the dance, OMG, when he sees me in my dress he'll be on his knees begging me to take him back."

I stuck my tongue out after she'd walked past. She was going to be so disappointed when he left her after one dance and spent the rest of the night with me. I couldn't wait to see that look on her face.

❖ ❖ ❖

The Homecoming game drew a larger crowd than I'd seen yet. Ezra had asked if I could also get some pictures of him escorting Casey, as well as the ones I'd planned to take of the game.

Apparently, the Homecoming procession was a big deal.

Personally, I didn't get it.

I'd agreed to take the pictures he'd asked for, even if the thought of photographing Ezra and his ex-girlfriend made my skin crawl, but he was right about the prestige. It wasn't only our town newspaper who had come to the high school to cover the big game. Several larger state papers had photographers crouching on the sidelines, and a Providence news crew was even there with video cameras. I guess the fact that Cedar Falls had gone undefeated that season and were probably heading to the District Finals in a few weeks had people interested.

I let Tori off the hook of going with me that night, because Mike had come home from college talking about nothing else but the game. I did remember to bring a thick, heavy blanket with me, though. After finding seats, Mike and I sat on the blanket first, before wrapping it tightly around ourselves. It was so cold that night that our breaths were showing.

I almost felt sorry for the queen candidates who were standing on the sidelines, shivering in their skimpy formal dresses.

Almost.

Secretly, I enjoyed watching Casey turn blue.

It took Mike all of about three minutes before he declared he was starving and ran off to get a hotdog and some nachos. "Want anything?"

"Hot chocolate, please." Maybe Ezra would come steal another sip.

"I'm on it. Be right back." He took off jogging towards the concessions stand.

Well, it turned out that Mike's 'be right back' took about twenty minutes. By the time he returned, the queens and their escorts were making their way onto the field.

"Sorry, I ran into a few people," was all he said as he handed me the hot chocolate and took a huge bite from his hotdog.

"A few?" I raised an eyebrow.

"Okay, a lot." Grinning, he pointed his hotdog towards the field. "Hey, there's your boy."

"He's not *my* boy." I spat.

"Yeah, yeah, just keep telling yourself that." He knocked his leg against mine.

"You're worse than Mom," I scoffed.

"Oh no, you take that back." He leaned away from me, pretending to be offended.

"Why? It's true. You're a little gossipy momma's boy," I mocked in the baby voice I knew he hated.

"Just take your stupid pictures." He took another bite, pretending to be angry.

I ignored the rest of his mumbling and focused on what was happening on the field. The previous year's Homecoming Queen, Lindsey Nelson, was standing on a raised platform at the end of a long maroon carpet that had been unfurled on the field. Each of the current year's nominees had removed their coats, visibly shaking as the band began to play.

The senior girls—which let's face it, were the most likely candidates to win Homecoming queen—were the last to march onto the platform, meaning Ezra and Casey were one of the final four pairs.

A twinge of nausea washed over me as I took in how closely the two of them stood together. She had one arm slung through his, while the other was holding a huge bouquet of roses. He kept tilting his head to whisper things in her ear. She would giggle and lean up on her tiptoes to whisper back. I felt like all the air had been sucked from my lungs while someone else punched me in the gut.

I snapped all the pictures I could stand of the two of them walking slowly across the field, climbing the stairs, and finally, Casey waving to the crowd from the platform. When the last queen nominee had been presented, the platform was carried off the field by several men and the long carpet was quickly rolled up. It was as if, within a matter of seconds, nothing unusual had happened.

The moment the boys took the field for the coin toss, I found myself actually interested in the game. I was starting to understand it better after the past few weeks, and the fact that I was more interested in Ezra made me heavily invested in what was happening. Every time our team had the ball, my chest would tighten in anticipation, and if he was the one running the ball, I forgot how to breathe until he scored.

Mike leaned over after about the fourth time I'd gasped out loud, and said, "so, explain to me again how you don't like him? I think I missed that part."

"Shut up." I smacked him on the arm and then stole his half of the blanket.

He shivered, hugging himself for warmth. "Okay, okay, I was wrong, You're not crushing on Ezra. Not even a little bit. You hate his guts."

I let him have the blanket back and he didn't say another word about my feelings for the rest of the game, which we won, by the way.

Mike yelled so loud he lost his voice.

Afterwards, we had barely hit the bottom of the stairs before one of his friend's spotted him and they started talking. I tried to be patient, but my brother seemed to be catching up with every person he'd ever known.

The rest of the stands cleared, the field emptied, the band packed up their instruments.

The other team's fans left, most of them already pulling out of the parking lot.

But Mike hadn't moved. He was still talking… to everyone.

The wind started blowing harder, and I grew so cold I began to shiver. Wrapping the blanket we'd brought around my shoulders, I ducked around the back side of the bleachers, hoping it would be warmer there.

It was. A little bit. At least the wind's ferocity was deadened.

Leaning against one of the bleacher supports, I watched as the football players emerged from the locker room, fresh from the showers and dressed in their regular clothes. A small group of girls were standing outside the doors, jumping up and down to keep warm while the waited for their boyfriends to emerge. As soon as they spotted them, they'd run into their arms, hugging and kissing them while showering them with praises and telling them how amazing they'd been.

I wondered if Ezra had already come out? It would be nice to see him and congratulate him on the win. I inched closer to the doorway, pressing myself against the bleachers.

The door opened and there he was. He was wearing a coat and beanie, pulled low over his ears and forehead. His hands were shoved into his pockets.

"Ezra," I called out, waving.

He turned at the sound of my voice, but someone else got to him first.

Casey Turner.

Frozen in place, I stood in the shadows of the bleachers, and watched her run up to him, arms spread wide.

"Congratulations," she squealed.

Ezra stepped into her embrace as if it it was no big deal, like it was something he did every day. She placed her hands on his chest, and I stopped breathing. I'd never touched Ezra in such an intimate way. The only time I'd laid a hand on his chest was that day in the hallway when I'd shoved him back against his locker. It had not been at all romantic. Not like the way Casey was touching him now.

I grit my teeth. I was the one he'd asked to meet him at the dance the next night. *He had asked me.* Not her.

I wanted to leave, to run away and not watch any more. I was torturing myself, but my feet were rooted to the spot. I couldn't stop thinking about the way Ezra had touched my hands at the farm that day, sending shivers down my spine in the best way possible. Yes, we'd been close enough to kiss, and for a moment, I thought he might want to.

I had been the one to pull away.

The one too scared to give in.

Maybe I had sent him a message that I wasn't interested in kissing him, or putting *my* hands on his chest. Maybe he was used to girls who just fell into his arms. Maybe he was regretting breaking up with Casey.

No!

Ezra had told me he had to dance with her once and then he wanted to meet up with me. *Me.* If he still liked Casey, wouldn't he just dance the whole night with her? Why would he have asked me to meet him there? Why would he have even bothered? He wouldn't have. There was no reason for him to get my hopes up, simply to shatter them.

I was overreacting. I had to be.

Then again, maybe not…

Before I could take a step forward, the unthinkable happened. Casey inched herself up onto her toes, grabbed Ezra's face with both hands and kissed him hard on the mouth.

I gasped, quickly covering my own mouth to keep any more sounds from escaping. I silently begged him to step away.

He didn't.

He reached out, laying his hands on her waist.

I couldn't watch anymore. It was too much to deal with, so I did the only thing I could. I turned and ran.

Grabbing Mike by the arm, I yanked him away from his friends. He started to protest, but as soon as he spotted the tears streaming down my face, he wrapped a protective arm around my shoulders and walked me home. He asked what had happened, but I couldn't tell him. I couldn't tell anyone. Not because I didn't want to, but because I couldn't form the words.

"Did something happen with Ezra?" He asked.

I just cried harder.

How could I describe the anguish I felt as my heart seized inside my chest? There was no way I could tell him that I was breaking into tiny pieces with every step we took.

When I got home, I ran up to my room, shut the door, fell into bed, and cried until my pillow was soggy with tears and I could only draw shuddering breaths. I'd said I would never cry over a boy, especially not Ezra, but I couldn't stop the tears and the pain.

I sobbed and sobbed and sobbed.

CHAPTER FOURTEEN

I STAYED IN BED the next day. I didn't want to see, or talk, to anyone. Mom came up to check on me and I told her I had cramps and wasn't feeling well. It was the one illness she never questioned. I felt bad for lying to her, but I couldn't face the truth. Ten minutes later, she brought up the heating pad, along with a plate of jam-slathered English muffins, and a large coffee with hazelnut creamer and extra sugar. I ate in bed while I watched tv. Mike came up to check on me too, but I still couldn't tell him what was wrong.

"If you need me to do the big brother thing and have a talk with Ezra," he smacked his palm with his fist. "Just say the word."

I started crying again, so he left me alone.

A few hours later, I texted Tori to let her know I wasn't going to the dance. There was no way I could keep it together if I had to watch Ezra and Casey hanging all over each other the whole night. She asked if I wanted her to come over, but I told her no. She said she'd come over Sunday and we could hang out all day.

I flung the formal dress that I'd hung neatly on my closet door into the far reaches of the closet and slammed the door shut. I didn't want to see it, or think about the dance at all. I knew I'd have to face Ezra at school on Monday, but I didn't have to torture myself before then. The last thing I needed was a visual reminder of what could have been.

The day dragged on forever and as the sun began to sink behind the clouds, I grew even more depressed. I should have been getting ready for the dance. Tori and I should have been fixing each other's hair and putting on our makeup.

Instead, my hair was piled on my head in a greasy, messy bed-head bun, and instead of a great navy blue dress, I was wearing pajamas and thick, wooly socks.

Around the same time I'd worked up the energy to reach over and turn on my bedside lamp, there was a knock at the door. Mom poked her head in my room. "Hey, sweetie, how are you feeling?"

"Still not very good." I sighed.

Slipping into my room, she sat on the edge of my bed. The first thing I noticed was that she was dressed in nice clothes. Not, stay at home on a Saturday night clothes.

"I hate to leave you alone, but Dad and I had made plans to go out to dinner with Jack and Susan tonight, and Mike's out with Marina. Will you be okay here by yourself for a while?"

"Sure." I tucked the blankets up around me. "Have fun."

As if the day hadn't been terrible enough, everyone in my house had a date that night.

Everyone, except me. *How could Ezra do this?*

"I've ordered you some Chinese food, and it should be here in a bit. Make sure you eat, okay? Feel better, sweetie."

I laid back and closed my eyes, wallowing in self-pity and misery as she left me alone again. I must have gone to sleep at some point, because when I next opened my eyes, it was much darker outside and the doorbell was ringing.

The food!

I jumped out of bed, remembered that I wasn't wearing a bra, and grabbed the hoodie hanging on the chair by my bed. Throwing it on, I ran downstairs, flinging open the front door.

My breath lodged in my throat and my heart stopped beating.

My food had arrived all right, but the delivery boy was the last person I'd expected to see standing on my porch.

"*Ezra!*" I gasped, frozen in place.

There he stood, dressed in a fancy suit, looking like a hot, young *James Bond*, holding take-out containers of chicken fried rice and crispy wantons in his arms.

"Looks like you've had a delivery. Are you okay?" He asked, concern etched on his face.

"Why do you care?" I blurted out before I could catch the words.

You would have thought I'd slapped him

across the face the way Ezra's mouth fell open. "I looked everywhere for you at the dance, but you weren't there. I waited and waited, and you never showed up. I finally found Tori, and she told me you had stayed home, so…I came to check on you. What's wrong?"

"Oh, I'm sure your girlfriend just loved you leaving the dance like that." I sneered.

Ezra's eyebrows shot so far up his forehead, they almost disappeared into his hairline. "Excuse me? What girlfriend?"

I took the Chinese food from him and stepped back inside the house. "Listen, you don't have to pretend any more. I saw everything last night, okay? Thanks for stopping by. See you at school Monday." I tried to shut the door in his face, but he thrust out a foot and stopped it.

"What are you talking about? What did you see?" He stepped forward, one foot inside the house.

"You and Casey, kissing after the game. Sound familiar? You should probably get back to her. I'm okay. Really. What was it you said to me that time? Oh yeah…you can't hurt me."

Ezra stared at the ceiling, running a hand over his face. "I didn't want anyone to see that."

"Well, we can't have everything we want, can we? Good-bye." I turned on my heel, hoping he'd get the message and leave.

He didn't. He followed me into the kitchen.

"I can explain," he said.

Opening the containers of food and taking out a plate and fork, I refused to make eye contact with him. "You don't need to explain anything. I get it. She's popular. She's a cheerleader, and you two looked great together last night. I've got the pictures to prove it if you want to see them. You're missing her and she clearly wants you back, too. I know how the world works, Ezra. You don't have to say anything."

"No, actually I think I do." He walked around the kitchen island until he was standing next to me. I still didn't look up at him. "You know I don't like Casey anymore. She and I are just friends."

"Funny, I don't usually go around making out with my *friends* after football games." I played with the fork in my hand, tears stinging my eyes.

Letting out a huge sigh, Ezra clenched his fists. "I was not making out with Casey. She caught me coming out of the locker room."

"So, I just imagined that I saw you kissing her?" I finally lifted my gaze to him, or rather, I scowled at him.

"Yes. I mean, no. I mean—*grrr*." He slammed both palms on the countertop.

"You can't have it both ways. Either you kissed her or you didn't." I inched away from him.

Ezra seethed. "When I came out of the locker room, she ran up, congratulating me on the win and I hugged her. *Hugged*. That's all I had planned on doing. But, before I knew what was happening, she was kissing me. I didn't want her to, and I did NOT kiss her back."

"That's not what it looked like from where I was standing." I put my hands on my hips and glared some more.

His mouth formed a thin line. "Which was where?"

"Behind the bleachers. I was waiting on Mike and I saw you come out. In fact, I—"

"Called my name?" He interrupted.

"Yeah."

"I heard you, or I thought I did, but then Casey was there and I thought maybe I had just imagined it." His chest heaved.

"That still doesn't explain how you *didn't* kiss her, because it looked like you were pretty into it." I crossed my arms over my chest.

"Well, you obviously didn't stick around or you would have seen me push her away." He lifted his arms, exasperated.

"No, I didn't stick around. When I saw you grab her, I left." My eyes and throat burned from holding back tears. Tears I did not want to slip out in front of him.

His brow creased. "I didn't grab her. What are you talking about?"

"You—" I fumbled about with my words and my hands, before I lunged for him, placing both my hands on his waist. "—you did this."

Ezra's entire body went tense. Lifting my eyes

to his face, I suddenly felt really stupid, but I couldn't pry my hands from his sides.

"I pushed her away." His gaze became intense, as if he could see straight into my very soul.

"That's not what it looked like." The tightness in my throat made it hard to speak.

His voice grew raw and gravely. "If I'd really wanted to kiss her back, I'd have done something like this instead."

I sucked in a breath as Ezra reached out and took my face in his hands. His thumbs gently caressed my cheeks and tugged me closer so that our lips were only an inch apart. Blood pounded in my ears.

Lowering his forehead to rest against mine, he whispered, "I swear to you, I don't like Casey. How could I, when you're all I keep thinking about?"

I bit my lip, my fingers digging into the fabric of his suit. "You keep thinking about me?"

He nodded. "I can't get you out of my head. I like *you,* and only you, in case I haven't been making myself clear." His breath tickled my cheek.

"You…" I couldn't find the words.

He pulled me closer. "Bailey," he whispered, his lips brushing feather soft against mine. I kissed him back, not sure if I was doing it right, but I didn't care anymore. I wanted his lips on mine and I figured if he wasn't complaining then I must be doing something right.

At the moment we broke from the kiss, I smiled. That was the first time Ezra had ever called me by my first name, and I loved the way it sounded on his lips. I wanted him to keep saying it and never stop.

"I'm sorry I didn't come to the dance." I uncurled my fingers from his sides, moving my hands to his arms.

His fingers moved down to my neck and then he smiled, tugging on the ends of my hoodie strings. "I thought you were going to give this back."

I glanced down.

I had put on his hoodie.

My cheeks burned. "Yeah, sorry about that."

Ezra inched closer. "Keep it. It looks better on you, anyway. Besides, it's kind of hot, seeing you wear my clothes." He wrapped his hands around my back and pulled me against his chest. Looking down at me, he licked his lips.

I rose slightly on my tiptoes, wrapping my arms around his neck. I closed my eyes. Puckered my lips.

A car door slammed shut in the driveway.

Ezra and I flung apart as if someone had set off fireworks between us. I jumped so hard, I tripped over a bar stool and had to catch myself on the edge of the counter.

"Get out." I shrieked, once I had gained my balance.

"What?" He said, breathless.

"You've got to get out. I'm supposed to be sick. I don't have time to explain." I rushed to the kitchen door and flung it open, glancing down the wraparound porch.

"Do you really want me to go?" Ezra appeared at my side.

"No. Yes. I'm sorry. I can't do this right now. Go, please." The front door opened.

Ezra grinned as I placed a hand on his chest and he let me push him out the door. "This isn't over." He winked.

"I know. Now go."

I closed the door, just as Mike walked into the kitchen. "Hey. Oh, Chinese food. I'm starving."

"Didn't you eat on your date?" I said, lunging for my food before he could steal it all.

Grabbing another plate from the cupboard, he grinned. "Yeah, but you know I can't say no to fried rice."

Snatching up the boxes, I wrapped both arms around them. "Mom ordered this for me. It's mine."

"Oh, come on, just a bite." Mike smacked his palms together and stuck out his bottom lip.

"Fine, but I get to fill my plate first." I opened the boxes and scooped out a large helping of chicken fried rice and placed three wantons on my plate.

"You feeling better?" He eyed me carefully, dumping the rest of the food onto his own plate.

"Yeah, I am. Much better." I smiled to myself.

"So you ready to tell me what Ezra did, or should I just go drag him out of the dance and rough him up a bit?" He shoved a huge bite into his mouth.

"No." I almost choked.

"Come on, I know he's the one who upset you last night. I mean, who else would have made you cry like that." He gave me a knowing look.

"I'm fine, Mike. Really, Ezra and I are good. I was just having a really bad night. Hormones, I guess."

"Okay." He held up his hands. "Enough said. Let's move on."

I couldn't believe how my day had completely turned around. Ezra had come to my house to check on me. He told me he liked me, and that he couldn't stop thinking about me. He'd kissed me in my kitchen. He'd told me I looked hot in his hoodie.

As Mike and I sat down in the living room to eat and watch a movie, the tightness in my chest began to ease, replaced by an entirely different sensation. I felt like I was floating. As if, at any moment, my heart would burst out of my chest.

I wished I'd gone to the dance. Ezra would have seen me in my dress and we would have danced all night together.

Then again, I wasn't going to forget what had happened in the kitchen any time soon.

I think I liked that memory even better.

CHAPTER FIFTEEN

I'M NOT SURE WHAT I expected the following Monday to look like, but it certainly wasn't Ezra waiting for me at my locker when I got to school. As soon as I rounded the corner into Senior Hall, there he was, sitting on the floor, doing his homework, completely unaware that everyone walking by was staring at him.

"What are you doing?" I said, squatting down next to him.

"Waiting for you." He grinned, leaning over to lightly kiss me. My cheeks burned as I imagined everyone in the hallway staring at us, even though there were only a handful of people around. I wasn't used to the whole kissing thing yet and doing it in public made me very self-conscience.

I couldn't help but grin like a fool. "Can I get in there?"

He slid to the side, far enough so that I could open my locker and deposit my coat and scarf. Dropping down next to him on the floor, I pulled out my camera. "Want to see what I got at the game on Friday?"

"Yes, please." He leaned closer, our sides

pressing together.

Flicking through the pictures, he pointed at them, making comments about what had been happening in the game at the time each one had been taken. The longer we sat on the floor, the more relaxed I became. I didn't mind so much that people were staring at us.

In fact, when our new Homecoming Queen, Casey Turner walked by and physically tripped over her own feet because her mouth was hanging open, staring at us, I felt a surge of pride course through my veins. I'm not ashamed to admit that I almost laughed and waved at her, but it wasn't necessary. Whatever she'd hoped would be rekindled between her and Ezra was shattered, and all I really needed to do was smile and lean my head against his shoulder as I watched her attempt to regain her dignity.

When the morning bell rang, I shoved the camera back into my bag, letting Ezra wrap his hand around mine and pull me to my feet. I expected him to let go, but he didn't. Dropping our joined hands between us, he laced his fingers through mine, making me tingle all the way down to my toes.

Leading me down the hall, he leaned over, his mouth close to my ear. "So, Halloween?"

"What about it?" Heat flooded my cheeks.

People were not just staring at Ezra and I, they were pointing at us as if we had tentacles instead of hands. I wanted to jump into a classroom and hide from them, but at the same time, wanted to shout for joy at the top of my lungs. Ezra and I were holding hands, walking down the hall together. We couldn't hide any more.

This was serious.

"Halloween is in two weeks and we have to get a photo of it for our project, right?"

"Yes." I was impressed he'd remembered.

"Well, I was thinking we need to have a plan. Either we're going to have dress up, or figure out a way to take pictures of little kids walking up and down the streets without it being creepy, or getting ourselves in trouble."

"Right. I assumed we'd take pictures of kids trick-or-treating, but you're right, we need to think how we're going to do it and still let them be anonymous." The wheels in my head began to turn.

I stopped walking. "What if we set up the shot so that we only got them from behind, in silhouette, against a lighted backdrop? It would take prior planning and setting up the shot, and I'd still want to ask the kids parents if it was okay first, but what do you think?"

"I like it." He squeezed my hand. "But, you know what I like even more?"

"What?"

"Food. How about you and me. *Taylor's.* Tonight?"

Was Ezra asking me out on a date?

"I love *Taylor's*," I said.

"Six o'clock?" He leaned in dropping my hand to wrap his arm around my shoulders.

With Ezra pressed so close, I could smell the wonderful cologne he wore. It made go a bit woozy. "Perfect."

"It's a date." He pressed his lips feather light against my temple, before turning down the next hallway.

Somehow, I managed to find my way into the correct classroom and sit down in my seat before my legs gave out from shock. I was going on a date with Ezra.

A real, actual date.

Even though I knew I would have to tell my mom the truth now, I was still more excited than I'd ever been about anything.

Except maybe applying to PSD.

It was funny, over the past few weeks, I hadn't obsessed over hearing back from them. I hadn't run to the mailbox every day after school with a knot in my stomach hoping to find a large, white envelope with Providence School of Design stamped on the front. Working with Ezra hadn't been the nightmare I'd imagined it to be. In fact, nothing had gone the way I'd imagined.

My heart clenched.

Hadn't I told Tori that the last thing I needed was a boy messing everything up for me? I'd been so prepared. I had planned for everything. Boys were never meant to be part of the equation, so why had I let that change? How had I gone from the girl who'd attacked Ezra in the hallway for not wanting to do the project with me, to the one sitting in a classroom all glassy-eyed over him?

Granted, he had turned out to be absolutely charming—but nonetheless? How had the idea of a date with him made me more excited than PSD ever had?

Was I letting myself lose sight of what was important? I didn't think so, but maybe Ezra had encouraged me to slack off and stop focusing on what was important during senior year—getting into college.

In so many ways, it felt like he'd helped me to expand my thinking, forcing me not to be so tunnel-visioned about my future. If anything, he'd helped relieve a lot of the stress I'd been under those last few months. His ideas for our project had all been really good, and I had high hopes for what we'd do for the rest of the photos we still had to take.

"You're worrying for no reason," Tori said, after I spent our first period American History class freaking out, instead of working on our project for the Revolutionary War.

"You think? I don't know, I'm just not used to this kind of thing." I lowered my voice when the teacher walked by.

"That's the point. You're less obsessed with college than I've seen you all year. Besides, Ezra is really great and he likes you. Don't ruin this by worrying yourself into a nervous breakdown." She squeezed my arm.

"I'm trying."

I couldn't remember the last time I had goofed off during an entire class, laughing and talking about boys. Probably when Tori and I were about twelve years old and she was in love with Lucas Smith, the new kid who had moved from California.

I'd told myself that I wouldn't rest until PSD was in the bag, but now I'd almost completely stopped thinking about it. Was I getting sloppy... in exchange for a social life?

Was Tori right and this was a good thing, or was I setting myself up for failure by allowing my focus to slip?

Did I even care anymore?

CHAPTER SIXTEEN

THAT EVENING, I walked out onto the porch to find Ezra standing at the foot of the stairs.

"Oh, I thought we were meeting there," I said, startled to see him.

"We were supposed to meet at the dance too, but you stood me up." He smirked. "I wasn't taking any chances this time."

I zipped up my jacket and walked down to meet him. "Were you really worried?"

Reaching his hand out to me, he grinned. "No, I just wanted to walk with you."

Lacing my fingers through his, we walked down the street, admiring all the house decorations and kicking up fallen leaves in our wake.

"So, have you decided what you're going to do with your pumpkin for the carving contest?" He asked.

"I think so. Mom and I planned it out a couple of days ago. Are you entering?" I didn't remember ever seeing him there before.

"No, I just help grow the pumpkins. I don't carve them." He laughed. "My grandpa does, though. He's won a few times, actually."

"So, why don't you enter?" I teased.

Ezra snorted. "I wouldn't want to scare the children."

"I'm sure it's not that bad."

"Trust me, no one wants to see my carvings. Last time I brought one home, my mom put it in the backyard, where only the dogs could look at it."

I giggled. "She did not?"

"Cross my heart," he said, mimicking the action across his chest, "ask her about it."

"Maybe I will." Of course it would mean meeting his mom, but if she and his dad were anything like his grandparents, I had nothing to worry about.

"I'm not lying." He raised our hands, twirling me under our arms as we turned onto the main square.

"We'll see about that." I spun again, coming to a stop with my hand against his chest. It reminded me of seeing him with Casey, and I pulled back.

"What's wrong?" His brows knit together.

"Nothing." I was being stupid, but knowing I wasn't the first girl to do that to him made me cringe.

"Come on then, let's eat." He steered me across the street and through the door of *Taylor's*.

Once inside, it was as if I'd never been there before. Don't get me wrong, I'd eaten at the cafe my entire life. In fact, I doubt if there was a table, or chair for that matter, that I hadn't sat at. I'd tried everything on the menu at least once, except the tuna melt—*eww!*—and Tori and I were on a personal mission to sample every single pie they served, including all the seasonal ones.

However, walking in with Ezra made me feel like it was the first time, especially when he pulled my chair out for me, before slipping into his own.

"Order whatever you want, but save room for pie." He rubbed his hands together. "I've had my eye on their pecan pie and tonight it will be mine."

I laughed. The whole dating thing seemed so easy for him, which caused me to worry, and my stomach to flop. How many girls had Ezra dated? Was he comparing me with all of them? I knew about Casey, but who else had come before her?

Trying not to think about it, or let my hands shake, I took a deep breath. It was only Ezra. I was comfortable around him. There was no need to worry.

Right?

When the waitress came over, Ezra ordered the bacon double cheeseburger, a *Coke* and a large plate of fries for us to share.

"And what about you?" The waitress turned to me.

"I'd like a cheeseburger and a *Dr. Pepper*, please." I was so hungry my stomach was growling.

"Coming right up." She turned on her heels and disappeared behind the counter.

I stared out the window, lined with yellow twinkle lights and fake fall foliage. "This is so pretty. It would make a great photo."

Ezra chuckled. "Do you think of everything in terms of how it would photograph?"

I turned to meet his gaze. "Not always. I mean, more so now with the contest and everything, but mostly, my mind goes to how I could paint, or sketch, something."

"How long have you known you wanted to be an artist?" He leaned forward in his chair, so interested in what I was about to say that he didn't even glance up when the waitress brought our drinks, setting them down in front of us.

"Since I was a kid, I guess. I've always loved to draw, and art was my favorite class in Elementary School. But, I think I really considered it as a career option when I found myself consistently choosing the artistic option for class projects. I didn't want to write about the battle of Valley Forge, I wanted to draw it, or build I model replica of it. So, I did, and I was good at it."

Ezra leaned forward, resting his chin on his palm. "I remember that replica from eighth grade. Mr. Morris kept it on his desk for the rest of the year. That was yours?"

I nodded, before taking a sip of *Dr. Pepper* and

continuing, "Then, freshman year, Mr. Shultz took a bunch of us on a field trip to visit PSD and I was hooked. I'd never seen any place like that before. I loved it and knew instantly that I had to go there. It's been my dream ever since." I paused. "So what about you? Has football always been your dream?"

Ezra stiffened, running a nervous hand through his hair. "Yeah, I guess. I mean, I've been playing football since I was a kid, too. It's all my dad and I have talked about for years. I kind of don't remember a time when it wasn't the plan for me."

I felt as if I'd stepped into something that Ezra wasn't ready to talk about, so I changed the subject. "So, what are you thinking for our Halloween pictures?"

"Oh." His face lit up, and his shoulders relaxed. "Well, I thought I could talk to my aunt and uncle, and see if they wouldn't mind us taking pictures of my cousins when they come over to trick-or-treat. I like your idea of doing it in shadow, from behind, but we might need to check on the lighting at my house before then to see if we'll need any more. We don't have a front porch, so it's not as bright as at your house."

"That would be great, if they'll agree to it." I was surprised by how much thought he'd put into the project.

We continued to share ideas back-and-forth until our burgers arrived.

Ezra shoved a handful of fries into his mouth. "I don't know why my aunt and uncle wouldn't agree to it. It's not like we'll be able to see the kids faces. Besides, if we can set it up ahead of time, then when they get there, it should go so much faster, right?"

"Yeah, and it beats having to stake-out in the bushes all night." I grinned, although the idea of hiding in the bushes with Ezra wasn't totally unappealing.

"Exactly what I was thinking. Oh, I also know that we need to get a nighttime, low light shot too. My mom has these old-fashioned lanterns that she lines our walkway with and only lights them up on Halloween night. I've always thought they looked a bit creepy, but they might be cool for that shot, if we turn off the front door light and do like a low-to-the-ground thing."

I must have had a concerned expression on my face because he stopped talking and his face fell. "Or not, it was just an idea."

"No." I reached across the table and took his hand without even thinking about it. "I love it. I was thinking we'd use a jack-o-lantern, or something, but I like the idea of real lanterns even better. You're right, they are a bit creepy, or at least I always thought so. Mike and I used to come to you house every year, because you guys had the best candied apples."

Ezra's gaze had fallen to our hands and then slowly moved up to meet mine. He rubbed his thumb up and down my knuckles. "My mom and Grandma still make them. They're always super popular. I can't believe you came to my house and I didn't know it."

My mouth watered just thinking about the apples. "You were probably out trick-or-treating, too. Do you think there's any way I could sweet talk your mom into letting me have one this year?"

His grin turned to a wide toothy smile. "I think we could probably work out some arrangement. I know where she keeps them."

"I'm so in." I let go of his hand and took a huge bite of my cheeseburger.

"When we're done here, we could go to my house and check out the lighting if you want?" He swirled the same French fry in ketchup four times.

Being the one who was typically nervous, it was cute to see Ezra squirming and not sure of himself. It was a side I'd not expected from him.

"I'd love to."

His shoulders dropped and he shoved the fry into his mouth with a grin.

After we finished our burgers, we went to scope out the pie counter. The staff changed them out every day based on the whims of the bakery crew.

"Yes, they have the pecan." Ezra punched the air with his fist.

"Can I help you?" The lady behind the counter

asked.

"Pecan, one scoop of vanilla ice cream, please." Ezra had the words out before she could even start writing it down.

Turning to me, she waited, her pen poised.

"Cherry please, also with ice cream," I finally said, although I wasn't completely sure of my choice. All the pies looked amazing.

We waited as she plated up the slices of pie and scooped the homemade vanilla ice cream from the freezer.

Ezra moaned loudly, his eyes closing as he took the first bite.

"Good?" I asked.

"So good." His eyes shot open. "Want a bite?"

My heart lurched at the thought of sharing food with him. Like the hot chocolate at the football game, but better. I nodded my head.

Ezra scooped another bite onto his fork and pointed it across the table. I opened my mouth and he gently placed it on my tongue.

"You're right. That is good." And it was. It was the best pecan pie I'd ever had, and I thought my grandma's had no equal.

"Told you." He shoved another huge bite into his own mouth, sighing.

"Want to try mine?" I offered.

"And ruin the good thing I've got going on over here? No way." He wrapped a protective arm around his plate.

"You don't like cherry?"

"No, I love it, but nothing is going to ruin this for me right now." He polished off the last of his pie and ice cream, leaning back in his chair and sighing in sheer bliss.

Once he'd paid for the meal, Ezra suggested we get two coffees to go. Taking our time getting back to his house, we wandered through the streets, cappuccinos in one hand and our fingers laced together on the other.

I grew more nervous with every step we took. I didn't know if I was ready to meet Ezra's parents. We'd only had the one date together. Were we at the *meet the parents* phase yet? I wasn't sure.

"Here we are." Ezra gestured up to his red brick Georgian house.

The lanterns were already lining the walkway, but like he'd said, they were all dark.

"Yep, here we are." I swallowed around the lump in my throat.

My palms began to sweat. I prayed Ezra wouldn't notice.

Then again, maybe it was my imagination, but I think his were sweaty, too. Was it possible that he was just as nervous as I was?

CHAPTER SEVENTEEN

EZRA'S GRIP ON MY hand suddenly disappeared as we approached the house. He took a deep breath, wiping his palms on the front of his jeans.

I hadn't realized how much I'd been relying on that connection between us to steady my nerves, until my own hands started to shake. Even though I kept telling myself that I had nothing to be nervous about, my heart was like a raging lion, ready to leap out and attack anyone who got too close. My anxiety only grew as we walked through the front door.

If I thought the outside of Ezra's house was impressive, it was nothing compared to the inside. Either the family farm business did much better than I thought, or his mom had very expensive taste. The entryway alone boasted marble tiles, a round table, which you had to walk around to get into the rest of the house, the top glistening like fine-polished obsidian, a huge gilded mirror, and a chandelier dripping with crystals.

I suddenly felt very under-dressed and embarrassed that Ezra had come inside our house. With its rustic, farmhouse decor that my mom loved, mismatched—but super comfy—furniture, and dirty dishes in the kitchen sink, he must have felt like he was back at the farm. I doubted if there had ever been a dirty dish in the O'Neill kitchen sink—let alone take-out containers or paper plates on the countertops.

Ezra slipped his shoes off right inside the door, and after seeing the pristine, arctic white carpet in the living room beyond, I did so too. Dirt had no place in his house. Not even a speck of it.

"Mom?" Ezra called after he'd stashed our shoes and jackets in the coat closet.

"In here." I pleasant voice answered from somewhere within the house.

Leading the way into the kitchen, Ezra stopped at the doorway, taking a deep breath. His obvious tension was not making me feel any better.

"Did you have a good time?" His mom glanced up from the planner and notebooks she had spread out on the table. "Oh. Hello. We weren't expecting you." Her expression became pinched when she saw me standing next to her son.

"It's nice to meet you. I'm Bailey." I could still be polite, despite the look I was being given.

"Bailey. So, you're the one my mom and dad keep going on and on about." A deep voice, belonging to Ezra's dad, came from the other side of the kitchen.

I flinched in surprise.

He walked over, handing his wife a cup of coffee, before leaning against the counter, crossing his arms over his broad chest. I'd seen Ezra mimic the same pose many times, but he had never looked so menacing.

I gulped.

Ezra broke the tension. "So, you know that Bailey and I are doing this photography contest for school, and we need to get some picture on Halloween night. If Uncle David says it's okay to take pictures of Elle, Cameron, and Oliver when they come to trick-or-treat, do you care if we take some shots of the front of the house?" He paused, sucking in a deep breath, but not relaxing his posture. "Oh, and one of the lanterns too?" He glanced at his mom.

"Oh yes, the art contest." His dad's voice dripped with sarcasm as he rolled his eyes.

My hands clenched into fists as the silence around us grew more oppressive. Ezra's mom finally spoke up. "Of course dear, as long as David and Kim say it's okay, we don't mind. Just give Kim a call tomorrow."

Ezra let out a short quick breath, which made me wonder how long he'd been holding it in. His body sagged a bit in relief. "Thanks, we're going to go out and check the lighting if that's okay?"

"Sure, whatever you need." She gave us a flat smile.

Every eye in the room was on me. I had to

say something. "Um, Ezra says you're making the candied apples again this year. They were always my favorite as a kid. My brother and I both loved them."

"Yes, they do seem popular with the children, and I take great pride in our traditions. When people expect you do something, it's not a good idea to disappoint them." Her smile grew syrupy, as her words hit me like a slap in the face.

I couldn't help but think that we weren't just talking about the candied apples.

"I'm going to get a flashlight out of the garage. I'll be right back." Ezra's eyes met mine and held for a fraction longer than necessary, as if to convey a message of courage and apology at the same time.

A few seconds later, I was left alone in the kitchen with his parents. Both of them stared at me as if I was something that smelled bad, or was going to get dirt all over their perfect house.

"So," his dad cleared his throat, "I know you've got my parents convinced that you're a lovely girl and perfect for our son, but I'm not so easily swayed. This whole art contest thing is turning Ezra's head, and I don't like it. He's never been concerned about anything other than football and college, but now he spends his time talking about photography, and you, and how this contest is somehow a good thing."

I forgot how to be polite, and interrupted him. "It is a good thing, Sir. If Ezra and I win, the prestige alone will make colleges take note. It will look very good on our applications."

"Just stop right there." He held up his hand. "Let me tell you a thing, or two, okay. Ezra is the star player on the football team. They're one win away from heading to District finals, and you know what comes after that? Regionals, and when he wins that, the State Championships. That's what impresses colleges, not some stupid art contest."

"Darrell, please." Ezra's mom tilted her head, giving her husband a pleading glance.

He ignored her. "Ohio State, Michigan, Alabama...they're looking for big wins in high school. Wins with my son's name attached. That's it. Period. And up until a few weeks ago, Ezra knew that. Now, you've turned his head and made him start thinking he could do something else. Maybe he is good at taking pictures, or maybe he's just pretending he is so he can get something from you. I don't know, and I don't really care which one it is, but he has changed. And that I do care about."

I must have seemed shocked, because he smiled and continued. "He's losing sight of what's important. But, don't, for one second, think that you have any chance of swaying him away from our goals. Football is what he's good at. Football is what he's meant to do and nothing is going to change that."

Tears welled in my eyes. I'd never been spoken

to like that before, especially by an adult—a friend's parent.

In the beginning, Ezra had fought with me about the contest, and now I knew why. But, he'd softened. He'd given in and seemed to actually be having fun with the project. Had he been pretending the whole time, to get what he wanted out of me?

My gut tightened when I realized that as soon as the contest was over and I gave him all the pictures I'd taken at his games, Ezra may never talk to me again. He could use me and then leave me.

I started to back out of the room, but his dad spoke again. "Take your pictures of Ezra's games. Give him what he needs, and then leave my son alone. He doesn't need you messing with his head. He doesn't need you at all."

I didn't wait around for Ezra to return, or to hear anything else his dad had to say. I turned and ran from the room. In the entryway, I wrenched open the closet door, grabbed my jacket and shoes and didn't even put them on. I flung open the front door and collapsed on the front step as tears streamed down my cheeks.

I'd never been so insulted in my life. I didn't know what to do. As I sat there, I thought of all the things I should have said, all the ways I should have defended myself, but in the moment, I'd been too shocked and upset to respond.

Pulling on my boots through blurry eyes, I wiped the tears away, threw my arms through the sleeves of my jacket, and took off down the walkway. The front door opened behind me, but I didn't turn. I simply marched forward, one foot in front of the other. I wanted to get home and forget the last ten minutes had ever happened.

A strong hand grabbed my arm and I turned so quickly I smacked hard against Ezra's chest. His arms came around me and I buried my face in his shirt and cried.

"What did he say to you?" His voice was strained.

I sobbed. "That I was ruining everything for you, making you care about something other than football. He said that was the only path for you and no one would care if we won the stupid art contest, or not. He said that as soon as you got what you needed from me that you would walk away. He told me to leave you alone."

"That's not going to happen." His arms tightened around me and I felt his Adam's apple bob. "I'm sorry, my dad is very opinionated."

"Opinionated?" I pulled away to look at him. "Ezra, he's got your whole future planned out for you, and you don't seem to care. He said you were going far, far away to college to play football. Do you want to leave your family, the farm, Rhode Island? Is that what you really want?"

"It's what we've planned for." His eyes narrowed.

"But is it what *you* want?" I placed both hands on his chest. It didn't feel weird that time. It felt right.

Blinking, he dropped his gaze, and for a long time, he just stared into my face. "I think so. I mean, I always thought it was what I wanted." His voice was so quiet, when he finally spoke I had to strain to hear him. "I don't know."

"Did I break you?" I winced at the implication behind his father's words.

Ezra flinched, violently shaking his head. "No. I was having doubts before this contest fell into my lap, but since I agreed to do it with you, I've been thinking more and more about my future. I like doing photography with you, and I'm good at it. I mean, I'm not saying I want to make a career out of it or anything, but for the first time, I feel like I have options. Like, maybe there's more out there for me than just football."

"There is Ezra. There are so many things you could do with your life." I eased my hands up his chest so they were resting on his collarbone, my fingers curling over his shoulders.

He shook his head. "It's too late. I waited until senior year to try to figure things out. I mean, I get good grades and all, but I've never let myself see if I was actually talented at anything besides football. It's all my dad and I have talked about for years. I can't disappoint him now. I just can't."

I blinked, swallowing hard. "Do you really want to move halfway across the country to play football? Do you want to leave your whole life behind to follow your dad's dreams?"

He pulled away from me. "It's not just my dad's dream. You act like I hate football. I don't. I love it. I'm good at it. It's been the thing I've dreamed of for longer than I can remember. Just because I'm starting to wonder if I could be good at something else, doesn't mean I want to give up my dream. Can't you understand that?"

Tears welled up again. "Yes, I totally get following your dreams, of course I do. But, what I don't get is, it seems like football is more your dad's dream than it is yours. Are you sure you're not just letting him push you the way that *he* wants?"

Ezra took a step forward. "How can you say that? You don't know anything about me, or my family. Yes, my dad is frustrated, but it's only because he cares about me. I'm sorry he said mean things to you, but you don't know the whole story."

"Maybe I don't, but here's what I do see. Your dad's convinced that I'm messing with your head, but maybe I'm the only one who sees your true potential. Maybe I'm the only one who's going to tell you that you can do more. That you're worth more." No matter how hard I tried to keep my voice steady, it eventually broke.

Ezra's eyes softened when the tears rolled down my cheeks, but the tension in his body remained. "It's not like I'm the only one with out-of-focus ideas here. What about you? You said Providence was the one-and-only option for you. You don't even want to apply somewhere else because you're so convinced you'll get in, but I'm not you. I need options. I don't get to have a dream school. I can't put all my hopes into one thing. That's what my dad wants for me, too. If I get into all the schools we've talked about, then I can decide which one I *want*—not before."

My throat tightened. "So, there's not one school that makes your heart beat a little bit faster when you think about it? Is there one whose catalog you flip through more than the others?"

He gave me a hard stare, but didn't answer.

I took a brave step forward. "Because it sounds to me like your dad chose the schools, and you're just going to wait, hoping you'll eventually fall in love with one once you get in. It shouldn't be that way, Ezra. You should apply to a school because *you* want to go there. Choose the one that offers you everything you would like to accomplish. Heck, apply someplace you think you'll never get into, just to see if you can."

Ezra ran both his hands through his hair, making it stand on end. "I want to believe you. I want to see the potential in myself. I want to explore other things that I'm interested in, that I'm good at, but it's too late." He kicked the ground with his shoes. "It's too late. The applications are ready to go. All I'm waiting on are your pictures."

"None of the schools are around here, are they?" A tear slid down my cheek. How could he do this? How could he just give up? Was it because he was too scared to stand up to his dad, or was he just wanting to please him so badly that he felt like he couldn't upset the grand master plans?

Ezra didn't say anything, and he didn't have to. The way his face fell as he chewed his lower lip and closed his eyes told me enough. *No.* Ezra would be moving far, far away from me. No relationship that I might have been hoping to have with him would ever last if I was here and he was off in Ohio, or Michigan. I felt sick.

"Boston College," he blurted out, shoving his hands into his pockets.

"What?"

Lowering his voice, he stepped closer. "You asked where I wanted to go. It's Boston College. They have so many classes and degree programs that I would like to explore, and their football team is currently number one in the Atlantic Division, but do you think I can walk in there and tell him that?" He pointed towards the house.

"Why can't you?" I took his hand in mine.

"My future's been decided." His shoulders sagged.

I grabbed his chin, forcing him to look me in the eye. "No, it hasn't. I know you want to make your dad proud of you, but if he loves you, he'll want you to go somewhere that will make you happy. You can't spend your whole life miserable because you did what someone else wanted you to do. Now is the time to step up and take control."

Our eyes locked and held, for minutes, hours, days… I'm not quite sure.

Ezra reached for me, pulling me close and hugging me tightly against his chest. His heartbeat thudded against my ear. "Thank you for believing in me," he whispered, "but this isn't as easy as you think it is. Things are decided. I'm sorry my dad spoke to you like that. I'll talk to him, and it won't happen again."

"Ezra—" I pleaded as we broke apart.

"I had a great time tonight. I'll see you tomorrow." He let me go and turned back toward his house.

"Ezra—" I repeated, my voice cracking.

He closed the front door before I could say another word.

CHAPTER EIGHTEEN

STRAINED. TENSE. UNEASY.

Those three words pretty well summed my life with Ezra for those next two weeks. Everything had changed that night at his house, and even though we hadn't really had a fight... we were different.

I hated different.

There were no more dates. We didn't hold hands in the hallway, and even working on our project was uncomfortable.

Sure, we got two more of the photos taken: acorns—because they were laying all over the ground outside the school, *so why not?*—and the decorated street scene, because after the Pumpkin Carving Contest that Thursday, the town was in full festive mode.

We went out just as it was getting dark and shot a few pictures around the town square, but it wasn't fun. Not like it should have been. Ezra suggested that we get coffees as we walked around, which we did, but the whole energy around us had charged. It was as if the slightest little thing might spark a fire, and I was worried that if that happened, we wouldn't be able to put it out.

Ezra and I hadn't talked about what happened that night again, no matter how much I wanted to. He really needed to be encouraged, but every time I thought about saying something to him, my mouth would go dry and I'd chicken out.

I didn't know what to do, or how to reach him.

As for the pumpkin carving contest, Mom and I both did okay, but my heart wasn't in it this year. Every time I looked at the white pumpkin Ezra had chosen for me, the burning behind my eyes would start up again, and I couldn't focus.

Afterwards, Mom and I carried our pumpkins home with only the blue "Thanks for Participating" ribbons, and stuck them on the front porch. I'd left mine with her to put a candle inside, because I really didn't care any more.

With every day that pushed us closer to Halloween, the knot in my stomach tightened. How was I going to go back to Ezra's house after the last time? How were we going to be able to work together if his dad was acting like a monster? I couldn't sleep, my appetite had practically vanished, and I found myself dreading one of my favorite days of the year.

That Friday night, I didn't go to the football game. I just couldn't. I know Ezra and I had a deal, and this was "the" game that would determine if they went to the District finals, but I couldn't chance another face-to-face meeting with his parents. Besides, things were so weird between us, I didn't know if he even wanted me there.

Instead, Tori came over and we hung out in my room watching tv and eating popcorn. Once, or twice, I opened the window to hear the score of the game, since the loudspeakers from the field echoed across the town. I even heard Ezra's name a few times, but each mention of him was like a punch in the gut. After a while, I stopped opening the window. I was only torturing myself.

After Tori went home, I was on my way back upstairs to run myself a long, hot bubble bath, when Mike poked his head out of the living room.

"Hey, Ezra's outside. He wants to talk to you."

I gulped. *Why is he here?* I braced myself for a fight I wasn't ready to have.

Making my way back down the stairs, my legs were like lead and my hand shook against the railing. Out on the front porch, Ezra was pacing. When I stepped outside and closed the door behind me, he almost jumped out of his skin.

Turning quickly, and heaving breaths as if he'd just been chased by a monster all the way across town, he locked eyes with me. "You weren't there."

"I'm sorry." I wrapped my coat around myself for warmth.

Ezra blew hot air into his hands. "I didn't know what to do when I looked into the stands, and I didn't see you. I played awful tonight. I couldn't get you out of my head. I'm sorry things have been weird between us. I know it's my fault and I'm trying really hard to work all of this family and college stuff out and make it right. I just…I needed you and you weren't there." His eyes were wide and his whole body rose and fell with his breaths.

"I didn't think you wanted me to come." I hung my head.

Ezra gripped both my arms. "How could you think that? Or course I wanted you there."

"I'm sorry I didn't get any pictures of the game?"

Huffing out a growl, he said, "I don't care about the freaking pictures. I care about you."

Gazing up into his eyes, my heart softened. "You've just been so distant the past couple of weeks. I figured if you had started to share your dad's opinions, then I was better off staying away."

He took my face in his hands, his cold thumbs drawing small circles against my cheeks. "Don't, for one second, think that I share his opinions, especially about you. It's taken me a lot of sleepless nights and deep soul searching, but I finally realized you were right. I don't want to move halfway across the country to play football when I could play here and be so much happier. I want to apply to Boston College. I want to stay in New England. I love it here. I'd miss everything too much if I left. This way, I can come home on weekends like Mike does. I can see my family. I can be near you."

My cheeks warmed beneath his touch. "What did you say?"

A smile crept onto his face. "I said I'd be near you."

"What changed?"

He pressed his forehead against mine. "You're my good luck charm, Bailey. How am I going to get you to come halfway across the country to watch me play if I leave?"

I smiled. "Ezra, not to hurt your feelings, but you do know I just go now to take pictures of you, right? I don't think I could stand having to go to all your college games, too. I mean it is football after all"

His lips were so close, I could feel his breath on mine. "You're missing the point."

I stilled. "What point?" I forgot what we were talking about.

"The thing I'm really trying to say here." He took a deep breath. "I like having you at my games but what I like most is you. I'm falling for you, Bailey, and I don't think that's going to go away any time soon. There's no way I could be half-way across the country and feel like a piece of my heart was missing."

"You're in my heart too, Ezra." Every nerve in my body was a live wire. I wanted to jump out of my skin.

"Don't give up on me," he whispered.

"Never." I didn't want to break the moment, but I pulled back enough to meet his gaze. "What are you going to tell your dad?"

Ezra's jaw clenched. "I don't know. He's going to be so pissed when I tell him. Maybe I should just apply to Boston and if I get in, then I'll tell him."

"Don't you think he'd want to know now?" I couldn't imagine pulling a switch-up like that on my parents, but then again, mine had let me apply wherever I wanted.

Shaking his head, he said, "no, he won't want to know at all, but why say anything until I know for sure that I've gotten in, and if there's any chance of getting a place on the football team. I mean, whatever else I may want to study and do, I still want to play college football."

"Do you have the application yet?" I asked.

Ezra shook his head. "I figured I'd get one from the Counsellor's office at school on Monday."

I took his hand in mine. "Come with me."

Pulling him into the house, I led him up the stairs to my room. My parents were in the kitchen and would probably say something about me taking a boy to my room, but we wouldn't be there long.

"Uh…" His eyes widened and a questioning expression came over his face as if he was wondering the same thing.

I grinned. "Don't get excited. I have something for you."

Leaning against the doorframe with his hands in his pockets, Ezra surveyed my room. I hadn't even thought to make sure it was tidied up before I brought him up there, but it was too late now. I went to my desk and opened the top drawer.

"Here." I walked back over and handed him the packet.

"What's this?" He turned it over.

"An application to Boston College." I grinned.

His mouth dropped open. "But…how?"

Shrugging, I said, "I picked it up after that night at your house. I was trying to find a way to encourage you to apply and was waiting for the right moment to give it to you."

"Has anyone ever told you you're the best?" He wrapped me up in his arms, the application packet crinkling against my back. He pressed his lips to mine.

"No, but I like hearing you say it." I whispered against them.

"Hey, what's going on up there?" Dad's voice boomed up the stairs.

Ezra and I shot apart, laughing. "Nothing. I'm just getting Ezra some paperwork he needed. We're coming."

Ezra said hello to my parents as we passed them in the kitchen. Mom was smiling, but Dad crossed his arms over his chest and sucked on a tooth as we headed for the front door.

Back on the porch, Ezra turned to me. "Hey, I forgot to tell you the other good news. We won the game, despite my pathetic performance."

"Oh, congratulations. So, this means Districts, right?"

"Yeah, anyway, the team is having a huge bonfire tomorrow night at Golden Park to celebrate. There'll be tons of food, s'mores, usually a scavenger hunt in the woods, I don't know what else…" He chewed on his lip. "Would you like to go with me?"

"Really?" I had never been invited to anything cool, and the football team's bonfires were legendary.

"Who else would I take?"

"Yes. Of course, I want to go." Heat flooded my cheeks at the anticipation of a party with the cool kids in the woods.

"Then I'll pick you up tomorrow night." He stepped closer to kiss me good-night, but Mike flung open the front door at that very moment.

He eyed Ezra up and down. "Hands to yourself, O'Neill. That's my little sister."

"Shut up, Mike." I yelled after him as he jogged to his car. "Sorry," I turned to Ezra.

"It's okay," he smiled, leaning over to give me a quick peck on the cheek. "Good-night."

"Good-night, Ezra."

CHAPTER NINETEEN

WHEN EZRA PICKED ME up the next night, I was the perfect combination of excited and terrified. I'd never been around the other football players. I mean, I'd known them all since grade school—Cedar Falls was a small town, after all—but we'd never socialized.

And that went for their girlfriends, too.

When we arrived at Golden Park, my stomach was doing somersaults, but it soon calmed down. The football team didn't seem nearly as intimidating without their pads and helmets on, and I was surprised to see that I was actually friends with at least three of the girls there. Kelsey, Becca, and Chloe were the kind of girls that you sit next to in class, and when the teacher makes you choose a partner for a project, or hands out a group assignment, you know they'll work with you and it never feels weird. Not really friends, but almost.

"Hey, Bailey." Becca ran over as soon as she saw us get out of Ezra's jeep.

"Hey," I said, reaching into the back seat and picking up the bags of marshmallows that Ezra had brought.

"It was *his* hoodie?" She half whispered—half shrieked—as soon as Ezra had walked away and was doing that fist bump, shoulder slap, secret hand shake thing guys do when they see each other.

"Yep." I couldn't help smiling.

"OMG! I cannot believe this. You and Ezra. Wow!" She gushed all over me as we walked to where the other girls were standing around a table piled high with shopping bags full of food.

Becca told everyone about me and Ezra, and I didn't mind one bit. Actually, it saved me having to do it myself. I still had to field tons of questions, but the girls were all super cool about it.

"So, what are we eating?" I glanced at the food on the table.

"Nothing, if Joel and Flynn don't get the fire going soon," Chloe huffed, "they keep telling us they know exactly what they're doing, but as you can see, it's getting dark and we still have no fire."

I watched as Ezra went to join the boys, helping them stack the logs in a different formation. After hauling a pile of old newspapers from the back of his jeep, he pulled some extra matches from his coat pocket and bent close to the wood.

Soon, there was a fire, blazing away.

Joel walked over and wrapped his arms around Becca. "See, babe, I told you we could do it."

"Yeah, good thing Ezra got here when he did, or we'd still be freezing." She reached up and patted him on the cheek.

"Hey, I had things under control." He squeezed her tighter. "Now, where's the food?"

"Right here." Kelsey pulled a dozen packages of hotdogs out of one bag. "Why don't you grab the sticks from Ben's truck and get cooking."

"Yes ma'am." Joel unwrapped his arms from Becca and threw Kelsey a salute, before scooping up the hotdogs and carrying them back to the bonfire.

The boys loaded as many hotdogs as they could onto the sticks and before long, they were blackened to perfection. The girls and I had piled the table with buns, condiments, and so many bags of chips and pretzels they were practically falling off. Two of the guys had arrived with huge coolers full of drinks, and for dessert, one end of the table was a mountain of marshmallows, chocolate bars, and graham crackers.

Once the hotdogs were cooked, we spread blankets and chairs around the huge bonfire and sat down to eat. Ezra and I sat on a blanket near the far side of the fire, a bit away from the others. It reminded me that we needed to get a photo of the bonfire for our project, as well as one of the marshmallows, or s'mores, if we could.

"Do you think anyone would mind if I took some pictures?" I asked Ezra as he slumped down beside me on the blanket and handed me a can of *Dr Pepper*, dripping with freezing cold ice from the cooler.

"I don't think so." He took a huge bite of his hotdog.

"Maybe I should do it now while the fire is really big." Setting down my plate, I pulled the camera from my purse.

Ezra thrust out the hand holding his hotdog. "Drop the camera. Now is the time for eating. We can take pictures later."

"But, I don't want the fire to die down too much and lose the light." I rose up on my knees.

Mimicking my every move, he said, "if the fire dies, I'll stoke it back up for you. Come on, eat."

"I don't know." I glanced longingly between him and the fire.

Putting on his best pirate voice, he shoved his hotdog at my chest like a sword. "Arr…listen here, milady, I don't want to hurt you, but I will if I have to."

Bursting out laughing, I grabbed my own hotdog, holding it out towards him.

Raising his other hand over his head, he grinned. "En guard."

"Really, you want to sword fight right here, right now, with hotdogs?" I snorted with laughter.

He swatted at my hotdog with his. "What's the matter, afraid you're going to lose?"

"No, I just don't want to humiliate you by kicking your butt in front of the whole football team" I swatted back, actually making contact with him.

"Not gonna happen." He lunged.

I tried to dodge him, but ended up falling backwards, his hotdog smashed against my cheek—ketchup-side down—as he fell over me, our faces impossibly close. For the longest time we laid there, staring into each other's eyes. The rise and fall of my chest against his had my blood racing through my veins.

Ezra leaned closer, licking the ketchup off my cheek.

"What are you doing?" I whispered into the space between us, as his tongue flicked out again against my cheek.

I could feel him grin as he said, "what do you think I'm doing?"

My entire body became alive in the moment. I turned a fraction, glancing towards the fire. Practically everyone was staring at us. Turning back to Ezra, I sucked in a breath and reached up to tap him in the side.

He paused, pulling away, his eyes full of question, and longing.

I jerked my head towards the fire.

Following my glance, he sighed and closed his eyes. Reaching for my hand, he sat back up, pulling me with him. Settling himself back on the blanket, he handed me a paper towel to wipe the rest of the ketchup off of my cheek.

I felt bad for having stopped him, but I still

wasn't ready for an audience. And, not just any audience. The entire Cedar Falls High School football team—and their girlfriends. My self-confidence was not nearly high enough for that.

After we finished our hotdogs, everyone grabbed the sticks again and started roasting marshmallows. Ezra and I were able to get a really awesome picture of two of them on sticks crossed like swords in front of the bonfire, the marshmallows still glowing with blue fire. Once we'd checked the camera to make sure we'd gotten what we wanted, we roasted ours, and used them to make the best s'mores I've ever had.

Licking all the sticky marshmallow and chocolate from my fingers, I took out the camera again and walked around the clearing, photographing the bonfire from several different angles.

Ezra came to stand behind me. "Let me take some. I have an idea."

Handing him the camera, I grabbed a graham cracker from the table and sat back down on the blanket, munching away.

Ezra went somewhere behind me. I guessed that it was to get more of a larger group shot with the fire, which, I had to admit, would look pretty cool. When he returned, plopping down next to me, he handed me the camera. I flipped through the pictures he'd taken, but they weren't of the football team.

He smiled. "I couldn't resist."

While I'd been eating the graham cracker, Ezra had taken a photo of me from behind, sitting on the blanket facing the fire. I couldn't see any details, or tell it was even me, for that matter. All I could see was a girl in silhouette, watching a bonfire. It was artsy and cool and…

"I love it." I gushed.

"Of course you do. My pictures are awesome." He thrust his chest out.

"You're getting pretty good at this." I leaned my head against his shoulder, as he wrapped his arm around me, letting his hand fall to my hip.

"Why, thank you," he whispered into my hair.

"You're wel—"

"Okay guys, it's time." Joel jumped up.

Standing in front of the fire, he shook the large bag he was holding.

Everyone else stood up at once and rushed toward him, pulling flashlights from the bag and taking off running though the woods.

"What's going on?" I shrieked, as Ezra—with a flashlight in one hand—grabbed my hand with his other and pulled me into the dark woods.

"The hunt?" He replied, turning on the flashlight and following the worn path through the trees.

"What hunt? What's happening?" I was so confused.

He slowed his pace, but didn't stop. "Whenever we come out here, the Captain of the team hides something in the park. He leaves clues scattered around, and the player who finds the prize and returns back to the bonfire first, wins."

"What's the prize?" My legs were stiff from sitting in the cold for so long.

"Don't know. Could be anything. Freshman year it was 100 dollars. Sophomore year it was the team hoodie we'd all signed after our first game. Last year it was tickets to a *Patriots* game. It's always something really good though." He twisted the flashlight all around, up into the trees, down to the ground.

We walked passed other couples, shining their lights around, frantically searching for clues.

"Have you ever won?" I asked, carefully trying to avoid stepping in a hole or tripping over a log.

"Nope, but I have a feeling about this year. I've got my good luck charm with me." He squeezed my hand.

Leading us away from the path, and the rest of his teammates, Ezra and I crept through the brush.

"There." I spotted something white nailed to a tree trunk in the distance.

We took off through the forest. Ezra got there first, reaching up high and pulling a thin piece of white paper from the tree. He handed it to me, holding his flashlight so I could read it aloud.

"Search in the place where lovers meet."

Ezra and I locked eyes, as we both gasped at the same time and said, "the bridge."

Taking my hand in his, Ezra and I tore off for the most famous landmark in Golden Park—Lover's Bridge.

As if the park wasn't beautiful enough, in the center of the forest was a deep gully, cut over many years by a wide stream that rushed over rocks and logs on its way to the ocean. Hanging across the gully was a wooden suspension bridge. I'm pretty sure every kid in Cedar Falls had spent hours of childhood on that bridge with friends, one of you jumping on your end and watching your friend bounce on the other, then waiting for the ripple of come back to you and doing it all over again, for hours.

When we got older, we understood why it was named Lover's Bridge. If two people met in the middle of the bridge, by the time they were close enough to touch each other, the wave of movement they had both created on their trek to the middle would be enough that the lover's couldn't help but fall into each other's arms.

I had never met a boy on the bridge before, but I'd heard stories from others who had. My heart fluttered at the thought of Ezra and I meeting in the middle. I didn't care about the football prize anymore, I wanted to see if the rumors were true.

When we arrived at the bridge, no one else was there yet. That was a good sign. Ezra shone his light across the gully. Nothing was there.

"Aw man, we lost." He slapped his hand against his leg.

Noticing something on the other side, stuck to the end post, I pointed. "What's that?"

Ezra took off across the bridge, making it shake so much, he stumbled three times before he reached the other side. When he got there, he plucked the white paper, or envelope—I couldn't tell which—from the post and held it up above his head. "Got it."

"What is it?" I called.

He opened it—it was an envelope—and pulled out a piece of paper. "Oh cool."

"What is it?" I repeated.

He looked over the gully, shining his light at me. "Dinner for two at the Clam House in Newport."

"Oh, I've always wanted to go there." I'd heard their crab cakes were amazing.

"Well, guess where we're going next weekend." Ezra pocketed the gift certificate and started back across the bridge.

It was time to put the rumors to the test.

Taking a brave step towards him, the bridge wobbled. He glanced up, smiling, and slowed his pace. With each step we took towards each other, the more I had to hang on to the sides to keep from pitching forward. My heart beat wildly in my chest, but I couldn't tear my eyes from Ezra.

When we were only a few steps away from

each other, he paused, panting. "I've never been on this bridge with anyone before."

"Me either." A wave of heat washed over me.

Ezra took a step, the vibrations on the bridge causing me take one too, just to keep myself from falling over. "I've always wondered if what they say about it is true." His eyes sparkled in the shaky beam from the flashlight.

"You have?" My voice was barely above a whisper.

We were only about four feet apart, and my hands were shaking.

He nodded his head. Then, his smile grew predatory. "This is your last chance to turn back."

"Not gonna happen." I gripped the sides of the bridge to keep me on my feet.

Turning off the flashlight, Ezra stuffed it into his back pocket. Then, he lifted his foot, but didn't shift his weight yet. His eyes locked with mine. "Good, because whether the stories are true, or not, I'm going to do something I've wanted to do since that moment you pushed me up against my locker in the hallway. I'm going to make out with you on this bridge, Bailey Grant."

A tiny squeal ripped from my throat as he put his foot down, moving towards me in such a swift motion that I didn't have to wait for the bridge to make me move too. I was in his arms, both of us swaying in the lowest point of the bridge before I could blink.

Ezra's hand gripped the rail to steady us as

I fell against his chest and his lips crashed into mine. I didn't care that we were bouncing around over a gully, or that we were stomping around together like two wobbly toddlers to keep from falling over.

All I knew was that Ezra O'Neill was kissing me on Lover's Bridge and it was the best experience I'd ever had. All those sweet, innocent kisses we'd shared up to that point paled in comparison as Ezra picked up where he'd left off earlier with the ketchup, and his tongue slipped into my mouth.

Wrapping my arms around his shoulders, my fingertips found the soft ends of his hair. As the bridge stilled, Ezra wrapped one hand around the back of my neck and placed the other at my hip, pulling me against him, kissing me harder, deeper, completely knocking the breath from my lungs. His hand slipped up, his fingers finding the bare skin beneath the edge of my sweater. His fingertips were calloused as he pulled me harder against him so that all of me was pressed against all of him.

When I finally gasped for air, I gripped the front of his jacket with both hands. My blood was like fire in my veins, warming me all the way down to my toes. Both of Ezra's hands were at my hips then, holding me steady on the bridge. We shared the same ragged breaths as we stood there staring into each other's eyes in the dark.

"This is the best bonfire I've ever been to." His

voice was hoarse and pitched low.

I smiled. "Because you won?"

He laughed, his chest rumbling against mine. "Well, there's that too, but no, I meant this moment right here, with you." He tugged me close, catching my mouth with his again.

That time, the bridge wasn't shaking. It was still enough so that we could kiss without the risk of falling. I don't know how long we stood in each other's arms, but kissing Ezra was the best experience of my life.

When we finally returned to the bonfire, Joel congratulated us on the win. We made more s'mores and sat down on our blanket while we waited for everyone else to give up and trudge back to the fire. Ezra sat behind me with his knees bent, pulling me down between them where I leaned back against his chest. He kept pressing slow, gentle kisses to my neck, making me shiver against him. He lazily traced his fingers across the backs of my hands and in the spaces between all my fingers.

If someone had told me at the beginning of the year that I'd be sitting with a boy like him—whom I'd just made out with on Lover's Bridge—at the football team's bonfire, happy, kick-my-feet giddy, and perfectly content all at the same time, I would have told them they were crazy.

Then again, maybe I'm the one who was crazy, but just like I've learned from many years of studying art, sometimes a little chaos actually makes for the best masterpieces.

I was anxious to see just what kind of masterpiece Ezra and I were creating.

CHAPTER TWENTY

THE NEXT WEEK SPED by so quickly, I'm not sure where the time had gone. Everything was a blur. All I knew was that Ezra and I were so happy together. We held hands in the hallways, stole glances at each other across the English classroom, and snuggled close in Photography Class as we worked on our project together.

But, as Friday grew nearer, Ezra grew more and more nervous. He was constantly wringing his hands and every time he sat down, his leg jiggled with way more energy than I'd ever seen him have before. It was as if he couldn't stop moving.

The District Final was an away game, in Helmsdale, which meant that as soon as I'd kissed Ezra beside his locker at the end of the day, wishing him good luck, he ran off to get on the bus with the rest of the team.

Tori and I also left right after school, stopping for food along the way, and making it with just enough time to grab seats on the front row and get set up for taking pictures.

It had finally gotten cold enough that I'd permanently swapped a jacket for my winter coat, hat and gloves. But, even then, it was so cold that night, that despite the three blankets we'd brought, Tori and I shivered against each other for warmth. The stadium at Helmsdale High was much bigger than Cedar Falls, and a lot more people had come out to watch the game, along with the newspapers and tv crews who were, once again, there.

As soon as the teams marched out onto the field, Ezra immediately jogged over to where Tori and I were sitting.

"Hey, you." He grinned, rubbing his hands together to keep warm.

"Nervous?" I asked. If he felt anything like me, there was a battle raging in his stomach.

"Not with you here." He winked.

Tori rolled her eyes. "Okay, it's hot chocolate time. Want one?"

"Sure," I said, as she unwrapped the blankets, pulled her coat tighter around herself and marched off for the concession stand.

"Come here." Ezra motioned for me to join him on the field. "Bring the camera."

I didn't argue, even though it meant getting out from under the blankets, too. He met me at the bottom of the steps and took my hand, ushering me towards the field.

"Okay, so we need a football shot for the contest, right?" He asked.

"Yeah, but I figured we'd use one I'd already taken of you." My shoulders knotted as I stepped onto the field. It felt wrong, like my feet were on sacred ground that I wasn't meant to touch, or something. The turf was extra squishy beneath my boots.

"Well, I had a different idea, and got permission from coach to do it, but we have to make it fast." He raised an arm over his head, signaling to Joel, who threw him a football. He caught it against his chest and jogged to the center of the thirty yard line.

I followed. "Okay, what do you want to do?"

"Helmsdale's color is orange, and the stands are packed with their fans." He pointed back at the bleachers.

My gaze followed, and sure enough, the crowd was wearing at least 90 percent burnt orange, as well as the stands themselves being painted that color.

"I thought the orange would work better with the rest of our pictures than if we shot one at Cedar Falls, since our field is mostly silver and white. So what I'm thinking is, I'll hold the ball on the line like I'm getting ready to kick it, while you get down low and shoot the ball with the orange stands blurred behind it. It's not an action shot from a game, but I bet no one else will have one like it. What do you think?" His breath hovered in a white haze in the cold night air.

"I think it's brilliant." I dropped down onto my knees in the freezing grass, lining the camera up for the best shot. "Can you move this way about three inches? You're blocking the light."

Ezra shifted his weight, squatting down close to me so that he was only holding the football in position by his fingertip. "Better?"

"Much." Making sure the focus was on the ball, and the crowd was blurred in the background, I took several shots.

"Got it." I stood up, letting the blood flow back into my numb legs, and showed him the pictures I'd taken.

Ezra walked me back to the stands where he leaned down and brushed a kiss across my frozen lips before winking and jogging back to join the team.

"Look at you two, being all cute and stuff." Tori teased when I sat back down.

"I know. What's wrong with me?" I wrapped the blankets around myself and took the hot chocolate she passed me in both hands, blowing across the top to warm my cheeks.

"Nothing," she knocked her cup into mine. "I actually think it's really great. I like seeing you happy. You are happy, right?"

"Yes." I took a sip of hot chocolate and caught Ezra's eye over the rim. "Very happy."

The game that night was the best I'd seen the boys play. Maybe it was because I'd gone to the bonfire and knew more of the players better than I had before, or maybe the game was just that much more exciting, but I was on the edge of my seat the entire time, cheering, yelling, clapping.

When Joel ran the final touchdown across the end zone, clenching the win for us, I leapt up so furiously I almost knocked Tori off the back of the bench.

Afterwards, we all ran onto the field to congratulate the team. Becca, Chloe, and Kelsey were jumping up and down, hugging their boyfriends. Tori and I weren't quite so excited, but we joined the circle around the team, who had all taken a knee as the coach talked to them.

"Holy crap." Tori pinched her nose as we got closer.

Giving her a hard look, I had to admit that the sweaty, musty smell coming off the team was a bit overpowering. It made me glad that this on-the-field celebration with the fans wasn't an every game thing. The boys all needed showers—*badly*.

Maybe I didn't even want to get near Ezra if he was going to smell that bad.

The coach praised the boys on the victory and rallied them for the next games to come. He told them that now they were working toward Regionals, which would be in another three weeks. The team stood to their feet when he was finished and dispersed among those of us standing around, seeking out family and friends.

I looked on as Ezra hugged his mom, dad, and grandparents, before scanning the rest of the crowd and locking eyes with me. He smiled, pulling away from them and making his way over to where Tori and I were standing.

"I'll go warm up the car." Tori hugged the blankets to her nose and walked quickly off the field.

"Okay," I said, turning back as Ezra jogged up to me. His hair was sticking up all over the place, wet with sweat and smelling like even his cologne I loved so much wouldn't help. My first instinct was to keep my distance, but as he got closer, he stretched his arms out and I jumped right into them, holding my breath, as he lifted me off my feet and swung me around in a circle.

He squeezed me so tightly I thought my ribs would crack.

When I was back on solid ground again, I smiled up at him. "I's so proud of you."

"I can't believe it." He couldn't stop grinning.

I stepped back a fraction. "I was so nervous for you, I forgot to take some of the pictures."

"Who cares? You're here. That's all that matters." He reached out, both hands fitting around my waist. He leaned down, and I must have wrinkled my nose, or winced, because he pulled back, his brows creasing. "I smell as bad as I think I do, don't I?"

I nodded. "You're the worst thing I've ever smelled in my life, and I live with Mike."

Ezra clutched his chest. "Oh, that hurts, Grant, that really hurts."

I almost felt bad, but the smile which broke across his face told me he wasn't upset at all.

"How about this, I'll go hit the showers, and I'll see you tomorrow." He leaped forward, kissing me quickly on the cheek, before he winked and ran off to join the rest of the team.

My palm pressed his kiss into my cheek as I walked off the field and went to find Tori.

◆ ◆ ◆

The next day was Halloween, and that afternoon, Ezra showed up at my house looking super hot in a flannel shirt rolled to his elbows and jeans. We'd decided not to dress up in costumes, since we would technically be working that night. Besides, it was one of those days where it was a bit warmer, but extremely humid. I had a feeling that I would be a sweaty mess if I'd put on a costume.

Ezra's eyes roved over me as we stood on my front porch, which made me feel giddy inside… that is, until he started laughing.

"What?" I put my hands on my hips.

He pointed at me. "Nice outfit."

My gaze shifted down, then back up at Ezra, then back down. It took me a minute to notice that he and I were wearing the same thing. I too had donned a flannel shirt—albeit a different color and pattern than his, but still.

I started laughing too. "Well don't we make a cute lumberjack couple?"

His eyebrows shot up. "Couple?"

My pulse started racing. "I just meant—uh—I didn't mean that you and I were—oh forget it."

Taking a step forward and wrapping his arms around me, Ezra whispered against my hair, "you're really cute when you're nervous."

"Oh yeah, I'm adorable." I mumbled against his shirt, my face burning.

"I think so." He rubbed his hands together. "Now, I know we've got work to do in a bit, but I've got a surprise for you first. Are you ready to go?"

"Sure, just let me tell my mom good-bye."

I didn't expect it, but he followed me back into the house. My mom's face lit up when she saw Ezra walk into the kitchen. I told her we were going to get some pictures of his cousins trick-or-treating, so I wouldn't be home for dinner. She waved us out the door with a huge grin on her face.

Ezra drove out of the city and towards his family's farm. Once again, he took the secret road through the hills, but instead of going down into the valley towards the farm, he turned onto a narrow lane which I hadn't noticed the last time we'd been that way.

Climbing higher into the hills, we came to a space in the road where the trees overhead formed a tunnel of bright orange around us. Ezra pulled over and turned the engine off.

"You coming," he called over his shoulder as he got out and went around the back of his jeep.

In the back, Ezra had spread out an old blanket, along with a wicker picnic basket and a cardboard drink carrier from The Magic Bean—two cups resting neatly inside.

"What's all this?" I asked.

"Well…" Ezra climbed into the back, offering a hand to pull me up. "I was up here a couple of days ago and the leaves were so pretty, I thought this would be the perfect place to take the foliage photos we need. But then…" He handed me one of the pumpkin spiced lattes. "…then I also had the brilliant idea that there was no better place in the whole world, than right here, to ask you a very important question."

The sip of coffee I'd just taken lodged in my throat. My heart pounded violently inside my chest.

"What?"

Ezra's voice shook and his fingers trembled as he reached for my hand. His Adam's apple bobbed when he locked eyes with me and said, "can we make things official between us because I'd really like to start calling you my girlfriend?"

Words escaped me and I just grinned like a fool.

He leaned forward. "Does that smile mean yes?"

Leaning forward too, our faces inches apart, I found my voice. "What do you think?"

Then I kissed him.

I had expected the whole kissing thing to get

less exciting the more Ezra and I did it, but it hadn't. Every time was just as thrilling as the one on the bridge had been, and even as we grew more comfortable with each other, the moment we connected never failed to send sparks of electricity all the way to my toes. Reaching up, I held his face in my hands.

Pulling me closer, he deepened the kiss.

Outside, the wind blew, throwing leaves across the road and into the back of the jeep. I shivered, pulling away. Ezra's eyes were heavy and glazed as he rubbed his bottom lip with his thumb in the moments after we separated.

A thunderclap outside drew both our attention. "I think it's going to rain. Should we get the pictures we need before it hits? I mean, there is food in there and I'm hungry, but I don't think the weather will wait." Ezra pointed to the wicker basket at my side.

My stomach rumbled, but he was right. I reached for the camera, just as large droplets of rain began to beat against the roof of the jeep.

"We're too late." He sighed. "I'm sorry."

"Not necessarily." I looked around, inside and out. "I've got an idea."

Moving to the center of the jeep, I turned so that my legs were pointed out the back. "Sit like I am," I said.

Ezra moved over and stretched out beside me. With my coffee in my right hand, I acted like I was going to make a toast with him. He got the idea of what I was thinking and did the same thing with his. With my other hand, I lined up the shot.

"Cross your feet at the ankles," I said.

With our makeshift picnic, the orange canopy around us, and the rain-soaked, leaf-strewn road stretching out the back of the jeep, I couldn't have set up the shot any better. It was artsy, and cool, and I'll just say it, romantic.

"Cheers." I pushed my coffee towards Ezra.

"Cheers." He did the same.

"This is better than what I'd had in mind, but now we're stuck back here." Ezra leaned over to look at the pictures I'd just taken, laying his chin on my shoulder, pressing little kisses against my neck.

My breath caught in my throat.

He pulled the picnic basket closer to us. "You hungry? I made some sandwiches and stole two of Mom's candied apples, in case she doesn't let us have some tonight." He sat up, crossing his legs beneath him and opening up the basket.

"You made me food?" No one had ever done anything so sweet.

I leaned over and kissed him, as he mumbled against my lips. "Don't get too excited. It's not that hard to make a couple of peanut butter and jelly sandwiches."

"I love it." I took the cling-wrapped sandwich he handed me.

"Well, if that impresses you, I also stole a bag

of *Doritos.*" He puckered his lips.

After that kiss, we ate the meal he'd packed while the rain pelted down on the jeep. The wind chilled around us, making me appreciate the hot pumpkin spiced latte he'd bought me even more. When he finally unwrapped the candied apples, my eyes rolled back in my head at the first taste. I savored every bite until all the remained was an apple core on a stick.

The rain finally let up, the smell of damp earth and wet leaves filled the jeep. "Come on, let's see if we can get some of these pictures," he suggested, shoving all our trash back into the picnic basket.

I grabbed the camera.

My initial idea for a foliage picture had been something similar to the one we'd taken with me and the apples—one of us holding a clump of colored leaves—but what we found was that the puddles which had formed on the road now had beautiful orange leaves floating in them. The effect was breathtaking, especially with the low lighting and reflections in the water. We took turns taking pictures up and down the road.

Before leaving to go back to Ezra's house to set up for our Halloween photos, we took one more picture. Ezra stood behind me, pressing me against his chest as he wrapped his arms around my shoulders. I reached up and gripped his exposed forearms.

Since we had both decided to wear plaid

shirts that day, we not only got the flannel picture we needed, but, we also took our first photo together as a couple. It was the picture I never thought Ezra and I would ever take together, but I think it was my favorite one yet.

CHAPTER TWENTY ONE

THE NEARER WE GOT to Ezra's house, the joy from our picnic began to bubble over into dread. I stared out the window of his jeep and took deep breaths, hoping it would slow my racing heart and swirling stomach. All I did was fog up the window.

"Hey, you okay?" Ezra asked as we turned onto his street.

"I'm just nervous. The last time I was here…" I didn't want to think about it.

Sighing, he reached over and clasped my hand. "Relax, my dad's not home. He hates Halloween and all the *fuss* that Mom puts into it. He's on his annual run-away-to-the-Cape fishing trip with his buddies."

I let out a strained breath, but I still wasn't totally calm. "What about your mom? She didn't seem too happy with me last time, either."

"Mom should be cool. Give her a chance." He pulled into his driveway and turned off the jeep. As we got out, the streetlights were just starting to come on, casting the front yard in an orange glow. I followed Ezra into the house, remembering to take my boots off at the door.

"Ez, is that you?" His mom called from the kitchen.

"Yeah Mom." He took my hand and led me into the house.

"Hey, will you—" She paused when she saw us together, her gaze drifting to our joined hands. Licking her lips, she continued. "Will you two mind carrying these to the table by the front door. She gestured to the trays of candied apples on the countertop.

"Sure." Ezra dropped my hand and picked up the closest tray, heading out of the room and leaving his mom and I alone.

I was pretty sure that I was going to have to break the awkward tension first, but to be honest, I had no idea what to say to her. Ezra's mom was so different to mine. She was dressed in office clothes, even on Halloween—and a Saturday no less. She didn't have a single hair out of place. Her nails were perfectly polished and she wore fine golden bangles around her thin wrists and pearl studs in her ears.

My mom was probably sitting at home wearing the garish pumpkin leggings she'd been thrilled to get on sale last year, a loose black sweater with a giant pumpkin appliqué the front and her house slippers. Mom always insisted on dressing Halloween-ish—*her words, not mine*—even if she didn't go full out with a costume.

"The kids like it when they come by trick-or-treating" she'd always said.

I took a deep breath, my brain grappling for something to say, but Ezra's mom spoke first.

"Listen, Bailey—it is Bailey, right?"

I nodded.

"I want to apologize for what my husband said to you the last time you were here. It wasn't kind. You have to understand that he just wants what's best for Ezra and he gets a little bit blind-sided sometimes." She fingered her pearl necklace.

I bit my tongue. It wasn't an apology. It was, at most, an excuse. But, she was still expecting me to say something.

"Thank you, Mrs. O'Neill. I appreciate that. I also want what's best for Ezra. I believe in him. He's got real talent and I would never do anything to jeopardize that. I promise."

I prayed that would be enough to ease her worries.

"I hope that's true. He seems to really like you, which makes me want to give you the benefit of the doubt." She half-smiled.

"Thanks." I hoisted the other heavy silver tray into my arms and carried it to the front door.

"How's it going?" Ezra slung his arm across my shoulders.

I snorted. "How do you think?"

He handed me my boots. "She'll come around. Come on, let's get set up outside."

In the front yard, we lit the lanterns lining the driveway, then positioned ourselves near the hedges bordering the road. It wasn't quite dark enough for the pictures we wanted to take yet, but it would be soon.

Families began to emerge onto the streets not long after that. Children were dressed as princesses, pirates, witches, and cartoon characters I didn't recognize. Their faces were painted in bright colors, and they carried plastic pumpkins they planned to fill to the brim with candy and treats.

Some of the parents were dressed up too, carrying smaller children in their arms, or pushing them in strollers. Ezra and I watched them come up and down the driveway, huge grins appearing on their faces when they received one of his mom's famous candied apples.

Before long, Ezra's cousins arrived, and we were able to take the pictures we needed. The kids lined up at the door and we shot them from behind—a witch, a little *Batman,* and a short, squashy pumpkin—holding out their buckets and saying trick-or-treat. Ezra's mom was the only person visible in the photo since she was directly in the light as she handed out the apples, but we planned to blur her slightly so that she too would be anonymous.

Once we had the pictures taken, including the ones of his mom's creepy lanterns, we headed back inside the house.

"You two want some hot cocoa?" Ezra's mom

asked as we pulled off our shoes and hung our coats in the closet.

"Are you serious?" I said before I could catch myself. Hot chocolate sounded too messy and ordinary for this house.

"Sure Mom, that would be great." Ezra eyed with a raised eyebrow.

She headed for the kitchen. "Get the door if anyone stops by. I'll be right back."

Ezra and I leaned against opposite walls, staring at each other. When the doorbell rang, he answered it, handing out three more apples. I watched the way he spoke to the kids, bending down to their level, complementing their costumes and smiling that charming smile that had melted my heart more than once.

I think it was at that moment when I realized just how much Ezra O'Neill meant to me. How much I was starting to fall for him.

How much I cared about him…and his future.

Pushing off the wall, I marched straight into the kitchen. Ezra's mom was pouring hot water from a kettle into three matching grey mugs. She glanced up when I walked in.

"Can I ask you something?" I gripped the edge of the counter to steady my nerves.

"Of course." She paused, placing the kettle down on a blue trivet.

"What college did you go to?"

She flinched slightly as if that were the last thing she'd expected me to say, but then she smiled. "NYU."

I swallowed. "Was it your dream school?"

Spooning cocoa powder from a fancy metal tin, she stirred the first mug. "Yes, it was. Why do you ask?"

"Did your parents approve of it, or did they want you to go somewhere else?" My voice shook, but it held.

Her eyes locked with mine. I wanted to turn away but I mustered up the courage not to. "No, actually," she said, lowering her spoon, "my dad wanted me to go to Yale."

"Yale? That's impressive. Did you get in?" I leaned forward on the counter, feeling more confident.

She pursed her lips. "Yes. What's all this about, Bailey?"

"Well, I need some advice, if you don't mind?" My pulse steadied inside my veins. So far, so good.

"Oh." Her shoulders relaxed. She picked the spoon back up and stirred the second mug. "Wouldn't you rather talk to your own parents? How could I possibly help you?"

I had her right where I wanted her. "No, see that's the problem. My parents both went to Connecticut State, actually that's where they met, and they've been talking to me about it for years. My brother Mike goes there, too. I know it's a good school, but my dream is to be an artist."

She jumped on that like a kid with a new

trampoline. "What kind of artist?"

"I really want to go into graphic design, maybe working for a major advertising agency, or possibly using my love of photography and become a photo journalist, or something. I don't really know yet. All I know is that if I want to follow my dreams, I can't do that at Connecticut State. My dream is go to Providence School of Design."

She raised an eyebrow. "That's a hard school to get into."

"I know. Believe me, I know." I smiled.

"So, what advice do you need?" She pushed a mug towards me, along with a crystal bowl full of soft, plump marshmallows.

I added a handful to the top of the mug, smiling. "How do I tell my parents? I mean, they both want me to go where they went, but do I give up my dream of Providence to do what they want? How did you tell your parents you wanted to go to NYU over Yale? I mean, were they mad?"

"Yes actually. When I told my parents I wanted to pursue a career in the fashion industry, they were furious, especially my dad. But, I explained that by living in the city, I would gain practical experience, more opportunities to intern at magazines, and that as much as I loved and respected them, and was proud at the fact that I could get into Yale, I had to follow my heart." She moved over to the table, pulling out a chair and motioning for me to join her.

Sitting down, I wrapped both hands around the mug. "Did they understand, or were they still mad?"

She chuckled. "I told them I wanted to give up an Ivy League university and go to New York City to study fashion. What do you think?"

"Good point." I took a sip and paused. I don't know where Ezra's mom had found that hot chocolate, but it was the best I'd ever tasted.

"Do you regret your decision?" I waited with bated breath for her response.

She didn't hesitate as she met my gaze. "Not for a second. I got a great internship at StyleCo. Magazine. I made wonderful connections in the industry, graduated with honors, and now have a job that I love as a design consultant for Front Row, one of the major fashion magazines in the country. I love my life."

That explained the opulent decor throughout the house.

"And you wouldn't have been happy if you'd gone to the college your parents were pressuring you to attend?" My heart began to pound.

She worked her perfect red lips between her teeth. "Of course not. Why are you so interested?"

"She's interested because of me?" Ezra appeared at my side.

I'm not sure how long he'd been standing there listening to us, but I prayed he wasn't angry with me for talking to his mom.

"Sweetheart?" She seemed just as shocked to see him as I was.

"Why have I never heard about Yale and how you turned it down to go to NYU? Why didn't you ever tell me about going against grandma and grandpa to follow your dreams?" He placed both palms flat on the table beside me. "I mean, isn't that the kind of pep talk that would help me make some really hard decisions right now?

Her face went pale. "Ezra, you have to understand that they just wanted what was best for me. My family had gone to Yale for decades. They thought I would want to go there too."

I could feel his body tense next to me. "But, you went against them. You made the decision that was best for you and never looked back."

"Yes, I did." Her face grew pinched.

"I don't believe this." He stood, running his hands through his hair. "I've been going crazy trying to figure out how to tell you that I don't want to go to one of Dad's football schools out west, and you've been holding out on me this whole time. You know exactly what I'm going through here, but didn't think I had the right to know that you understand me."

His mom's eyes grew as wide as saucers. "You what?"

Ezra pulled out a chair, flipped it around backwards and plopped down on it. "Mom, I don't want to go to Michigan or Ohio, or wherever else Dad wants me to go."

"But what about football? What about all the hard work we've put in?" She clenched her mug so hard her knuckles turned white.

"I still want to play football, but I want to do other stuff, too. I want to study things I'm interested in, like business and art and computers. I want to stay here. I like it here. I don't want to be thousands of miles away from you guys, and grandma and grandpa and the farm. This is my home."

I reached under the table and laid a comforting hand on his knee.

"Where do you want to go then?" Her face was tight, like she was trying hard to keep everything together.

"Boston College." His voice cracked as he finally said it out loud. "I want to go to Boston. Their football team is good right now. They're ranked first in the Atlantic division. If I got in there, I'd still be playing for a good school, but I want to do more than that. Can you understand?"

His mom clutched her pearl necklace. "Of course I understand, sweetheart. I'm sorry you were scared to tell us this. Boston's a great school, and you know I wouldn't mind having you stay close-by. We thought you wanted to go somewhere else. We thought that was your dream."

"So did I, but then I started working on this project with Bailey." Reaching under the table, he squeezed my hand. "I realized that I'm good at more than just football. I want to go to a school where I can study new things. I'm not going to play football forever. I want a real job when I graduate, but I need to find out what I'm good at, what excites and inspires me. I need football to be a part of my college experience, not the entire focus."

As we clung to each other under the table, I'm not sure if he or I were more surprised when a smile worked its way onto his mom's face.

"Ezra, your father and I never meant to pressure you like this, and I'm sorry you felt like you couldn't talk to us about it, but I want you to go to the college that you want to attend."

"Really?" Ezra's face broke into that wide, dimpled grin I love so much.

"Of course. Apply to Boston College if that's where you want to go. I want you to be happy."

"What about Dad?" Ezra tensed again.

"You let me handle your father, okay? He wants you to be happy too, even though it may not seem like it. Everything will be alright. I promise."

"Thanks, Mom." He shot out of his seat and threw his arms around her neck.

I was giddy inside watching everything unfold before my eyes.

"We love you. We never meant to hold you back." She patted his back.

The doorbell rang at that moment and he

took off sprinting for the front door. When his mom and I locked eyes again, she was giving me the strangest pinched expression.

Ice fell into my stomach. "What?"

"Do your parents really want you to go to Connecticut State?"

I smiled. "They did, but they also fully support my decision to go to Providence."

She stood up and walked back to the kettle, pouring more hot water into her cup. "You know, Bailey, if this whole design thing doesn't work out for you, you might consider a career in law. You make a pretty good negotiator."

"I'll keep that in mind," I said, as Ezra came back in and plopped down beside me, resting his hand on my knee.

His mom turned around. "And, if PSD does accept you, I might know a few people in the biz who'd be interested in working with an up-and-coming photo journalist, or design major."

I almost spit hot chocolate on the back of Ezra's head. "Really?"

She laughed. "Yes. I admire young people who know what they want and go after it. Besides, I do have a few connections."

"Wow, thank you." I couldn't believe she was offering such a thing.

She smiled. "Maybe I should be the one thanking you."

The doorbell rang again, and that time she went to answer it.

Ezra turned to me, a grin on his face. "Okay, so I missed a lot there. How did you do that? What did you say to her?"

"I just asked her for advice on how to tell my parents I didn't want to go to the college they both wanted me to. I asked her if she'd had any experience with it, and by sheer luck, she had. She started talking. I thought if I could maybe soften her up by making her think we were talking about me, I'd figure out a way for you to tell your parents about Boston. I had no idea it would go this well, or that you'd walk in, in the middle." I took a sip of hot chocolate.

Ezra shook his head. Reaching up, he laid his palm against my cheek.

I leaned into his touch. "I had to do something."

He inched forward, but his mom returned then, so the kiss would have to wait.

For the rest of the night, we helped hand out all the candied apples, except for the two we stole from the tray and snuck outside to eat. After helping his mom clean up the kitchen, we showed her the photos we'd taken that day.

"These are really good." Her gaze shifted between Ezra and I. "What are you thinking for the overall design?"

I told her all about our ideas and about the other pictures we'd taken.

"I like it. You definitely have an eye for this, Bailey," she said.

"Thanks, but a lot of those ideas were his." I pointed to Ezra.

She nodded her head as if she already knew.

As Ezra walked me home later, his steps were lighter, his mood had improved, and it made my heart swell to think that I'd had a part to play in his future happiness. The fact that his mom and I were getting along better, too, may have put a little lightness in my own steps.

CHAPTER TWENTY TWO

TUESDAY MORNING, I woke up to a text from Ezra, telling me that he wouldn't be at school that day. He'd started running a fever the night before and then woke up that morning with a sore throat. His mom said it looked like strep, so she was calling the doctor and he was staying in bed.

I'm kind of ashamed to admit that my first thought wasn't for his well-being but rather, I hope I don't get it. I did kiss him a lot two days ago. The last thing we needed was for both of us to get sick right as the project was nearing its deadline. There was still so much to do.

What I said to Ezra, though, was to feel better and let me know what the doctor said.

It felt weird to go to school without him. I mean, I'd walked the halls of Cedar Falls High by myself for the last four years, but without Ezra's hand in mine, it was as if I was wandering around in a daze.

What was happening to me?

I had never been like that before. I used to laugh at those couples who walked around like they were joined at the hip, and yet, I'd somehow become one of them. As much as I liked being with Ezra, it also scared me. Was I depending on him too much?

My doubts only got worse when I went to Photography Class and he wasn't sitting beside me. There were only three weeks left to get our project completed and sent off for judging, and all we'd done so far was color-grade the photos and collect a few bits for the display.

Because a lot of our photos involved food of some sort, we had decided to make models of the pieces we wanted to showcase, since using real food wasn't an option. Ezra and I had gone to The Magic Bean and asked for an empty to-go cup, with the idea of cutting it in half and attaching it to the boards somehow. It would represent the picture we'd taken of our picnic in the back of Ezra's jeep.

Using my free time in some my other art classes, I had started work on crafting a fake candied apple, a few other smaller cellophane-wrapped candies, realistic-looking roasted marshmallows on sticks, and the front of a 3D lantern, which I made to look like the ones lining the walkway to Ezra's house.

I had also spent days drying out pumpkin vines and leaves in our garage, as well as cleaning up the acorns and twigs we'd collected. When my mom had decided to go to the fabric store in town to get some Christmas material for some craft project she was working on, I had gone with her, and bought two yards of a soft brown and orange flannel to use as a major portion of our backdrop. I'd even kept one of the newspaper articles about the District football game to add as our memento for the photo we'd taken on the field that night.

Ezra had taken the old fruit crates home and pulled them apart so that we had slats of wood instead of boxes. He'd spent a long time making sure all the nails were removed so as not to damage any of our props or photographs.

The only pictures we still needed to get was a picture of us baking something, as well as one from a corn maze. The best maze around was in the nearby town of Wrightsville, and we'd planned on visiting it as soon as we got a free moment.

I went to one of the computers and pulled up all the pictures we'd spent the better part of two weeks meticulously color-grading. Each new photo was easy to slot in with the rest once we'd decided how we wanted them colored.

I knew I should have waited for Ezra, but I had nothing else to do, so I started to work on the arrangement of the photos.

"Nice work." A voice behind me made me jump.

I turned around to see Mr. Shultz standing there, staring over my shoulder.

"Thanks."

He leaned down, getting a better view of the screen. "I like these, but they're not really your usual style, are they?" His eyebrows rose in question.

My breath caught in my throat. "What do you mean?"

"Well, I know the kinds of pictures you like to take. You like to plan everything out and make it look perfect. You're not this spontaneous. These seem more impulsive, less staged. Except for this one." He pointed to the apple cider photo. "This one looks like you, but what about the rest of them?"

When it dawned on me what he was implying, it was as if someone had poured ice water into my stomach. Hadn't I fought with Ezra in the beginning about my ideas and how I was the artistic one, not him? And yet, most of the photos we'd taken for the project had been his ideas, not mine.

Not mine.

"No." I admitted with a gulp. "Ezra came up with a lot of them. I took most of the photos, but they were his ideas."

Mr. Shultz smiled. "I told you not to count him out. I knew this project would be good for you. Keep it up. I'm excited to see what the final piece looks like." He waved his hand over the screen.

Turning back to the computer, I shut my eyes tight, biting the inside of my cheek. He was right. The project I'd set my hopes and dreams on was barely even mine anymore. I'd let Ezra suggest most of the photos. What was I thinking?

Had I really believed that his ideas were so much better than mine, or had I become so obsessed with *him*, that I'd let him talk me out of my better judgement?

Opening my eyes, I looked more critically at the photos on the screen. They were impressively shot, I had to admit. They captured all the required elements, and I felt like each one told a story. The longer I stared at them, I started picturing Ezra's face. The photos we'd taken weren't just ticks off a checklist, they were pictures which represented us.

Everything we'd done. Every moment we'd had together had involved taking pictures. I remembered the giddy butterflies I'd had as we took those first apple photos. It was the first time Ezra had touched my hands in a way that sent electricity coursing through my body. I thought about our picnic date in the rain, and the fallen leaves that had surrounded us.

The photos weren't images, they were memories. *Our memories.*

I wondered if the judges would feel what I felt when they looked at them, or would they see a sub-standard attempt at art that had been led by an amateur?

If Providence compared this project with the portfolio of work I'd submitted with my application, would they be impressed? Something deep inside told me I'd let my head get caught up in a boy, allowing him to push his ideas to the surface—while drowning my own—and I hadn't stopped it.

I had given in without a fight, not letting my artistic ability lead the project as I had planned all along, but instead, I had spent so much time and effort concerned about convincing Ezra that he could do more and be more, that I had suppressed my own talent.

It was too late to go back and retake all the photos, and if we did, it would crush Ezra. I couldn't explain to him what I had discovered, without hurting him, but it was *my* future on the line here, not his. Could I honestly turn in a project that didn't scream… ME?

Mr. Shultz seemed to like the pictures, so maybe I was overreacting. Even if most of the photo ideas weren't mine, if we won, would it matter?

The answer was no, it wouldn't, but the seed of doubt had been planted inside me and it was starting to take root.

At some point over the last few months, I had become a girl with two lives: *Before Ezra* and *After Ezra*.

Before Ezra, I had been focused. I knew exactly what I wanted and was determined that nothing was going to stand in my way of getting it. I obsessed over colleges, praying I'd hear back from PSD, anxiously checking the mailbox for large white envelopes with my name on them. I spent my free time drawing, painting, and taking pictures. Those were the things that made me happy.

Unfortunately, my creative life after Ezra had collapsed. Instead of dreaming up a new painting, I had spent my time thinking about him, wondering when we'd see each other again. I had once dreamed about Through the Lens, but now I was more concerned about the boy I was working with than I was about the project itself.

I couldn't remember the last time I picked up a paintbrush or my sketch pad. I didn't go out on solitary walks to take pictures, and I certainly wasn't as concerned about Providence as I had been.

As I should have been.

Unable to look at the pictures anymore without a lump forming in my throat, I pulled the memory card out of the camera I'd been taking Ezra's game photos with, and sorted through them instead, editing the best ones and saving them to a flash drive so he could select the ones he wanted to use. I decided to drop it by his house after school so he could finish his applications and get them in the mail.

There was still time left once I'd finished with that, so I grit my teeth and pulled up all the project photos again, arranging them into pairs and groups which I felt looked best together.

Every choice was mine, and mine alone. I decided how the pictures fit. I decided what I wanted.

I was glad Ezra wasn't there, even though the thought made me feel sick.

His ideas had been good, and they had worked out well for us up to that point, but I had to regain control of the project. My future depended on it.

I prayed he would understand, or that I could take back over without him even realizing what was happening, because the last thing I needed was for our relationship to suffer because of this, but I had to put PSD first.

Above Ezra.

Above everything else.

Without him ever knowing anything about it.

CHAPTER TWENTY THREE

AFTER STOPPING BY HIS house to drop off the flash drive, I messaged Ezra. He said it was strep, and I have to admit, a small part of me felt relieved.

Was I a terrible person because I was glad to have another day, or two, to work on our project by myself? The way my stomach flipped upside down at the thought told me I probably was, but I couldn't help it. I needed to gain some perspective, not only on the project design, but on myself, and more importantly, myself with Ezra, and what that was supposed to look like now.

He and I talked on the phone every evening until his voice gave out, and then we'd spend the rest of the night texting until one of us fell asleep—usually him. Despite the feelings I'd been grappling with, I missed Ezra so much it hurt. I needed him in my life, but I had no idea how to balance everything that was weighing on my heart.

The first day he came back to school, he surprised me my running up to my locker and throwing his arms around me. I turned, falling into his embrace and inhaling his cologne.

"Why didn't you tell me you were coming back today?" I breathed.

"I wanted to see the look on your face when I surprised you." He pulled back to meet my gaze, squinting and pursing his lips to the side, before nodding and smiling. "It's a pretty good face."

I smiled back, the worry that had been consuming me over the past few days, dissolving before my eyes. Ezra wasn't trying to ruin my future with Providence, or our chances at winning Through the Lens. His ideas had been good, and the more I'd worked on the layout of the photos, the more I saw the story we were trying to tell. I could feel the progression of our relationship each time I stared at them.

Lacing his fingers through mine, Ezra walked with me down the hall, and once again, everything felt right and true.

Why had I been so worried?

❖ ❖ ❖

The week passed quickly and before we knew it, the football team headed out of town for the Regional Finals. Ezra was more nervous than I'd ever seen him before. He paced back and forth as he stood by the lockers, he wrung his hands together in class, and his hair stood permanently on end, as if he couldn't stop running his fingers through it.

The night of the big game, I convinced Tori to come with me again, which she agreed to, even though she and the rest of the drama club were only a week away from opening night of *Into the Woods*. They didn't have rehearsal that night, but she had been looking so tired from all the late practices. I know she would rather have stayed home—probably sleeping—but being the good best friend she was, she came along. I didn't even mind when she fell asleep as I drove.

The game itself was nail-biting, but Ezra and the team played hard, and won—barely—but a win is a win. They were headed for the State Championships, something Cedar Falls High School hadn't done in more than a decade.

The whole town rallied behind them, hanging posters in store fronts and hung signs suspended between the street lamps on the square. There was even a parade in their honor, with floats from most of the school clubs, including the art club—we made a huge football helmet from chicken wire and paper mâché, painting it maroon and white. It had taken a lot of time that I didn't really have to give, but we did our best to support the team, and I was happy to do it for Ezra.

After the parade, Ezra and I drove over to the Wrightsville corn maze. Standing outside his jeep he rubbed his hands together. "So, I was thinking that we should maybe find a spot in the maze where no one else is, and try shooting from different angles, like low to the ground, high above if I can reach that far, and maybe even bury the camera in the middle of the stalks and see what kind of shot we can get." He grinned, expecting me to agree to his ideas immediately. He wanted me to tell him they were good.

My chest tightened. "No," I said firmly.

Ezra's eyes widened. "What?" His entire body tensed.

I let my arms fall to my sides, gulping. "I said no. I don't like that idea."

"What's your big plan, then?" His mouth formed a thin line as he crossed his arms over his chest.

Pulling my hat tighter over my head and wrapping my scarf around my neck, I gazed up into his eyes. This was the first time I'd told him no since the project began. The first time I'd pushed back.

Taking a deep breath, I said, "The color of the corn and the evening light won't provide any contrast if we only photograph the corn. We need something else in the picture to provide a visual break-up."

Even though I hadn't meant it like that, he visibly flinched when I said *break-up.*

"So, what do you suggest, Miss artist?" His body was tense, his mood suddenly sour.

"Are you mad, or something?" I grabbed his arm, forcing him to meet my gaze.

"No, why would I be mad?" His mouth said one thing, but his eyes said another. They were strained, tight. They didn't sparkle.

I licked my cold, chapped lips. "Because I told you no."

Ezra sighed. "You've never done that before. I thought you liked my ideas."

"I do," I said, reaching for his hand, "but we haven't taken one picture yet that was *my* idea. They've all been yours. I thought we were in this project together?"

He turned to me. "So, that's what this is about? It's not that my idea was bad, it's that you're upset that you haven't gotten your way this whole time, like you planned from the beginning? You wanted to have all the ideas and take all the pictures and for me to just stand around and do what, hand you stuff? Isn't that what you said that day in the hall? And now you're mad because it didn't work out that way, aren't you?"

Jerking my hand away from him, tears burned the backs of my eyes. "That's not fair. Weren't you the one who said we were in this project together? Well, so far it's been all you. *Your* ideas. *Your* plans. Even Mr. Shultz noticed that I wasn't having a part in this. Some of these ideas need to be mine, can't you understand that?"

"Yeah, sure. Whatever." He stuffed his hands into his pockets.

"Look, I didn't mean to start something here. I really just feel that I have a better idea for this one. It's not like I hate everything else we've done, I just don't think your idea is going to work this time. It's not personal."

Why are we fighting?

I didn't get it. I'd only made the suggestion to take a different photo and he was acting like I'd ripped his football jersey into tiny pieces and thrown them into the ocean. After I stomped all over them.

Stepping away and turning my back to him, I wondered what I was going to do next, because expressing my opinion had been the worst idea ever. This was a side of Ezra I'd never seen before and I wasn't sure how to handle it.

I did know one thing for sure though…I didn't like it, not one tiny bit.

Arms came around me from behind as he buried his face in the spot between my neck and shoulder. Groaning into my hair, squeezing me tightly, he said, "I'm sorry."

Reaching up, I gripped his forearms with both hands and leaned back into him. "It's okay." I just wanted the fight to be over.

"No, it's not." Ezra lifted his head so that his breath was now tickling my ear, making my whole body tingle. "I shouldn't have gotten so mad. It's not even you I'm angry at."

My brows met in the center of my forehead as I turned in his arms to face him. "What's wrong?"

He dropped his gaze. "My dad found the application."

A knot worked its way between my shoulder blades. "To Boston?"

Nodding, he chewed on his bottom lip.

"What happened?"

Finally, he looked up, shrugging. "He told me if I wanted to go against his plans then I better get Boston to come watch me play ball. He said I had to get some sort of athletic scholarship, otherwise we wasn't going to pay for me to go. He thinks I only want to go there to party. I sent the application in last week, along with the others, but he's so mad. He accused me of messing with the plans and not thinking clearly."

"Didn't your mom talk to him?"

"She did, but it didn't help. His mind is made up, and doesn't really care what I want." He shook his head. "I'm sorry. I didn't mean to blow up at you. Forgive me?"

"Of course. I wish you'd told me about this. Maybe I could have helped." I wrapped my arms around his waist.

"There's nothing you can do." He leaned his forehead against mine. "Come on, let's go get our pictures. What were you thinking for the shot?"

Leading the way into the corn maze, I didn't let go of Ezra's hand. When we found a place where we were alone, I handed him the camera. "Take a picture of me pulling you through the maze. Just get me from the back, but make sure you also get our joined hands."

"Oh, I see. This'll be cool." He took the camera and did as I'd instructed.

There should have been a surge of pride inside me, for taking back the control I'd been craving, but there wasn't. Ezra was so miserable with everything going on at home that his heart wasn't in it, and even though we got the exact picture I'd been imagining in my head, we both left the corn maze feeling worse than before we'd gotten there.

I thought I'd helped him by talking to his mom and getting her on our side. But, instead, it was as if someone had started to pick apart the thread binding Ezra and I together? Even though neither of us was upset with the other, there was a tension between us that shouldn't have been there, and I had no idea what to do about it.

All I could do was reach over and take his hand, and hope that would be enough.

CHAPTER TWENTY FOUR

AS EZRA AND THE rest of the football team geared up for the State Championship, he and I found it really difficult to spend any time together. Which was bad enough on its own, because I just wanted to be with him, but we also still needed to take the last photo on the list—the one involving baked goods—and it was starting to seem like getting it might be impossible. I'd asked, several times, if he wanted me to bake something with my mom and take pictures of it, but he kept saying no, insisting that he wanted to be there.

On top of everything else we had going on, the situation with his dad hadn't gotten any better. Even though Boston College had notified him that they would be at the State Championship to scope out the best high school players in Rhode Island, Ezra's dad still thought he wasn't taking any of it seriously. I felt so sorry for him, but didn't know how else I could help.

He agreed to come with me to see *Into the Woods* that Friday night. The cast did a really awesome job. Tori was hilarious as *Cinderella*, and Ezra had fun pointing to the stage and whispering about *Milky White* the cow, whenever he saw it. I held his hand through the entire show, remembering the day we'd stood on that stage together.

The day everything about us shifted. The day I got his hoodie and started seeing him in a different light. It felt like a lifetime ago, rather than just a couple of months.

❖ ❖ ❖

One morning, the following week, Ezra slumped against my locker, bags under his eyes, looking as if he'd picked his clothes that day from his floor, instead of out of his closet.

He sighed. "Can I come over after school?"

"Don't you have practice?" I said, grabbing my books and closing the door.

He shook his head. "Not today, and I don't want to go home until it's absolutely necessary. I don't have it in me to go another twelve rounds with my dad."

"Sure." I wrapped an arm around his waist. "Want to try to get our baking photo done? I make some mean snickerdoodle cookies."

Ezra's eyes lit up. "I love snickerdoodles. I'm in."

"Good. It'll be nice to hang out with you. It's been forever," I said, rising up on my tiptoes to kiss him lightly on the cheek.

Tilting his head to plant an answering kiss on

my temple, he smiled. "Tell me about it. Coach has never pushed us this hard. I'm sore in places I didn't even know I had."

"Well, that's what you get for making it to State, and Boston will be there watching, don't forget that." I suddenly grew nervous for Ezra. I couldn't imagine what he was going through. "It'll all be worth it in the end." I tried to sound encouraging, but they just felt like empty words.

"I know. It's the only thing that's keeping me focused right now. Well, that, and knowing you'll be there cheering me on." He squeezed my hand.

"I wouldn't miss it."

"You better not. I can't play without my good luck charm."

"I know." I wrapped both arms around his middle. "Don't worry. I won't let you down."

◆ ◆ ◆

After school, Ezra met me at my locker and we walked to my house together. Mom was reading and enjoying a large cup of tea in the living room when we walked inside.

"Oh, hello, Ezra. What brings you by?" She asked—a little too sweetly.

I didn't let him answer. If she started talking to him, we'd be there all afternoon. "Do we have the stuff to make snickerdoodles?"

She sat her book down. "We should. I just stocked up for all the Thanksgiving baking. Do you need my help?" Her eyes lit up with anticipation.

"Not right now." I threw my backpack on the floor by the stairs. "We have to get a baking photo to finish out project. I may need you to come take some pictures in a bit, but I'll let you know."

"Sounds fun." She eyed Ezra in a way which told me she wanted to ask him so many questions, but she was trying to be polite. "Holler if you need me."

"We will." Grabbing Ezra's arm, I dragged him away from her and into the kitchen.

While I went around opening cabinets and pulling out ingredients, he smiled and leaned against the island, looking tired but just as hot as ever. When I sat the sugar and flour on the countertop, his grin turned wolfish.

"What?" I walked past him to grab two aprons from the hook in the pantry.

His hand came around my wrist and he pulled me to him, lowering his voice. "I was remembering the last time we were in here."

"Oh yeah?" I was suddenly very hot in the kitchen and I hadn't even turned the oven on yet.

My mind rushed back to the night I'd skipped the dance and he and I had stood there, tension building between us, me in his hoodie, surrounded by the aroma of Chinese food. I grinned just thinking about it. Our first kiss.

He lifted an eyebrow. "I'd been wanting to kiss you for a while, but standing here, you were so upset thinking I wanted to get back with Casey, thinking I'd kissed her, and I was just like 'screw it' and finally gave in."

"I remember. If Mike hadn't interrupted us..." My cheeks burned under his intense gaze.

Ezra's hands found my waist and he pulled me to him slowly, his fingers curling around my back. "Mike's not here now," he whispered.

"But my mom is," I whispered back.

"I'm not worried." His gaze fell to my lips.

Wrapping my arms around his neck, I leaned up on my tiptoes. Dipping his head, Ezra brought his lips to mine. We were both hungry and frantic, more aggressive than usual. I dropped the aprons on the floor as his hands crawled up my back and into my hair. Pushing me backwards, we stumbled across the room until my back slammed into the refrigerator. Ezra kept moving, pressing himself fully up against me, more than he'd ever done before. His hands slid back down to my waist, fingertips grazing the skin beneath the hem of my sweater, lighting me on fire.

"How's it going in there?" Mom's voice pulled us apart so fast, I almost fell to the floor without Ezra there to support me.

"Fine," I called, my voice ragged, "just getting set up."

I caught Ezra's eyes, which were glazed over and heavy. He bent down to pick up the dropped aprons, handing one to me while throwing the other over his own head.

I grinned at him. "That was close."

"That was great." He winked. "So, what do you want me to do?" He rubbed his hands together.

Pushing a bowl towards him I showed him the recipe. "Start measuring the sugar, I'll put in the butter."

"Aye, aye, Captain." He saluted me before pulling the lid off the sugar canister and diving in with the measuring cup.

Over the next hour, Ezra and I made tray after tray of snickerdoodle cookies, covering the kitchen countertops—as well as ourselves—with layers of flour, sugar and cinnamon. We had formed a mini assembly line in which I formed the dough into balls and passed them to Ezra, who would dip them in the cinnamon sugar mixture and place them on the cookie sheets.

When the sheets were filled, I plopped them in the oven and we started all over again. Mom's cooling racks were scattered around the kitchen, holding cookies in various stages of the cooling process.

We had decided to wait until we had all the cookies baked before taking any pictures, because I didn't want to risk getting flour or butter on the camera lens.

"I'd like to do a flat lay for this one, because I think it would best capture the theme." I said, clearing off the ingredients we no longer needed, and scooping up the broken egg shells before tossing them into the trash. "What do you think?"

"I don't care how we shoot it, as long as I get to eat these when we're done." Ezra swiped a cookie from the cooling rack and plopped it into this mouth.

I playfully smacked his hand. "If you don't stop eating them, we won't have a picture at all."

With his mouth full, he mumbled. "Then I'll just have to stay here all night so we could make more."

His words made me grin. "Nice try."

He swallowed. "What's the matter, are you getting tired of me already?"

"No, but I don't want to have to spend all night making more cookies because you ate them all."

"Fine, okay, I give up. But can I at least stay for dinner?" Lifting his eyebrows repeatedly, he reached for another cookie.

I did smack him that time, and then pointed a wooden spoon towards him like a sword. "Stop it."

Raising his arms in surrender he stuck his bottom lip out. "Hey, I'm in training for the big game here. I need all the calories I can get. Coach says."

I began to plop cookies down onto the already floured countertop and arrange them with wooden spoons, measuring cups, whole—unbroken—eggs, a small bowl of cinnamon and sugar, and a bit of burlap ribbon I'd stolen from Mom's craft cabinet. "Oh please, you're making that up."

"I am not. I'm hungry. Don't you know you can't make delicious food in front of a guy and then not let him eat any of it?" He acted like he was going to go for the cookies again, but I jumped in his way.

Holding up my arms to block him, I said, "okay, help me get this shot and you can have all you want."

His face turned wicked as he grabbed for me, wrapping his arms around my waist. "What if I just want you?" Pushing me back against the counter, I waited for him to kiss me like he'd done earlier, but instead, he reached around me, grabbed a cookie and jumped back before I could stop him.

"You are evil." I laughed, somewhat hurt that his words had been used to distract me and not to seduce me.

Laughing too, he shoved the cookie in his mouth. "I was desperate. Besides, you have more than enough for the photo."

He was right. Grabbing the camera, I peered through the lens to check for placement. I moved the ribbon and spoon slightly into a different arrangement, then snapped the final photo.

"Let me see." Ezra hugged me from behind, resting his chin on my shoulder.

Holding the camera up, he reached around me to take it, flicking through the pictures. "Perfect."

"You think so?" I leaned against him, letting his warmth wash over me.

"Yes. So I guess this means we're done then, like done, done? That was the last one we needed."

My breath caught in my chest. "Yes, I guess it does."

I didn't want to be finished. This project had brought Ezra and I together, and part of me wondered if not having it would cause us to drift apart.

Closing my eyes, I tried to banished the worry from my heart.

"Hey, what's wrong?" He kissed my cheek. "You went all quiet."

I opened my eyes, steadying my voice. "Nothing. I'm being stupid."

Moving around to face me, he gripped both my upper arms. "Tell me. What is it?"

I shook my head and averted my eyes. "You're going to think I'm crazy."

His hand moved to my chin, lifting my face to look him in the eye. "Not possible. What's the matter?"

Taking a deep breath, I sighed. "I was just

worrying that now that the project is over you might not want to spend time with me anymore."

He chuckled. "Why would you think that?"

My cheeks burned. "Because the only reason we started to spend any time together in the first place was because of this project, and I'm wondering if you'll still want to do stuff with me now that it's done."

He was grinning.

"I know I'm being stupid. Forget I said anything." I tried to find something else in the room to look at other than Ezra, but he was all I could focus on.

His hands found my face, fingertips grazing my cheekbones. "Bailey, I'm not going anywhere. I don't care if we never take another picture again, I want to be with *you*." He bent down and kissed me. He reached behind my back and stole yet another cookie. "Now that I've reassured you of my affections, there's still one more big question which needs answered."

I laughed. "Yes, you can stay for dinner."

He punched the air with his fist. "What are we having?"

I pulled back, my eyes narrowing. "Does it matter?"

"Nope." He reached for another cookie. "I told you, I'm not going anywhere. Even if your mom serves me liver." He chewed for a moment. "Please tell me it's not liver."

"It's not."

"Excellent." He ate five more cookies while I rolled my eyes at him.

CHAPTER TWENTY FIVE

THE NEXT DAY, we added the final baking pictures and then spent the rest of the week color-grading, editing and fine-tuning our entire project. All that was left was for us to assemble it.

Ezra had, somehow, convinced his dad to help him glue and clamp the crate pieces together into our backdrop. When he told me they were going to work together, I raised a questioning eyebrow at him.

"It'll be fine." He'd reassured me. "Maybe it will give us some time to talk."

But, halfway through their afternoon together he sent me a message. It contained no words, only an emoji of a face with smoke coming out of its head. Clearly, his big plans to mend the bridges of communication with his dad had not gone well. Two hours later, Ezra showed up at my house, his face strained and his eyes had dark circles beneath them again.

"That bad, huh?" I said when I opened the door and he was leaning against the post on the porch.

He blew out a harsh breath. "I never should have thought he'd see things my way. Maybe I should just give up on the idea of Boston and go out west. I can't live the rest of my life with my dad and I at each other's throats."

My breath caught in my chest. "But you can't give up. Surely, it's not that bad." I reached for him, wrapping my arms around his waist.

He let himself go, the weight of his stress falling onto me as he hugged me back. "It is that bad. My dad and I used to have a great relationship and now he only talks to me to tell me how disappointed he is in my life choices."

Leading Ezra to the porch swing, I pulled him down next to me. He flopped back, covering his eyes with his forearm.

"What about State? Isn't Boston supposed to be there? Your dad can't think that you're not serious if they come, see you play, and offer you a place, right?" I ran my hand through his hair, pushing it up and between my fingers, enjoying its softness.

Uncovering his eyes, Ezra stared at me, so intensely I almost turned away.

"Maybe. But it's a big gamble." He sighed.

"Have you been scouted by the schools your dad wants you to go to? Have any of them offered you a place?" I asked.

He shook his head. "No, I've sent in my applications, but they've not sent anyone to see me play. I keep telling Dad that's what sets Boston apart from them. They're here. They can come to the games. They can watch me play, and if I get a place with them, I might even get offered a better position because they've seen me in action."

"And he doesn't see that as a good thing?" My jaw clenched. How could Ezra's dad be so cruel?

"Nope." He rubbed his temples. "I don't know what to do. I hate fighting with him, but I don't want to go to any of the schools he wants me to go to."

Tucking my legs up beneath me, I took Ezra's hand in mine. "I know it's hard right now, but once Boston sees you play, they'll offer you a place. I know they will. Then, you'll have a decision to make. Wherever you want to go, go there. Whether it's here or there, whether I like it, or not, you do what makes *you* happy."

He looked at me with pain in his eyes.

I carried on. "But, don't, for one second, go off to a college just because someone else is pushing you that way. You'll be miserable. Trust me."

He squeezed my hand. "I'll be even more miserable if this breaks my dad and I apart, Bailey. Thanksgiving and Christmas are almost here. How's that going to be for us if we can't even stand to be in the same room together?"

It killed me to see him hurting and upset. I bit my lip. "Lots of families fight."

Letting go of my hand, Ezra sat straight up. "How can you say that? How can you say lots of families fight? I don't want that kind of life. We're not like other families. We don't fight. I know that's supposed to make me feel better, but it doesn't."

My chest was like a deflated balloon. I felt completely helpless, and useless. My jaw began to quiver, and my voice shook. "I was just trying to help. I'm sorry I don't know what to say. What can I do? Tell me what will make this better?"

"Could you do it?" He spat.

"What?"

The tone in his voice rose, growing higher the more angry he got. "Could you make a choice that went completely against your parents, against Mike? Would you want me to sit here and tell you it's okay to make your family your enemy. That it's more important to follow your dreams than make peace with the only family you have?"

"I don't know. I'd want you to be there for me, but I don't know what I'd want you to say. I can't imagine what you're going through right now. I wish I could help. I wish I could do something that would make a difference. I don't know what to do, Ezra." A lump formed in my throat.

Leaning forward, he rested his elbows on his knees and laced his fingers together behind his head. He sat that way for a long time while my heart pounded inside my chest. Finally, he let out a long sigh before lifting his head, redness rimming his eyes. Turning, he leaned his head over onto my lap, curling his arm around my crossed legs. "Just let me lay right here and tell me it's going to be alright."

My fingers found his hair again, and I lightly traced over the shell of his ear as I whispered, "it's going to be alright," over and over again.

Ezra closed his eyes and squeezed my leg in response. I don't know how long we sat like that on the swing, but it grew dark and the streetlights began to flicker. Mom came out to tell us dinner was ready, and once again, Ezra stayed and ate with us.

❖ ❖ ❖

That night, a cloud of doubt fell over me as I lay in bed, my mind running through everything that had happened, or didn't happen, or could happen. I don't know why I only seemed to ponder the great mysteries of life when I should have been sleeping, but there it was.

I was so worried about Ezra. I knew what choice he needed to make and if he didn't he'd live a miserable life, but I also couldn't imagine fighting with my own family because of my future.

There had to be something I could do to help him, but I couldn't think of anything.

Some girlfriend I was.

When my pillow grew damp from the hot tears flowing down my cheeks, I sat up in bed, hugging my knees to my chest. How had I gotten into this mess? Two months ago, it was PSD that kept me up at night worrying. That's what had twisted my stomach into knots.

Now, I spent my nights worrying about a guy. Not that I didn't like thinking about Ezra, but he was consuming my every thought. If he and I had never been partnered up, I wouldn't have taken any notice of him in class. I wouldn't have thought that he had even the tiniest bit of artistic ideas floating around in his head. I wouldn't have found out that I actually liked going to his football games.

But, most importantly, I wouldn't have discovered that Ezra O'Neill filled a place in my heart that I never realized was empty. Tori had said to find my silver lining, and I had. It was Ezra. I cared about him. I might even love him, and I needed him so much.

But what if he didn't stand up to his father? What if he took the easy road and went out to Ohio or Michigan? What then? Would our relationship survive being stretched over that many miles? I couldn't see how it would.

Tears welled behind my eyes again. Is this how all girlfriends felt when their boyfriends were in trouble? Is this where I was supposed to be placing all of my attention?

I knew the answer, but didn't want to admit it to myself.

I couldn't put all my hopes on a boy who might leave me. The closer he and I grew together would only make it that much harder to say good-bye if he chose to do what his dad wanted.

Maybe I should wait until the contest was over, and then break things off with him. Maybe I should end it before I got hurt.

Before either of us got hurt.

But, then again, what if he stayed? What if he stood up to his dad and got into Boston? Could he and I actually get a happily ever after?

I didn't know.

I couldn't know. No matter how much I wanted to.

Life was a gamble, I guess. I couldn't hurt us both because I'd let my emotions run away from me. I wouldn't let myself get so scared that I ended up throwing away something really good. But I did need to make sure that my number one focus was still on PSD. I hadn't been accepted yet and I needed to do everything I could to ensure that I got in.

Which meant winning Through the Lens.

The prize was mine, and nothing was going to stand in my way.

Of that, I was more sure than I'd been in a long time.

CHAPTER TWENTY SIX

EZRA BROUGHT THE FINISHED backdrop to my house the next day so that we could begin gluing on all the pictures and props we'd collected, along with those I'd made in my other art classes.

It really didn't take as long to arrange them as I thought it would. We didn't argue once, and within an hour or two, the piece was finished. It looked amazing. We had created a real winner, and I didn't see how we could possibly lose. Now, all it needed was a name.

I stepped back and stared at the display for a long time, biting my lip and running ideas around my head.

"Pumpkin Spice and Everything Nice," I said after a while.

Ezra tilted his head to the side. "Excuse me?"

"Oh, sorry." I wrapped my arm around his waist. "I think it's the title of the piece. I want to drink that coffee. I want to take a walk in those leaves. I want to go to your farm and eat apple and pick pumpkins. It makes me feel cozy and it reminds me of you. Our partnership started over pumpkin spiced lattes, if you recall?"

"I remember." He squeezed my shoulder. "I

love it."

"Then let's get this to the school so Shultz can send it off."

We gently carried the piece outside and loaded it in the back of Ezra's jeep. The projects were being sent off the next morning, so we had to deliver them that afternoon. Mr. Shultz had said he'd stay in the art room until six o'clock.

It was four-thirty.

When we arrived at the school, Ezra pulled up to the side door nearest the art room. Slowly and carefully, we carried the project through the doors, down the hallway, and into the classroom. I was glad to see that, while we were't the first project to be delivered, we also weren't the last.

I couldn't help but walk around the room, scrutinizing the other pieces. Maybe I was being a bit prideful, but none of them held a candle to ours. They were okay, I guess, but not winners.

"Scoping out the competition?" Ezra leaned against the doorframe, watching me.

"What competition?" I lowered my voice, not like any of our classmates could hear me, but still. "These are terrible."

"That's a bit harsh," he said.

"I'm just being honest.

"I don't think they're so bad." He shrugged his shoulders.

"Trust me, ours is much better," I said, as we closed the door and stepped back into the hall. I wasn't sure where Mr. Shultz had gone, and I didn't feel safe leaving our project unattended. "Let's wait a minute."

"Whatever you say." Ezra leaned against the lockers, stuffing his hands in his pockets, while I paced.

About halfway down the hall, a poster for the State Championship caught my eye. There were pictures of Ezra and the rest of the team. I found him in every photo. Then my eyes fell to the bottom of the poster, and my heart stopped beating.

"No, no, no, no, no!" I shrieked, gripping the sides of my head with both hands.

Ezra ran up beside me. "What? What's wrong?"

I pointed at the poster, my mouth hanging open.

"What?" Ezra pressed.

Turning to face him, a wave of nausea washed over me. "Why didn't you tell me?"

His gaze volleyed between me and the poster. "Why didn't I tell you what? I don't understand."

"The date," I squealed, in a tone so high I'm sure only dogs could hear it, "look at the freaking date, Ezra."

Shaking his head, he stared at the poster, then shrugged his shoulders. He read it out loud, "November twenty-seventh. What's the problem. That's next—" His eyes grew wide.

"Yeah. Next Saturday. The same day as the showcase." I wailed, pounding my fists against the wall. It hurt so badly tears welled behind my eyes.

"I forgot the date of the showcase," he said, "I—I hadn't made the connection."

"Me either." I admitted. "I've been staring at these posters for a week now and never bothered to notice the date. This is a nightmare."

My eyes brimmed with silver, threatening to slip over the edges.

"How did this happen? How did we not see it?" Ezra kicked the wall beneath the poster.

"I don't know, but what are we going to do? You can't go to the game *and* the showcase. It's impossible."

Ezra paced back and forth across the hall several times. "Maybe, not," he finally said, "both are in Providence, right? Maybe I *can* do it."

"Look." I pointed to the poster again. "The game is at one o'clock. The showcase starts at two. There's no way you can be both places at once."

We stood silently in the hall for what felt like hours, walking back and forth, not meeting each other's eye. My stomach was so twisted, I didn't know if I would ever feel like eating again. I couldn't see a way around this. My dreams were shattering before my eyes and all I could do was watch as the broken pieces slipped through my fingers.

"I have to go to the game." Ezra's voice made me jump.

Whirling around to face him, my jaw clenched. "What?"

He stood there, feet separated, hands in his pockets, and repeated the words I didn't want to hear again. "I have to go to the game."

"But, you can't. What about the contest? If we're both not there for the showcase, we can't win. It's in the rules." My vision grew blurry and my hands started to shake.

"I know." He pressed his palms into his temples. "But, this is my one chance of getting Boston College to watch me play. If I'm not there, they may offer the place to someone else. If I have any chance of my dad taking me seriously, I have to be there. I have to play. It's my only shot."

"But this is my shot at Providence. This was what the whole project was about. If we're not both standing there when the winners are announced, we forfeit." My mouth had gone completely dry.

"I know," he said, "and I know that I promised you I'd be there. I know how important this is to you, I really do, but this is important to me, too. I have to play in this game."

"The team can win without you." I spat.

Ezra scowled. "It's not about whether or not we win, it's about Boston seeing me play. Don't you get that?"

"Of course I do." I took a step towards him. "But Through the Lens came first. We've known about this for two months." My voice caught and broke. "You promised."

He took a step too, backward. "So did you."

Our eyes met and held.

"You promised you'd be at my game. You promised you'd support *me*." He grit out.

My hands clenched and unclenched at my sides, and my feet fought the urge to run down the hall and out the door. "I know I did, but I have to get into PSD, and this is the best way to impress them. This contest is everything. I have to think about my future."

"What about my future?" He snarled. "Just yesterday, I sat on your porch and you asked me what you could do to make things better. Well, this is it, Bailey. This is what you can do. Give up this contest and come to my game. Be there to support me."

I huffed a series of harsh breaths in and out. How could he be asking me that? "And throw away my own chances at getting into the college of *my* dreams?"

Raising his hands in desperation, Ezra advanced on me. "Oh, come on, Bailey. You know you're going to get in. You're a good artist. I'm sure they've already looked at your application and portfolio. You don't have to win this contest to impress them any further."

Tears spilled down my cheeks as I stared into his eyes. "Yes, I do. I need this."

"No, *I* need this." He thrust his finger into his own chest. "This is my one-and-only shot. There are no more games after this. There's no other way for Boston to see me. My application might not be enough, but I'm sure yours is. Don't be so selfish. Think about what this means to me."

I knew what it meant to Ezra, but the next words that poured from my mouth with no filter to rein them in were, "I don't care. I have to think about myself."

Ezra acted like I'd slapped him with a brick. "What did you say?"

I turned around, unable to meet his gaze any longer.

"Because it sounded to me like you said you didn't care?" He rounded on me, forcing me to look at him. "What do you mean by that? Do you not care about me getting into the college I want, or do you not care about me?" His own voice shook.

"Does it matter?" I was breathing so heavily my lips began to tingle.

"Yes, it matters!" His roaring voice shook me to my bones. "Have you just been pretending this whole time? Was it all a big game to get me to work with you? Pretend you like me, but inside you really don't care about me at all? Is that what this is?"

"No," I sobbed, "of course this wasn't a game. I wasn't pretending."

"Do you care about me?" He locked eyes with me.

"Yes. So much." Tears streamed down my

cheeks.

"But not enough to let me have this opportunity." He reached up and gripped both my arms.

I stared through blurry eyes, trying to focus on his face. "It was my opportunity first. I can't give it up."

"Neither can I." Dropping his hands, his fists clenched tight, Ezra gazed hard at the floor.

I wrapped my arms around myself for warmth and protection.

When he glanced up again, his focus was set. "I'm going to the game."

"I'm going to the showcase," I said in response.

He pursed his lips. "Even if you know that, without me, you can't win, you'd still rather go there than come support me?"

I swallowed hard around a huge lump in my throat. "Yes. Maybe I can get them to change their minds if we win. Maybe they'll still give me the title, even without you."

Ezra stood up tall, crossing his arms over his chest and setting his jaw. "Bailey, I really like you, and I thought we were here to support each other. I thought we'd found something that was real, and special, and important. But if you can't see that you're being incredibly selfish by asking me to give up the one chance I have at getting what I want, then you're not the girl I thought you were."

"What are you saying," I blubbered, "that you want to break up with me?"

He shook his head, staring up at the ceiling. "I'm saying I need you to see the bigger picture here. See that between the two of us, I have so much more to lose than you do. Realize that sometimes when you care about someone, you have to make sacrifices for them."

I stepped up to him and wrapped my arms around his neck. "I can't give up Providence."

Pulling me close to him and resting his chin on my forehead, his voice softened to a whisper. "And, I can't give up Boston. Not after everything I've gone through to get to this point. Not after you told me not to give up. I have to take this chance."

My tears began to stain the front of Ezra's shirt as we stood in the hallway, holding each other.

"I'm sorry, but I've made my choice." He let me go and took a step away.

"You're choosing the game over me." My voice completely gave up, the burn in my throat all-consuming.

He nodded his head, his eyes asking me questions I couldn't answer. My tears were replaced with a rage like I'd never felt before.

"Fine," I spat, "if that's all you care about then maybe we should be done."

Ezra stiffened. "Is that really what you want?"

Reaching up, I wiped the tears from my

cheeks. "What I want is Providence, and nothing is going to stand in my way, not even you. I'm going to the showcase, and I'm going to win, with or without you."

Ezra set his jaw and marched past me. Turning at the door, he said, "Looks like we've both decided what's most important then."

"I guess so."

He stopped and turned back around, desperate hope in his eyes. "I need you, Bailey. I need you at the game. I need you in my life. Boston wouldn't even be coming if it hadn't been for you. But, I'm not going to beg. You need to decide what you want. I hope you figure out that I mean as much to you and you mean to me." He flung open the door and left without another word.

I slumped to my knees and bawled my eyes out in the middle of the school hallway. It had only taken a moment for Ezra and I to fall apart.

I suddenly regretted ever letting myself like him in the first place. How had I been so stupid? I'd said I would never let anyone come between me and PSD. I'd been so focused for so long, but I'd let him influence me. I'd let him into my heart, and because of it, I'd lost perspective on everything.

The only hope I had left was that if I did win, the judges of Through the Lens would allow me to claim the prize on my own—*without him.* Maybe I could explain that Ezra was in the State

Championship. Maybe they would understand, have pity on me, and bend the rules this one time.

It was all I could cling to. The empty hole Ezra had filled in my heart was blackening the more I thought about him.

Ezra O'Neill had ruined everything.

CHAPTER TWENTY SEVEN

MONDAY AT SCHOOL, I felt like everyone was watching me, as if they knew what had happened. I mean, it was pretty obvious that Ezra and I were fighting. Especially when he didn't come to my locker, walk with me in the halls, or sit with me at lunch.

Since our project was already finished and sent off to Providence, Ezra and I didn't have to sit next to each other in Photography class anymore, either. He sat as far across the room as he could and refused to look at me, so I plopped down by myself and tried to hold back the tears that didn't want to stay inside me.

English class was even worse, though. My gaze kept wandering over to where Ezra was sitting, and sure enough, he was always staring at me, too. But each time we made eye contact, he would turn away so quickly, it was as if he hadn't even seen me.

The worst of all, though, was the way people walked past me with their noses wrinkled up as if I smelled bad. Like it was all my fault that Ezra was unhappy. Only Casey Turner grinned each time she walked past me in the halls, and made a big show of waiting by Ezra's locker after school. The fact that he walked off alone was the only moment that made me feel like maybe there was still hope.

The next two days were no different, and by the time I walked home that Wednesday afternoon, my legs were like lead, there were purple bags under my eyes, and I'd cried so much that my cheeks and bottom eyelids felt dry and cracked.

The delicious scent of fresh-from-the-oven pumpkin pies and homemade bread washed over me as I walked in the front door. Thanksgiving was the next day, so Mike was home from college for a long weekend. His shoes were piled by the front door and I could hear him in the living room laughing at whatever he was watching on tv.

I didn't even say hello to him. I just ran straight up to my room where I flopped down onto my bed, face-first, wishing I could pull the covers over my head and hide from the world. My heart ached as if someone had ripped it from my chest and stomped on it.

I cried until I fell asleep.

When I heard the doorbell ring, I woke up from my nap, rubbing my eyes as I slumped down the stairs to see Mom carrying two large pizza boxes.

"I didn't want to cook anymore," she said,

meeting me at the bottom of the stairs.

I plopped down next to Mike on the sofa, thankful that he valued his life enough not to ask me how I was doing.

"So, what should we watch while we eat?" He asked instead, flipping through the tv channels with the remote.

I thought for a moment. "Something with a lot of action." The last thing I wanted was to sit through a sappy rom-com. That would only make me think about Ezra, and the more I thought about him, the more I would miss him.

My heart hurt so much already that I didn't need to see happy couples on the screen laughing, holding hands and giving each other those longing glances that he and I had shared so often. I didn't need reminded of any of it.

"*Star Wars* it is." Mike chuckled with glee.

"Which one?" I asked, pulling a blanket from the basket under the end table and wrapping up in it.

"Uh, *Return of the Jedi* because it's the best." He got up and went over to the shelf where we kept all our DVD's. The box was almost falling apart from being watched so many times.

I grabbed the pepperoni pizza from the kitchen and two cans of *Coke* from the fridge, then watched the movie with Mike, grateful that I had stopped thinking about Ezra for a while.

But, that night I dreamed about him.

We were back at his family's farm, walking hand-in-hand among the pumpkins. He looked so good I just kept staring at him. We drank apple cider and jumped in piles of leaves like little kids. When we landed in one of the piles, side-by-side, he gazed over at me, but he wasn't smiling.

"What's wrong?" I asked him.

"You," he replied in a far away, dreamy voice which wasn't his own. "You are wrong. I needed you, but you refused to be there for me."

I sat up, reaching for him, but I couldn't touch him. No matter how far I stretched, he was just beyond my fingertips.

"Ezra?" I could hear panic edging my voice.

"It's too late, Bailey." He stood up and walked away, disappearing into a mist which rolled across the pumpkin patch. "It's too late." His voice echoed in my head. "You made your choice, and now I'm gone."

"Ezra?" I called after him, unable to move from the leaf pile.

"Why didn't you choose me? Why was I not important enough?" His voice was disappearing.

"You are important," I cried.

He didn't turn around.

I awoke with a start, panting and sweating. Sitting up in bed, I tucked my knees up under my chin.

Was Ezra right?

Had I made a terrible mistake?

CHAPTER TWENTY EIGHT

BY THE TIME I fell back asleep, the sky outside was growing lighter. I woke up a few hours later to Mom banging on my door. It was mid-morning and the family would be arriving in a few hours. I got out of bed, took a shower, and wandered downstairs.

The kitchen smelled so good. Mom had already put the turkey in the oven and was busy making stuffing and peeling potatoes.

"I hope that's not what you're planning on wearing?" She glanced up and gave me the once-over as I walked into the kitchen, grabbing a bowl and filling it to the brim with *Cocoa Pebbles* and milk.

I'd thrown a sweatshirt on, but I was still wearing pajama pants and wooly socks. "No, I'm going to change in a bit."

"Good. You know how your grandmother is." She chopped the potatoes, tossing the pieces into a huge pan. "You doing okay?"

My eyes burned, but I didn't want to start crying, so I shook my head and said, "Yeah, sure. Everything's good."

"Mm-hm," she said.

"Really, Mom. I swear." I swirled my spoon around in my bowl.

"Well if you're so good then, would you please go set the table in the dining room. I've put everything out. Make it look pretty." She pointed with the knife towards the formal dining room we hardly ever used.

"Sure." I finished off my cereal, put the bowl in the dishwasher, poured a cup of coffee and headed off for the dining room.

My family members began arriving not long after, so I ran upstairs to change clothes, returning just as the people in the living room were finishing watching the *Macy's Thanksgiving Day Parade*. Santa Claus was making his way down the street and everyone was cheering.

After the meal, the women all congregated in the kitchen to wash dishes and chat, while the men gathered in the living room to watch the football game. I didn't feel like fielding a million-and-one questions about school, my love life, my college plans, or anything else that would make me cry, so I stayed away from the kitchen.

However, I soon found that sitting with the men watching football was equally as painful. It made me think of Ezra and my chest grew tight again.

Getting up, I moved to a chair by the window, put in my earbuds, turned up the music, grabbed a book, and disappeared for a while. No one bothered me, and I ignored them.

Before long, I found myself staring out the window. The sun was setting, and the leaves were blowing across the front yard in waves. I was seriously considering stealing another piece of pumpkin pie and escaping to my room when something caught my eye.

Or, I should say...*someone*.

Slamming the book shut, I ran, grabbing my coat and throwing it on as I opened the front door. Ezra turned suddenly, halting his pacing back and forth across the driveway.

"What are you doing here?" I asked, zipping up my coat.

"I... I didn't know where else to go. Things at home aren't good. My dad and grandparents are arguing about me and college and stuff. I couldn't take it anymore so I just left." His cheeks were red from the cold. "I'll go." He turned around.

"No, wait." I hurried down the steps.

Ezra stopped, but he didn't turn around. I walked down the driveway until I was standing in front of him. I ached to reach out and touch him, but I stuffed my hands into my pockets instead. "I'm sorry you're having such a bad day.."

His gaze shifted to meet mine. "It hasn't just been today."

Biting my lip, I flinched. "I know. Listen, I..."

He held up a hand. "I don't want to hear it."

My blood boiled. "Hey, you came to *my* house.

The least you could do is let me apologize."

"Fine, you want to apologize, apologize, but it's not going to make a difference, is it? You're still choosing the showcase." His eyes held none of the sparkle I loved.

I swallowed. "And, you're still going to the game."

"Of course I am. I have to." He crossed his arms over his chest.

"I never meant to hurt you." I took a step closer to him.

"Yeah?" His eyes lifted. "Well, what hurts the most is that you're so good at it."

I sucked in a breath. "That's not fair."

"Why, because it's the truth?" He spat. "Maybe if more people started telling you the truth, you wouldn't be so selfish."

Crossing my own arms over my chest, I took a deep breath. "Go home, Ezra."

"I never should have come here in the first place." He shouldered past me.

I had to say something, but all I could think was, "happy Thanksgiving."

Ezra snorted. "Whatever," he mumbled as he turned at the end of the driveway and headed down the street.

Why had he come? Was it possible that he was missing me as much as I was missing him, or had he come, expecting me to change my mind about Saturday?

Either way, I knew two things for sure:

One, I wasn't over him at all, and missed him so badly it made my chest hurt, and two, neither of us were going to give up our shots on Saturday, which meant that our relationship was only hanging on by a thread now...if that.

CHAPTER TWENTY NINE

SATURDAY MORNING, I arrived at the school at eleven o'clock with a travel mug of coffee, a stomach ache, and tightness in my chest.

Ezra.

He was supposed to be sitting on the school bus with me, sharing my coffee, holding my hand and telling me that everything was going to be okay. Instead, we were on separate busses—headed to the same city, of course—but for two very different reasons.

While I waited for the rest of the photography class to show up, I watched the football team load up their bus. Spotting Ezra almost instantly, I couldn't help but march across the parking lot, walking right up to him.

"Hey, Bailey," Joel said, when he saw me.

At the sound of my name, Ezra whirled around. His eyes first went wide, then narrowed, as he walked over to me. He led me away from the bus and all his friends.

"Where are we going?" I asked.

He lowered his voice. "If you're going to yell at me, I'd rather you not do it in front of the rest of the team.

"I wasn't going to yell at you." I gripped my mug with both hands.

"Oh." He cleared his throat. "Well, what do you want? We've got to get going."

I swallowed around the lump in my throat. "I just came over here to wish you luck. I really do hope you guys win today, and I hope that Boston is very impressed by you."

He ran a hand through his hair. "Thanks, I guess. I'm hoping I can play well enough that they offer me a place. Then maybe this whole mess with my dad can be over."

I reached for his arm without thinking. "You will. You'll be great."

Glancing down at my hand, he closed his eyes and bit his lip. I jerked my hand back so fast you would have thought it was on fire. "Sorry."

When he opened his eyes, he said, "I'm sorry. I didn't want to let you down, but I thought you'd understand how important this is to me."

The backs of my eyes burned. I opened my mouth several times to tell him how I felt, that I didn't want to fight anymore, but I didn't have the strength.

I mustered my courage to finally say, "good luck, Ezra."

Clenching his jaw, he half-turned before whirling on me and stepping so close that we were sharing the same breath. My pulse began to race and I wanted to push up on my toes and kiss him so badly I had to curl them to keep myself on the ground.

Leaning forward, his lips brushed against my ear. "You're the best good luck I've ever had, and you're not going to be there, no matter how much I need you to be, so while I appreciate you coming over here, you're riding on the wrong bus."

He pulled back, locking eyes with me.

My breath caught in my throat. "I can't."

"I know," he said, his voice cracking, "I can't compete with PSD. I've been trying to for the past two months, but no matter how much I might have been falling in love with you, you'll always choose Providence over me, and I don't like to come in second place. I want to win. I thought I could win with you, but it feels like I can't, and it's killing me. You're killing me, Bailey, and I don't know what to do." Ezra turned away and jogged back to the bus.

I gasped. He was starting to fall in love with me?

What?

I needed to say something. I searched for the right words, but nothing came out. *Run after him.* I told myself, but my feet were cemented in place.

Legs like lead, I finally moved one forward.

"Bailey!" Mr. Shultz voice rang across the parking lot. "Time to go."

No. I couldn't leave now. Not after what Ezra had just said. How was I supposed to get on the bus and leave him?

"Bailey!" My teacher was waving me over and pointing to his watch.

It was now or never. If I didn't get on the bus, I definitely was going to kiss Providence good-bye.

I guess I would have to deal with Ezra later. There wasn't time to say, or do, anything now. I growled to myself, clenched my fists and ran across the parking lot and straight onto the art bus. All the other pairs were sitting together, but I sat in a seat alone. Scooting over and pressing my face against the window, I watched as Ezra got on his bus.

I pulled out my phone I wrote at least a hundred messages to him.

I deleted them all.

What was I supposed to say? How could I tell him what I was feeling over the phone?

The entire ride, I replayed his words over and over in my head. Had he really meant what he'd said? We'd only dated for a few weeks. Had he really started to fall in love with me? More importantly, had I started to fall in love with him, too?

My legs were like jelly when I stepped off the bus at the Providence Civic Center. I still clung to the travel mug full of coffee, which I'd been too distracted to drink during the ride. The concourse areas inside of the Civic Center was covered with hundreds of Through the Lens pieces. My eyes flitted over the competition.

Many of the displays were very good, but none compared to mine and Ezra's.

At the thought of him, my jaw clenched.

"Okay class, if you want to wander around for a bit that's fine, but you need to be standing next to your projects by two o'clock." Mr Shultz said, catching my eye as everyone else dispersed. "I'm glad you came today, Bailey, to support the rest of your classmates. I'm sorry you and Ezra won't qualify. Your project really had a shot at winning."

My heart stopped beating. "What do you mean support everyone else? Do you really not think the judges would make an exception if I tell them why Ezra's not here? Do you think they'll not even consider giving me the win?"

His eyes conveyed a level of pity that made me want to cry again. "You know the rules, Bailey. Both partners have to be present to win. You're the only one here. You won't qualify. I'm sorry. They'll probably announce you, if you win, but you'll have to forfeit. That's the rules."

I took a deep breath before saying, "Sir, with all due respect, I plan to plead my case with the judges. They can't ignore quality and design. If our project is the best, surely they will understand that and take the circumstances into consideration."

He hugged the clipboard he was carrying to his chest. "I hope you're right. I really do, but if not, I hope you can still be here to support everyone else. If any of us brought home the trophy, it would be a huge win for Cedar Falls." He turned and walked away, leaving me standing in the middle of the convention hall all by myself.

Can I really do this?

Even my teacher didn't think I had any chance of winning without a partner, no matter how good our project was. This was all Ezra's fault, and he had the nerve to tell me he was falling in love with me. What did he think his declaration was going to do, make me change my mind?

Grrr. I huffed off to find my project, which, I was happy to see, was already gathering a crowd of people.

"This is excellent," a woman said to the man standing beside her, "I wonder who made it."

"I did." I stepped past them and took my place next to the display.

"Oh." The woman smiled. "The design is most impressive, dear. I love the use of the props. Very unique."

"Thank you." I smiled back.

"Where is your partner?" She leaned closer to the name plate attached to the project. "Ezra O'Neill. We'd love to congratulate him as well."

My face fell. "Oh, he couldn't make it today."

The woman pushed her bottom lip into a pout. "Oh, that's a shame. You had such a good chance of winning, too. Well, good of you to come anyway."

I gave her a tight lipped smile in return. Even she thought I had no chance of winning. Our project was good, very good. It had to win. End of story. All I could hope for was that the judges would think differently.

After another five people came by expressing the same feelings—*great project, no partner, oh too bad*—I couldn't take it anymore. Stowing my coat behind the display and grabbing my purse, I wandered off. The concourse was packed with students, art teachers and parents milling around all the projects. I kept walking until I found an empty bench and plopped down on it. Leaning forward, I lowered my face into my hands.

I thought I was all alone, until I felt someone sit down next to me.

"Are you alright, dear," a gentle voice said.

Glancing up, I saw the woman who had been admiring my project earlier. She was giving me a strained smile.

I normally would have lied and said I was fine, but for some reason I didn't. "No," I said.

She reached over and placed a slender hand on my shoulder. "What's the matter? Is it the contest? Is it your partner?"

My eyes welled with tears. "Yes. See, it's my dream is to get into Providence School of Design and I was counting on this contest to help impress them and make my application stand out. My partner...boyfriend...I don't even know anymore... we worked so hard, but then our school got in the State Football Championship, which is happening right now and he had to go play in the game because scouts from Boston are coming to watch him.

"It became clear that we both valued college more than our relationship so he's at the game and I'm here. I thought maybe I could convince the judges to let me win without him, but I don't think I can now. It's over. I've lost the contest and I've lost Ezra because I didn't get on the other bus. I didn't show him what he means to me."

I had messed up so badly, and I felt like an idiot. "I was stubborn and stupid and I've let him down. Now, neither of us is happy and it's all my fault. I'm stuck here with a project that doesn't stand a chance at winning, and he's across town, wishing I was there." I gazed up into the woman's caring eyes. "And then this morning, he said he'd started to fall in love with me. How do you spring that kind of thing on a person and then turn around and walk away? What was he thinking?"

"My, my," she said, "it sounds like you've had quite the time."

I nodded.

She smiled. "He said he was falling in love with you?"

I blew out a tense breath. "Yep."

"And, how do you feel about him?" She smoothed her skirt over her knees.

I shook my head. "I don't know. There were

times when I thought it was possible, but how do you know for sure if what you're feeling is love?" I lowered my head back into my palms.

The woman gently patted me on the back. "I asked that very same question a long time ago, and I'll tell you the answer I was given."

I took a deep breath and lifted my gaze to meet hers.

Smiling, she said, "love is one of the hardest things in the world to define, because it looks different for everyone. There is no secret checklist, no list of rules, no universal blueprints. But, as you search your heart, look past the way he makes you feel. If all you're getting is simple stomach flutters, it's most likely not love. But, if he occupies a place within the depths of your heart, and you find yourself wanting to put his needs above your own then it's possible that love has blossomed. I would recommend listening to what your heart is telling you."

I nodded. "But that's just the thing. Neither of us wanted to put the other's needs above our own, so doesn't that mean that we don't love each other?"

"Not necessarily. You're still young. You're both just learning about life and love, but if you didn't care about his needs you wouldn't be sitting here right now talking to a complete stranger about him."

I shook my head. "I have no idea what my heart's trying to tell me."

"I think you do know what it's telling you." She stood up, adjusting her jacket. "Look at yourself. Of all the places you could have gone in this entire building, you chose one near the only television screen that's covering his football game."

I whirled around. Sure enough, the State Championship was on the tv, and Ezra was running the ball towards the end zone.

Turning back to her, my mouth gaped open.

"Let me ask you one question which might help you decide what you should do. If I told you that you have already been accepted into PSD, and that winning this contest wouldn't change anything, where would you be right now?"

I didn't even have to think about it. "I'd be at his game."

She grinned. "This contest has rules, and they will not be modified for any reason. No matter how great your piece is, you will not win it alone."

My gut clenched.

"But, I've also been around this competition enough to know that, while Providence sends reps to scope out the winners, they base their admission decisions on applications and portfolios. Whether you get in, or not, will not depend on the outcome of today."

"Really?"

She nodded. "I hope you find your way, Bailey Grant, and I wish you all the best. Trust your heart. It won't fail you."

I stood up, extending my hand. "Thank you, Mrs…?"

"Carmichael." She grasped my hand. "Debra Carmichael."

"Thank you Mrs. Carmichael. Thank you so much."

She let go of my hand. "Your project really is remarkable."

I watched her walk away for a few seconds, then whirled back around to face the tv screen. Ezra and Joel were passing the ball back and forth as they ran down the field. As Ezra dove over the end zone and scored a goal, I screamed—so loudly that people stopped what they were doing to stare at me.

"Keep your voice down." Someone scolded me. "This isn't a sporting event."

"Yes, it is, and I'm missing it." I turned a ran out of the Civic Center.

CHAPTER THIRTY

RUNNING TO THE NEAREST taxi, I flung open the door and hopped in the back. "To Camden Field, please," I said to the driver as I yanked the door closed.

The driver pulled out onto the road and we took off across town. My heart raced and my palms grew sweaty as I clutched my purse and stared out the window. Within about ten minutes, the football stadium came into view. The driver pulled up outside and I hopped out, paying him quickly, before turning and running to the ticket booth.

"The game's halfway over." The guy in the booth said when I asked for a ticket.

"I know, but I still want one, please." I was breathing heavily.

He rolled his eyes. "Whatever. Five bucks."

With the ticket in my hand, I ran into the stadium. The stands were packed far more than I was used to. Scanning the crowd, there were no available seats except for extremely high up in the stands. I didn't want to climb all the way up there. I needed to be down by the field, so I stood by the stairs and leaned against the cold metal bleachers.

Within a few minutes, it started to sleet. The pellets were so cold I felt instantly chilled to the bone. Pulling my hood up and slipping my gloves on, I marched in place and wrapped my arms around myself for warmth, hating myself for wearing a skirt that day, even if my tights were thick and cosy.

Everyone in the stands began pulling out umbrellas and ponchos, but it was the players I felt sorry for. The rain and sleet pelted down on their hot, sweaty bodies, causing steam to rise from them as they ran up and down the field. Their cleats slipped on the wet grass and water cascaded down their helmets.

There was a tunnel to my right, which led down to the locker rooms beneath the stadium. I dove into it to hide from to storm.

Before long, the officials called a time out due to the ferocity of the storm and the players were herded off the field in soggy, slippery masses. This was my chance to catch Ezra, but what would I say?

The closer the teams got to me, the more nervous I became. I didn't know what to say to him. *I can't do this.* Turning on my heels, I ducked my head, but didn't get very far before someone grabbed my arm.

Closing my eyes I turned around slowly.

"Bailey?" Ezra gasped.

I opened my eyes, lifting my head to meet his gaze.

"Hi." I managed to squeak.

He grabbed my other arm too, pushing me against the wall of the tunnel. "What are you doing here? Is something wrong? Did you win?"

I pushed my hood back, out of my eyes. "I doubt it. No one seemed to think the judges would bend the rules for me."

"Then why are you here? Did something else happen?" He was shivering from the cold.

"You need to go inside and get warm." I reached out, and sure enough, his arms were like ice.

"Don't worry about me. Why are you here?" His eyes searched mine.

I bit my lip. "Why do you think?"

"O'Neill," his coach shouted down the corridor, "get your butt in here now."

"Go." I nodded my head in the direction of his coach.

Ezra's gaze shifted between the coach and me. His tongue darted out between his lips. "We're not done here."

I smiled. "I'm not going anywhere. Go, we'll talk later."

A deep growl came from his throat as he turned and jogged away from me, disappearing into the locker room.

Huddling against the concrete for warmth, I stayed in the tunnel until the sleet subsided and the officials decided to resume the game. Walking back out, I took up my place by the stairs again.

When the teams reemerged, Ezra paused next to me, reaching down to squeeze my hand. "I'll find you after the game."

"Then win it quickly." I grinned. "You know how much I hate football."

He smiled back. "I'm on it."

Maybe I truly was Ezra's good luck charm because the way the team played after the weather delay was night and day to what I'd watched them play before it. Ezra ran as if he had been given super powers. He was so fast, no one could catch him. He scored the two touchdowns the team needed to tie up the score, with only a few seconds left on the clock.

All they needed was to kick a field goal and they'd win.

I was on my feet, jumping up and down, screaming along with the rest of the fans who had come to support Cedar Falls. The boys lined up, the kicker hit his mark, and just like that, we became the State Football Champions of Rhode Island.

The crowd exploded in the stands around me, no one's spirits dampened at all by the weather. We screamed and screamed until our throats burned and our voices became hoarse. Newspapers from all over the state had been there to cover the game, and news crews stood on the sidelines where the reporters were announcing the final results into the cameras.

The gleaming gold trophy was hauled out to the middle of the field and presented to the team, who raised it above their heads as camera flashes went off all around them.

Once the presentation ceremony was finished, we all rushed onto the field. I ran out onto the soggy ground, very glad I'd worn my boots that day. Through the crowd, I searched for Ezra, but there were so many maroon jerseys that it was hard to tell one player from the other.

"Bailey!" His voice found me.

I turned around, but didn't see him.

"Bailey!" He was closer, then.

Breaking through the crowd, Ezra charged towards me. A few steps away, he ripped his helmet from his head and tucked it under his arm.

"Congratulations." I grinned from ear to ear.

Breathless, he grinned back. "Thanks."

I opened my mouth to say something, but was interrupted.

"Ezra O'Neill?"

He turned. "Yes."

A man held out his hand. "I'm Marcus Rigby from Boston College."

My heart stopped. This was Ezra's big moment. I could feel him stiffen beside me as he shook the man's hand.

I found his other fingers with mine and gave

them a reassuring squeeze.

"Mr. Rigby, thank you so much for coming." Ezra's voice shook.

"That was an impressive game, young man." Mr. Rigby pulled out a clipboard and began flicking through the pages. "We love to see that kind of dedication to the game and sportsmanship on the field. I wanted to let you know that I'll be submitting my recommendation for your acceptance into Boston College, and if you choose to sign with us, we would love to see you play for us next fall."

As speechless as Ezra was, he still managed to mumble, "thank you so much."

Mr. Rigby's eyes flitted to me. "Go, have some fun. You have a lot to celebrate today. We'll be in touch." He shook Ezra's hand one more time before nodding to us both and walking away.

Turning to me, Ezra's eyes grew wide and his mouth dropped open. "What just happened?"

I threw my arms around his neck. "That was all your dreams coming true. I'm so proud of you, Ezra. So, so proud. I knew you could do it."

He didn't hug me back.

Dropping my arms, I took a step back.

"Why are you here?" He asked, closing the gap I'd created. "What happened at the showcase? Why did you leave?"

I hugged myself, staring at the ground. "I choose you, Ezra. I'm sorry for being such an idiot. I was selfish and stupid and thought that what *I* wanted was more important than you. The only thing I've let myself care about was getting into Providence, and I didn't care what I had to sacrifice to do it. I thought that Through the Lens would give me everything I needed. I pushed you and stressed myself out, and yes, our project was awesome, everyone at the showcase thought so, but there was no way the judges were going bend the rules for me to win by myself. This is where I should have been the whole time. I should have been here for you." I said.

His fingers wrapped around my chin and gently tugged upward, so that our eyes locked. "So what about PSD?" Dropping his helmet to the ground with a thud, his cold palms found my cheeks.

"My application will have to be good enough." I reached up and wrapped my hands around his forearms.

Ezra inched closer. His thumbs traced my jaw. "This is what you want?"

"Yes." Swallowing hard, my heart threatened to leap out of my chest. "I love you, Ezra, and I'm sorry it took me so long to understand what that meant."

His pupils grew large as a smile broke across his face, and his hands found my waist. Lifting me into his arms, he pressed his frozen lips to mine. I caught my hands up in his sweaty, messy hair and kissed him back as he spun me around and around in the middle of the football field.

When he set me back on my feet, he rested his forehead against mine. "I love you, too."

He kissed me again, as the sleet changed into snowflakes that landed in his hair.

Suddenly, Ezra jerked back, his eyes flitting around. "What time is it?"

"Uh," I said, pulling out my phone, "four-thirty."

Bending down to pick up his helmet, he grabbed my hand. "How long did it take you to get here?"

My eyes narrowed. "Ten minutes or so, why?"

"Come on." He started running across the field.

I held on tight, trying not to fall on the wet, slippery ground. "Where are we going?"

When we got out to the front of the stadium, Ezra raised his hand, motioning for one of the taxi drivers. "We have a competition to win."

CHAPTER THIRTY ONE

THE TAXI PULLED UP and Ezra jerked open the door, ushering me inside. Sliding in next to me, he slammed the door shut. "The Civic Center, please, and hurry," he told the driver.

"We'll never make it in time." I held on as the driver pulled out of the stadium, taking a sharp turn, causing me to fall against Ezra.

He wrapped a protective arm around me. "Yes, we will. The judging is at five, right?"

"Yeah, but I haven't been there for hours. There's no way we'll win." I didn't want to get my hopes up.

Ezra grinned. "Yes, but the rules stated that both partners had to be present at the time of *judging* to qualify. It didn't say that we had to be there all day. As long as we're standing next to our display at five o'clock, we don't forfeit."

"I wish I had your optimism." I groaned.

When the driver pulled up in front of the Civic Center, Ezra had the door open before the car had completely stopped. His face fell and he gasped. "Oh, no. My wallet's back in the locker room."

"I got it." Stepping around him, I handed the

driver the money. "Come on." I grabbed his hand, and that time, I led the frantic running. I pulled him up the stairs and along the concourse level. Our project came into view as soon as we stepped off the stairs. There was still a crowd gathered around it.

Breathless, he and I skidded to a halt on either side of our display, ruffling the people standing there, and making one woman gasp and clutch her chest.

"Time?" Ezra asked.

Pulling out my phone, I said, "Four forty-seven."

"We made it." He dropped his helmet behind the project and bent forward, clutching his side. "Hey, can I use your phone?"

"Sure." I handed it to him.

Ezra poked around on the screen for a few seconds before lifting it to his ear. "Hey Mom," he said, "so, I still had time to make it to the art showcase after the game, but I raced off so fast I didn't get my stuff from the locker room. Could you find Joel and have him grab my clothes, wallet and phone, please?"

He was silent for a few moments, nodding his head and closing his eyes, before finally saying, "I know Mom, but this was really important too and if I'm not here, we can't win."

More silence and nodding.

"I'm at the Civic Center, the judging is about to start. Please can you get my stuff and meet me here? Oh, the guy from Boston said they want to offer me a spot on the team for next fall." He turned his head away, but I could still hear her screaming through the phone. "Thanks. So, can you meet me here? Okay, see you in a bit. Bye."

He handed my phone back, smiling. "They're on their way. Maybe I should have led with the whole Boston thing."

"You think?" I grinned.

"Are your parents here?" He asked.

"No, they've been to so many contests, I kind of prefer it if they're not hanging around making a big fuss." I reached over and took his hand. "Besides, I've got you here with me and that's all that matters."

Everyone who walked by gawked at Ezra in his dirty, stained, football uniform, but I didn't care. We were both there and we could still win. The seconds ticked by until it was five o'clock.

A voice came over the loud speakers, breaking the silence and tension in the corridors. "All Through the Lens contestants, please make your way to Conference Room B on the lower level where the judges will be announcing the winners. All contestants, please make your way to Conference Room B."

"That's our cue," I said.

"Let's go."

Filing into the conference room with all the other contestants, Ezra and I found seats, while my stomach began doing somersaults. Ezra reached over and laid his hand on my knee, which I hadn't realized was bouncing up and down like crazy.

"Easy," he whispered, "it'll be okay."

"Sorry." I let out a long, slow breath.

The judges walked up on the makeshift stage, clipboards in hand. A table behind them held trophies and envelopes filled with prize money.

Someone squeezed my shoulder.

Ezra and I both turned to see Mr. Shultz standing behind us. "Glad to see you made it Ezra. Bailey could never have gotten here without you."

His gaze shifted between me and Mr. Shultz. "I wouldn't let her down, Sir."

"So, did we win?"

Ezra's face lit up. "Oh yeah."

Mrs. Shultz's fists punched the air. "Yes, yes, yes! I knew you guys could do it. Well done."

"Thanks," Ezra grinned.

The judges were still conferring on the stage, their muffled voices echoing across the conference room. After several long minutes, a man stepped up to the microphone.

"Welcome to the twentieth annual Through the Lens Competition. Congratulations to all who took part this year. The designs were outstanding. You all really got on board with our theme and delivered some exceptional work, but of course, there can only be a few winners today. So, without further adieu, the three runner's up, in which each partner will receive five hundred dollars in prize money are: Lexi Carter and Jin Le from Helmsdale High School, John Waters and Simon Fuller from Cedar Falls High School, and Missy Blake and Margo Sanchez from Simon Chase High School here in Providence. Let's give a big round of applause to our runner's up."

The room exploded with cheers and clapping. Ezra and I whistled for John and Simon as they walked up onto the stage to receive their trophies and prize money, as well as pose for pictures. Their project had been really good.

"And now for the grand prize, which includes one thousand dollars for each partner and the honor of having their design on display at the Providence School of Design Museum for the next three months is…"

I squeezed Ezra's hand so hard he jerked his head towards me, hissing.

I eased up a bit.

"…Bailey Grant and Ezra O'Neill from Cedar Falls High School."

Mr. Shultz was on his feet yelling and clapping us on the back before we could even stand up. The rest of our class quickly followed as Ezra and I slowly stood. We rushed up to the stage, hand in hand.

As the judges presented us with our trophies and envelopes, the smile on my face grew wider and wider. I couldn't believe that Ezra and I had actually pulled off the win. I'd been so determined, that I'd lost sight of all the other things which were important. I'd let Ezra and I almost fall apart because I was too selfish to put anyone else's needs above my own. If I'd had a lot more faith and lot less tunnel-vision, neither of us would have spent the last week miserable.

I scanned the crowd for Mrs. Carmichael, but couldn't see her. I desperately wanted to thank her for everything she had said to me.

"Congratulations to all of our participants, and especially our winners. If you would please all go back and stand next to your projects so that those who wish to can come around and congratulate you. Winners, the Providence News-Leader will be taking pictures of you with your projects for tomorrow's paper, so make sure you stay here until the photographs are taken, then you're free to leave. You two," he turned to Ezra and I, "a representative from the Providence Museum will be coming by to collect your project as soon as the pictures are taken. Well done to both of you." He shook our hands again as the crowd moved for the doors.

Mr. Shultz met us at the bottom of the stairs, taking the trophy from Ezra. It would be on display in the case at the entrance to the high school from now to eternity, once the Through the Lens committee engraved our names into the plate on the base. "I am so proud of you both." He beamed from ear to ear. Turning to me he said, "see, I told you this would all work out for the best. I'm proud of you for giving it a chance and making one of the best display projects I've ever seen."

"Thank you for not giving me what I wanted."

"Never." He waved his hand. "Now, go. There are a lot of people who want to meet you."

As we walked away, Ezra leaned towards me. "What was that about?"

"Oh." I slung my arm through his. "I asked him to give me a new partner because I knew you were going to be terrible, but he said no."

Clutching his chest in fake injury, he gasped. "Really? Was that before, or after, you assaulted me in the hallway."

"Before, but I'm glad he said no."

"Me too." He stopped in the middle of the hallway, took me in his arms and kissed me.

I have no idea how many people came by to shake our hands and congratulate us, but there were two which stood out far above the rest.

Ezra's mom had tears in her eyes when she and his dad eventually showed up, carrying his backpack full of all the things he'd left in the locker room.

"I can't believe you two did all this." She breathed. "It is truly remarkable. You have real talent." Her eyes locked with her son's. "I mean it, Ezra, you have a gift I never knew about. I'm so happy for you. And I'm especially happy about Boston. We are so proud of you." She hugged him tightly, before turning to me. "And, you will do great things at Providence. Of this, I am sure. Congratulations, Bailey." She wrapped me up in her arms too, squeezing tightly.

I watched over her shoulder as Ezra's dad clasped his hand. "Son, I'm so proud of you. Forgive me for being so blind. If you want to go to Boston, you have my blessing."

"Thanks, Dad." Ezra's voice shook as he stood before his father.

When his dad's dark eyes turned to me, I stiffened. "Forgive me for my behavior the first time we met. You're welcome at our house anytime, Bailey." He gave me a tight-lipped smile.

"Thanks." I smiled back.

"So that's where all my old crates went." Another deep voice broke through the crowd behind Ezra's parents.

"Hi," I said, as Ezra's grandparents stepped closer. "Thanks for all your help."

He winked at me. "They've never looked better."

"Is that one of my napkins?" His grandma leaned close, her nose pressed against the display.

"Um…" My chest tightened.

"I don't think so, Grandma, they probably just look the same." Ezra said.

She reached up and touched the napkin. "Are you sure?"

"Yeah, I'm pretty sure." He turned so she wouldn't see the grin on his face.

Ezra's mom edged closer to me. "Bailey, we were all going to take Ezra out to dinner to celebrate his win at the game, and now, this too, I suppose." She gestured to the display. "Would you like to join us? This is also your victory."

"Thank you, Mrs. O'Neill." I said. "I'll have to check with my parents, and Mr. Shultz, since I'm supposed to ride back on the bus, but I'd love to." I couldn't believe she was actually inviting me along on a family meal.

After the newspapers came by to take our pictures—even more interested in our win after seeing Ezra in his uniform and discovering that he was also the state champion—a short discussion with Mr. Shultz, and a call home to get the okay from my parents, I found myself sitting in the backseat of Ezra's parent's SUV on our way to a steakhouse in Providence.

Ezra had gone into the bathroom and changed clothes before we left, his football uniform tucked in the back of the car. He held my hand the entire way to the restaurant, most of the way through dinner, and all the way home.

The dinner itself was unbelievable. I've never eaten a steak that tasted so good, especially with the side of shrimp Ezra and I had decided to share. His grandpa ordered us all dessert and by the time I'd stuffed myself with steak, shrimp, and then strawberry cheesecake, I didn't think I'd ever be hungry again.

When we got back to my house, Ezra walked

me up to the porch, kissing me quickly before saying good-night. Mom and Dad both greeted me at the door, throwing their arms around me and jumping for joy.

"I knew you could do it." Mom shrieked. "Congratulations."

"Well done, Squirt." Dad threw his arm over my shoulders and led me back into the house.

I fell asleep that night feeling happier than I had in a long time.

CHAPTER THIRTY TWO

OUR THROUGH THE LENS trophy appeared in the school's display case a week later, perfectly timed with the first official snowfall of the season.

A few weeks later, Ezra got his acceptance letter from Boston College, and Cedar Falls High arranged for a newspaper to come take a picture of him as he signed on with their football team for the next year. I went with him to the school library, sitting alongside his parents as he smiled for the camera and signed the papers.

Christmas was fast approaching, and I was really looking forward to spending it Ezra. I'd asked his mom for gift ideas for him, and she'd been very helpful.

Who knew he liked LEGO and was a huge Star Wars fan?

Once Mike found out, the two of them had decided to marathon the entire franchise while Mike was home on Christmas break before Ezra and I, along with the rest of the Senior Class, headed off to New Hampshire for the senior ski trip.

Walking home from school on the last day before Christmas break, Ezra and I checked the mailbox, like we always did. But that day, I stopped breathing when I opened the door and spotted a large, white envelope poised inside. Pulling it out, I screamed at the words:

PROVIDENCE SCHOOL OF DESIGN

Ezra let out a low whistled as I tore it open right there in the front yard, shoving the envelope into his outstretched hands. My eyes scanned over the letter.

I had been accepted!

I was in!

I was going to PSD!

I read through the letter three times, searching for any surprises. I didn't find any, except the signature at the bottom, which made me both smile and grow blurry-eyed at the same time.

It was signed:

Debra Carmichael

Dean of Admissions, Providence School of Design

It was *her*.

The woman who had talked to me at the showcase, who encouraged me to go after Ezra. She'd known all along that I'd already been accepted, and where I really needed to be that day. Clutching the letter to my chest, I made a mental note to find her on campus and thank her one day. Not only for the acceptance letter, but for the talk we'd had at the showcase.

I would thank her for her kinds words, for taking the time to care, and for helping me fix my relationship with Ezra. But mostly, I wanted to thank her for helping me see what love really looked like, and just how blind I had been to it.

As Ezra swept me up in his arms, spinning me around, we both squealed with delight.

I wished that someone had been there to photograph the moment, because I couldn't have imagined a better image to capture our Happily Ever After.

BAILEY AND EZRA'S
SNICKERDOODLES

Ingredients
* 1/2 cup butter, room temperature
* 1 1/2 cups sugar
* 1 teaspoon vanilla
* 2 eggs
* l/4 cup milk
* 3 1/2 cups flour
* 1 teaspoon baking soda

For Coating
* 5 tablespoons sugar
* 2 tablespoons cinnamon

Recipe
Preheat oven to 375°F/190°C. Grease 2 cookie sheets

Cream butter with electric mixer until light. Add the sugar and vanilla. Mix until fluffy. Beat in the eggs, then milk.

Sift the flour and baking soda over butter mixture and stir to blend. Refrigerate for 15 minutes.

For the coating, mix sugar and cinnamon. Roll tablespoons of the dough into balls and then roll the balls into the coating.

Place 2 inches apart on the cookie sheets and flatten slightly. Bake until golden brown, about 10 minutes. Transfer to wire rack to cool.

ABOUT THE AUTHOR

Sarah Cantrell

I am a girl of two worlds. I am a dual citizen of the USA and UK, but I'm also a girl who loves both reality and fantasy, which is why I write YA in both genres. I live in the UK with my husband and two children. Together, we enjoy exploring ancient ruins, castles, small-town coffee shops and used bookstores.

BOOKS BY THIS AUTHOR

The Tale Of Visions & Vengeance

A Curse Of Wings And Ice

Printed in Great Britain
by Amazon